Audia

Audia

Christopher Schaal

Library of Congress Control Number: 2010912700
ISBN: Hardcover   978-1-4535-6652-7
                Softcover   978-1-4535-6651-0
                Ebook   978-1-4535-6653-4

To order additional copies of this book, contact:
Xlibris Corporation
1-888-795-4274
www.Xlibris.com
Orders@Xlibris.com
76115

*I would like to express a special thank you to
Jennifer Ballard, without your assistance,
I could have never gotten this far.*

*Friends and family, for their time and patience
and every one in my life for their understanding.*

*Without each and every one of you,
this project of mine wouldn't have seen the light of day.*

Thank you for believing in me!

Prologue

S tanding before a barren wasteland of a planet, the mighty and powerful Rezorin looked down upon the view of nothingness. "I shall bring life to this dissolute world and make life in my image. I will teach them my ways and they will worship me, but I will treat them as my equal." And with his great power, Rezorin raised his hands, and with a flash of light, the planet began to shift and move. Clouds gathered and rain fell from the skies, filling the land with lakes and oceans. Plants and trees began growing from soil, sprouting foliage and bringing oxygen for life. Rezorin then took his mighty power to destroy one of the surrounding moons; the debris created a ring around the planet, leaving only one moon untouched. "This ring shall bring everlasting beauty to signify my love for all who live here." The power from Rezorin slowly drained him to complete the new world. "With this new world finished, I shall call it Vianna after my love that will always live within my soul." And with a burst of light and energy, Rezorin shed the last bit of energy he had remaining to fully finish Vianna.

With Rezorin's strength almost depleted, he slowly made his descent to the nearest landmass of Vianna. Trying to rest and regain his strength, Rezorin looked around to see nothing of beauty around him. "With this new world I've created, I shall make it a utopia, free from everything that had plagued my recent world. I will make perfect what once was flawed." Rezorin took his finger and cut his palm down the center to release a flow of blood, each droplet hitting the ground and soaking into the soil as if the blood itself was feeding the ground. A large hunk of ground started pushing from below; a hand made its way toward the surface and then an arm until finally a female, fully draped in a white shroud, appeared from the ground. Rezorin placed his hand upon the newly born, fully grown female, a light emitted from his hand toward her forehead. "You shall be called Audia, and I am giving you the power to make this world beautiful and to fill the air with music. You are the first of four whom I will grant the power to watch over and guide the people of this world, once I've created them." The newly created woman looked around at the world in which she was destined to make into her image of beauty, and with a swift motion of her hand, a bundle of roses grew directly from the ground and started surrounding her body, wrapping itself around her feet. The surrounding area began transforming into something colorful and amazing; vines of flowers wrapped around each tree with colorful pulps popping up in all directions, colorful birds and cute mammals flooding the landscape. Rezorin walked over, and with his hand on her shoulder, he said, "You please me with what you've done here. Now go forth and make this world into something of beauty!" Audia began her descent in the world to cover its landscape, making this new world into her own image.

"With all I see within this world, I have great hope for all who live here, but before I create the ones who will live here, I need a few more *spirits* to guide them on their way." Rezorin opened his palm once again to throw droplets of blood in three different locations in front of him, and each drop that hit the soil brought a new soul into the world. The three stood in front of Rezorin; they stood waiting for their orders, each covered in the same white shrouds as Audia. Rezorin walked over to the first being from the left. "You are Ewar, and you will make sure my rules are followed. You will keep everyone in line, and if I need to punish anyone, you will be the one I send." Ewar, still standing before Rezorin, began to kneel. "Yes, my lord. I will serve you well!"

Rezorin stepped aside to the right. "Idivant, you will be the keeper of all animals of this world. You will work alongside Audia from time to time, but you are solely responsible for all animals. You will also bring the seasons to all the land." Idivant kneeled before Rezorin. "As you wish, my lord!" Rezorin finally stepped toward the last remaining *spirit*. "Evony, I entrust you with the most daunting task of the rest. I'm putting you in charge of teaching the settlers of this world. You will teach them my ways, and when I deem them worthy, I shall grant them the powers of being a *spirit*." Evony kneeled before Rezorin. "All praise be to you, Rezorin! I will not let you down."

Rezorin set out his new disciples into the new world. With their eyes and ears, this world should live in harmony. Looking into the sky, he said, "I've created this world, and now I must create the place in which I and my *spirits* shall call home." Rezorin lifted his arms into the air, and with a mighty energy coming from his hands, a streak of light began to rise into the sky. Suddenly, within a flash, Rezorin vanished from Vianna and reappeared within a new location. "I shall call this Olma, a place where me and my brethren can rest and watch over all who worship." And with a swift hand motion, Rezorin opened a portal for viewing on the floor, watching as his new creations served him. He watched as new animals were born and named, the beautiful creations sprouting all over the land.

The day came to an end, with Rezorin still watching as this world breathed anew. "Come to me, for this day is at an end and there is much to discuss." Within a flash, his four disciples appeared in Olma, standing before him. "You have done well! Everything is coming together just as I've hoped." The four kneeled before Rezorin while looking up to view the face of their creator. "Before I create the beings that will inhabit this land, I need to go over how things will work." Rezorin talked to the four, telling them the rules that would govern this world. Each rule brought forth a means to a great society, free from everything that plagued Rezorin's previous world. He would go into great detail involving the hierarchy of the society, where he remained up top while *spirits* remained below him. The list also went into full detail of all classes below *spirits*: Adalum, Tormed, Incio, and lastly, Ement. Adalum would act as the assistants to the *spirits*, working and learning from them in any shape or form. Rezorin would speak of how Adalum could only gain the rank of *spirit* through him or through the act of at least four *spirits*. The Tormed students are very skillful in the Art of Knowledge, the knowledge Rezorin promised to share among his people, but are still not as skillful as all Adalum students. Next on the list is the rank of Incio, which means the beginning of great knowledge; only the most promising are held to this honor. Ement would be the last of the remaining ranks. Everyone in the land are highly encouraged to learn the basic skills that are taught at the level of Ement, and only the ones with high marks and a will of dedication can move up to the level of Incio, but like all ranks and classes, the only ones deemed worthy by the *spirits* or Rezorin shall move up.

The four *spirits* listened intently as the powerful Rezorin talked of what he expected from his disciples and the many tasks he bestowed upon them, the knowledge flowing into each *spirit* everything Rezorin wanted them to know. Each one was like a newborn child with the inability to communicate words into sentences but with the knowledge to do everything asked of them.

"And the time has come for my creations to have siblings to watch and guide. They shall be formed from my image but none of the power." Rezorin flew into the sky and, into the midst of dusk, began to give off a blinding light. "From the very essence of my being shall I create my followers that shall live their lives in peace and happiness!" Rezorin spinned in place, still giving off a bright light; from a distance, Rezorin looked like a bright star in the sky. His spinning gained speed until Rezorin blurred into a huge blob of light. Small tidbits of bright debris began falling from Rezorin in all directions; it was a sight to be seen as tiny bits of light scattered throughout the land. Each piece of light would slowly float down to the ground like tiny little fireworks in the sky. The tiny things of light finally reached the ground, each light soaked within the soil of the land; and with each droplet, a being would emerge from the ground.

Each soul looked around curiously, and with dusk still upon them, they watched in amazement as the darkening land littered their mind with sights they had never seen before. Rezorin slowly came out of his spin and floated down to speak with his new followers. "Do not be afraid, for I'm the one who created you. I've given you life in exchange for your love. Within this world, you will remain safe by my side. I shall watch over you and guide you throughout your lives. With me are four beings called *spirits*, each one with a name that you shall learn later. I will grant you shelter and the means to live and learn all that I have to teach. I also took the liberty of creating your soul mates so that this will not be the only generation to live on this world." Rezorin lifted his hand toward the distance; the land began to shake as small cottages lifted from the ground behind the newly created followers, each cottage large enough for a family but with a quaint sense of appeal to each of them; toward the side of each building stood a small shack used for farming tools and other such utensils. Rezorin floated back up to Olma, but before leaving, he turned to face the followers. "I have not given you names, for I am giving that pleasure to your spouses. Now be at peace and enjoy all that I have given you." And with a bright light, Rezorin vanished into the sky.

Back in Olma, Rezorin looking through the portal to watch over his people. "I love watching them. They're so simplistic like my ancestors before the Knowledge was ever learned." Audia, with a new sense of conversation, replied, "If you don't mind me asking, my lord, but where do you come from?" Rezorin's smile slowly vanished while still watching the portal on the floor. "A distant world that no longer exist. That's all you need to know and that's all I will be sharing with you. I've given you all the knowledge that I wish for you to know, even the coming of the Andemous, which has the power to kill me, something I wish for all of you to teach the new citizens of this world in due time. I don't want them scared, so give it some time. Come now. Share with me this wondrous feeling." The four now stepped closer until they stood side by side with their new lord. "Tomorrow I would like for all of you to greet them, and, Audia, surprise them with something beautiful when they wake. I want their first full day to be remembered in the back of their mind forever."

Chapter 1

𝒯 he day started out the same as before for young Eiades, who knew nothing of the news about to be bestowed upon him. Before he could begin his daily lessons from the Art of Knowledge, he would have to finish his daily chores. Once finished, young Eiades would head toward the side of the yard to sit down at his favorite spot to study under a medium-sized tree with a large root sticking out from the ground to rest and read against the trunk. Thinking of nothing besides the book in front of his face, Eiades sat reading, not paying attention to the beautiful woman standing before him, watching him read so intently. "Oh, so anxious to learn, young Eiades?" Eiades looked up, shockingly standing up in a panic to rightly greet the woman standing before him. "I'm so sorry, Audia. I had no idea you were near, or I wouldn't be so disrespectful in your presence. Please forgive me!" Audia, with a smile on her face, walked ever so close to Eiades. "No worries, my child. I've come to bear you with good news. You shall be the youngest Incio in history." Eiades, with a giant smile on his face, ran toward Audia and gave her a hug. "Thank you so much!" Eiades let go as quickly as he gave the hug. "I'm sorry, I let my excitement get the better of me. I promise I will control myself better." Audia, with an innocent laugh, stood next to Eiades and placed her hand on his shoulder. "You think showing emotion is something to be ashamed of? Please honor me with your excitement. We are all connected by what we feel, so you feeling happy spreads like wildfire to others." Eiades put his hand on top of Audia's hand that still rested on his shoulder. "I can't thank you enough for all this. I dreamed of this moment, but never did I dream that the beautiful Audia would deliver the message." "You should be thanking Rezorin. He's the one who saw greatness in you. He saw all the hard work and dedication you have been showing the last few years. Your graduation shall be within a week.

Rezorin wanted to bestow the honor of making you an Incio himself. Now go and celebrate this glorious day. You've earned it, young Eiades." Audia stepped back from Eiades, a bright light opening behind her; and within seconds, she vanished and the light she walked into now gone without a trace.

Eiades's father, chopping wood for the changing of the seasons, said, "Eiades! Come here. I need your help. I keep hoping Idivant will give me a break and postpone the changing of the leaves until I have enough wood for the cold." Eiades, still with a giant smile on his face, said, "Father, you won't believe who came to see me!" The axe went up and, with a powerful motion, came down to split a log in two, the two pieces of wood slump to the ground; his father, wiping the sweat from his forehead, stood attentive, resting against the handle of the axe. "I was studying underneath my tree when Audia came to speak with me." Now with full attention placed on his son, he said, "Please tell me you didn't do anything to upset Rezorin!" Getting down on both knees with his head placed upward and gazing upon the sky, his father said, "Please forgive my son, Rezorin, for he knows not what he does!" Eiades, grabbing his father by the hands to lift him up, said, "No, Father, she came to congratulate me on being the youngest Incio in history! I get to meet Rezorin in person for my celebration. Audia said he wants to honor me with this rank in person." The father now stood in front of his son, his eyes glazing over as he opened his arms and gave Eiades a big hug. "I'm so proud of you, my son. You have made it further than anyone in our family. Your mother will be so proud. You can tell her when she comes back from the market." Eiades, grasping in the emotions being shared, thought to himself that Audia was right that everyone is connected through emotions and that he can feel the happiness coming from his father. "I want to help you, Father, but would it be okay if I gave you a rain check on the gathering of the wood? I want to go out and celebrate." Letting his son go, wiping the sweat from his forehead again, he said, "Of course, my son, you deserve it."

Eiades, heading out into the woods, took in all the sights and sounds of nature, most of which Eiades praised Rezorin, Audia, and Idivant for having graced him with. Eiades walked along a few creeks and brushed his hands across a few flowers, which he knew wouldn't be here for long with the changing of the seasons. Soon, this whole land would be filled with multicolored trees, and most of the animals would be gathering food for the winter. A large rock within the distance invited Eiades to come sit while taking in all the sights and sounds of the land, birds flying over head in a V formation. A gentle breeze hit Eiades's face like a hand running its fingers across his skin, the feeling so tantalizing that he never wished it to stop.

The light from the evening began to dim as night slowly took over. The planet's ring still gave off a small hint of light from the sun, the multitude of colors layered on top of one another, something Eiades couldn't help but stare at every night. Eiades thought to himself that life couldn't get any better than this, that all his dreams were coming true, and now he gets to meet his idol, Rezorin.

A small noise broke Eiades from his relaxed state; startled, he began to walk toward the noise while holding his hand to cast a spell that would bring a blinding ball of light into his palm. Using his hand as a flashlight, Eiades began investigating his surroundings. "Hello? Who's there? It would be wise to show yourself and stop playing games. This isn't funny!" The noise never repeated itself, and Eiades couldn't seem to find the culprit, so he easily gave up and began walking home. But what Eiades didn't realize was that there was a person watching him; a young female who couldn't have been older than fifteen had been watching him that night but was too shy she couldn't muster up the courage to say anything, and so her best idea was to remain hidden among the trees This young female had been watching and learning everything she could about young Eiades; she loved the way he studied, she loved the way he was eager to learn anything and everything; and she couldn't help but feel curious over how dedicated he was. She would dream of the time she could finally say something to maybe strike his fancy, but nothing would ever come from it. This was a day to remember within her own thoughts; this had been the first time she had been almost face-to-face with him. The only way for her to ever watch Eiades was through the portal her mother, Audia, would ever allow of her. This young girl was the daughter of a *spirit*, and she was about to be in big trouble by her parents; they forbade her to ever go outside Olma until she grew older, but this young girl didn't seem to care, for her only thought was to finally see Eiades and to maybe say something like she had always dreamed of doing. The time had come, and even though she knew she would have to hear a lecture, she thought it to be completely worth the risk, but it was her time as well to start the journey back home to Olma.

Back in Olma, both Ewar and Audia stood waiting as their daughter, Puri, tried to sneak her way in. "Puri! Where did you go? Why did you not tell us you were going to leave Olma?" Puri began to stare at the floor. "I guess because I knew you would never let me go." "Do you not understand how vulnerable you are right now? You may be a *spirit*, but you aren't fully mature. If anything were to happen, then you could die!" Rezorin walked up to Puri. "I know you're curious, my little one, but you must understand the importance of what your parents are saying. Without your body being matured to the state of being a full *spirit*, then anything can kill you. You're not part of the chain yet, and so we all have to take extra steps in securing your safety. Do you understand?" Puri looked into Rezorin's eyes. "Yeah, my curiosity just got the better of me is all." Audia and Ewar, still upset, closed in on her to secure her with a group hug. "Promise me you'll never go outside of Olma until you're fully matured. Promise both me and your mother." Puri looked into both her parent's eyes. "I promise."

Eiades walked toward the cottage, looking through the window to witness his mother stirring something within the pot on the fireplace and his dad sharpening the axe he had used earlier that day to chop wood. He made his way to the door but had to wait to remove the smile from his face from the exciting news he had just received that day, his mother still clueless as to who had visited him, and so Eiades would try to play it off as if nothing had happened. Walking through the door, Eiades was greeted with his mother saying, "And where have you been?" Eiades quickly responded, "Nowhere, just out." His mother, not at all pleased with the answer she just received, said, "How do you expect to become an Incio? I find your book lying about with you out doing whatever you please." Eiades, unable to keep his joy to himself, broke out with a smile on his face; his mother, on the other hand, did not find amusement in this new expression. "You better hope Rezorin will have mercy on you for ditching the Art of Knowledge." "Mother, you don't understand. I was visited by Audia today. She came to congratulate me on being the youngest Incio in history. I'll be meeting with Rezorin in a week so he can personally give me the honors!" Eiades's mother, standing in shock, began to smile and then grabbed a hold of Eiades with a hug. "I can't believe this. My son has become the first Incio within the family. Our son will meet Rezorin and has seen Audia. Please tell me, son, what was Audia like?" Eiades walked over to the table to sit down. "Well, you know how everyone says that

Audia is the most beautiful being they've ever laid eyes upon? Well, that's an understatement. She literally glows with beauty. She smells of flowers, and her eyes share both colors of green and gold. The very sight of her gave me a warm feeling inside." Eiades's mother stood in amazement as her son gave off the description of her favorite *spirit*, wondering the day that she may meet the wondrous Audia for the first time.

That night after supper, Eiades sat outside on a log, looking up at the stars and thinking to himself, *Nothing will be the same. Everything is changing in my life. All my dreams are coming true, and I'm only thirteen. I can't believe I'm going to meet Rezorin. This has got to be the greatest day of my life!* Meanwhile, both Eiades's parents were talking among themselves. "Did you get a glimpse of Audia?" the mother asked the father as they both climbed into bed. "Actually no, I didn't." "Then how are we to know whether or not he's making all this up? I mean, for all we know this is just a means of getting out of studying for a week." Giving his wife a glimpse of displeasure, he replied, "Just because I didn't see the boy with Audia doesn't mean he's lying. I was concentrating on chopping wood and nothing else." The mother, now getting into bed, said, "I don't mean to doubt him, but whoever heard of a thirteen-year-old Incio? All I'm saying is that he has always had a wild imagination, and this could just be a way for him to take a break." "Well, if the boy wants to take a break, then maybe he should have one. The boy does work so hard every day, and he is still young. Maybe it's time we give him a little break here and there." The mother, making herself comfortable, said, "You're right. Maybe he does need a break. But the least he could do is be honest with us and not make elaborate stories as to get his way. He'll be an adult soon, and it's time he started acting like one." The two parents, about to turn out the candles near the bedsides, turned to each other to wish the other sweet dreams.

Eiades, still outside, basked in the thought of being a Incio, each thought bringing a bigger smile on his face—him staring at each of his books, remembering the sleepless nights before class where he would practice and practice until his concentration was gone, each spell in the back of his mind like second nature, thinking of all the advanced spells he would learn in the coming months, feeling like the same little kid that was introduced to the Art of Knowledge eight years ago.

Rezorin looked through the portal in Olma while Ewar stood beside him with a look of concern. "Rezorin, do you think it wise to make him an Incio?" Rezorin, with a small laugh, stepped away from the portal and faced Ewar. "You doubt me, dear Ewar?" Still standing over the portal, Ewar stared at Eiades. "I don't mean to doubt you, Rezorin, but he's too young to train as an Incio. I'm only thinking of his safety." Sitting down at his throne, Rezorin turned to Ewar. "I've been watching him for the last few years, and his dedication is so strong that I see him as a *spirit* within the next five years. He has shown me the kind of commitment needed to be one of the few to bear the name *spirit*." Stepping away from the portal, Ewar walked toward Rezorin to kneel before his lord. "I'm so sorry for doubting you. I only think of the young boy's health. Please forgive me!" Rezorin placed his hand on top of Ewar's head. "Think nothing of it, my dear Ewar. I'm glad you keep young Eiades's health in such high regard, but trust in me and all will be well."

Eiades's excitement turned into tiredness, his eyes beginning to hang low while yawns came every few minutes. "Even though I never want this day to end, I'm afraid it must." Eiades now headed inside to climb into bed; sleep still not taking hold of him while each thought of what has happened and what still will happen lingered in his mind until, finally, his eyes could take no more, and Eiades found his way into dreamland.

Eiades stood upon a hill with a blackish dead tree rotting before him, the wind blowing wildly and leaves floating all around in a scene of chaos. A voice called out from nowhere, "They will betray you! Trust no one!" Eiades looked confused. "Who said that?" The voice called out again, "I shall be the one to show you kindness and redemption. They will ruin everything you love. Trust no one!" Eiades looked wildly around as the wind began to pick up speed. "Show yourself and explain! Who will ruin everything?" The voice spoke out once more, "Nothing is as it seems, for love will bring tragedy, and friends and family will show coldheartedness. Trust no one!"

Eiades woke from what seemed to him like a horrible dream, but also a very vivid and confusing dream at that, something he should probably talk with his teacher to see if she could make sense of it. So Eiades put on some fresh clothes and sat down at the table for breakfast, but something didn't seem right; both his parents were sitting there with not so much as a smile on their faces. Eiades looked at his dad. "What's the matter? Why isn't anyone talking?" The father looked over at Eiades. "Oh, nothing. Me and your mother just didn't get a whole lot of good sleep last night is all." Eiades dug into his meal while still talking to his father, "I know what you mean. My night went pretty badly as well. I had a really weird dream that I need to speak with one of my teachers about." Looking over at his son, he said, "I'm sure it's nothing. Probably just a lot on your mind is all."

Eiades finished his breakfast to head out to the local Lage in hopes to speak with his now-former teacher. Class had not begun yet, so Eiades had a few moments alone with his teacher. "Excuse me, Mrs. Nepris. I was wondering if I could ask you a question or two about a dream I had." The teacher slowly looked up from a book she had been reading all that morning. "Ah, if it isn't my favorite Incio. What can I do you for, my child?" Eiades began to become flustered. "Oh, so you heard about that. Well, I need help determining what my dream meant from last night." The teacher placed a thin piece of wood within the book before closing it. "Sure, I love dreams and what they stand for. So go ahead and start from the beginning." Eiades grabbed a seat and began telling his teacher all about the dream he had from last night and how utterly confused it made him. "So you see, I have no idea what any of this stands for. Can you give me some insight as to what I'm supposed to make of it?" The teacher placed her hand upon her chin. "To be honest with you, Eiades, I haven't the slightest idea. The only thing that came to my mind is the fact that you are dealing with a lot at the moment and maybe that might make you have dreams of this sort." Eiades began to stand up. "That's funny because my father spoke of the same thing." The teacher grabbed her book once again. "Well, you know great minds think alike. But before you go, Eiades, is it true that you met with Audia?" Eiades, who was walking out the door, stopped in his tracks and turned around to his teacher. "I sure did, and everything you heard about her is true." The teacher, with a gasp of air, sunk down into her chair. "I wish I could have met her. She seems so amazing." Eiades thanked his teacher before heading out the door.

Before heading home, Eiades decided to visit the one place he always went from time to time—a flower garden in the middle of the woods. When Eiades first discovered the garden, he couldn't help but wonder where such a beautiful area could come from; he always just assumed it had something to do with Audia, so he went there only to marvel at its existence. Eiades stared at all the beautiful colors and admired the person who could create all this. A small noise broke his concentration once again. Eiades looked over into the bushes where the noise originated from but could see nothing. "Look, this isn't funny! Whoever you are, show yourself!" Eiades walked ever so closer to the bushes where he could see a small bit of white from behind the bushes. Eiades stood before the bush, pushing through, fanning out the branches to its side so that he may finally get a look at the creature or try to scare him. The white would finally reveal a young female squatting down so as not to be seen. When the realization hit that she was found, she quickly stood up to start running. Eiades reached out to grab her hand. "Please don't run. I just want to know why you were spying on me." Eiades's hand slowly let go of the young woman while she stopped in her tracks from his touch. The young woman turned around to face Eiades. "I'm sorry. I didn't mean to disturb you, Eiades." Eiades, with a shocked look on his face from his name being mentioned from a person he had never seen before, said, "How exactly do you know my name? If I'm not mistaken, I've never met you before." The young woman began to turn red from the embarrassment. "I must admit, I've been watching you for sometime. I find you fascinating—the way you treat everything as if it's special in some way, the way you stare into the night sky as if it were the first time, the way you look at the flowers in this garden as if you just discovered beauty." Eiades started to smile. "Because I look at everything and wonder on the person who created it all, how anyone could create something of such amazing beauty and how I can aspire to be like that person." The young woman started making her way toward Eiades. "My name is Puri. Again, I'm sorry for spying on you. I just love watching you." Eiades thought to himself, *How have I never met this wondrous person before? She's so beautiful and the way she speaks is like nothing I've heard.* The day was filled with the two talking to each other. They two sat down on a stone that was weirdly shaped like a bench as they watched the sun go down. Day would turn to night, and the young Puri placed her head upon Eiades's shoulder. "I never want this day to end!" Eiades gently placed his head upon hers. "I don't know what I've done to deserve all this greatness at once." Puri chuckled, "You consider me greatness?" Eiades, with his head still resting upon hers while staring at the great ring that covered the sky, said, "I've only known you from today, but I feel like I've known you my whole life. I don't know how to explain it, but I feel so close to you!" Puri, with a smile upon her face, replied, "I feel the same way!"

A startled Puri jumped up. "I have to go!" A confused Eiades said, "What? Why?" Puri gazed into Eiades's eyes. "I want to see you again, but right now I have to go. I'll explain later. Will you meet me here tomorrow?" Eiades, still having no idea of what was going on, said, "Yes I will meet you here tomorrow, but why can't you tell me what's going on? Why you have to leave so suddenly?" "I can't tell you now, Eiades, but I promise I will explain later." And with that last sentence spoken, Puri ran into the woods, leaving young Eiades behind.

The solitude breached Eiades's sense of being; with Puri there, everything seemed right, but as soon as she left, things seemed empty. With nothing else left to do or say, Eiades made his way back home where he would have to explain his whereabouts. The more he thought, the more he decided to leave Puri a secret until the time was right, for he knew that distractions were not welcome when trying to learn the Art of Knowledge. In Eiades's world, relationships were highly discouraged unless you were not to become an Incio, and since Eiades was well on his way up in rank, he thought it might be best if he left certain details of his life in the dark.

Eiades nervously walked toward the cottage, slowly making his way near the door, when suddenly, the door busted open with his mother storming out. "This has got to stop, Eiades! Do you know how worried your father and I were just waiting for you to come home? Now get inside!" Eiades, without a sound, walked into the cottage and sat down at the table. His mother paced back and forth in front of Eiades. "Well, what were you thinking?" His father just sat back, watching the show as it presented itself. Eiades stared at the floor. "I guess I wasn't thinking. I just lost track of time." His mother stopped pacing and stood in front of Eiades. "Your father had to do your chores for today, so I only think it's fair that you do his and yours tomorrow." Eiades looked up at her. "I agree. I will get up early to do both mine and his." Eiades's mother looked over at the father. "Try and talk some sense into him. I'm beat from all the worrying, so I'm going to bed." Doing as his wife asked, he got up from his chair to sit next to Eiades. "I know a lot is happening at once with you, son, and I know how hard it is to concentrate on one thing at a time with you about to meet Rezorin, but promise me you'll use better judgment next time." Eiades looked up at his father. "Don't worry, I just lost track of time is all. If I'm going to be out like that, I will be sure to let you know." Giving a look of concern, his father asked, "Are you planning on being out like that a lot?" Eiades, sensing he may have messed up meeting with Puri again, replied, "I just like going out into the woods and practicing my lessons in peace." His father's concern now washed away with a look of pride. "Why didn't you say something before? If your mother and I knew that's what you were doing, then I don't think you being out late would be that big of a deal. Do you at least understand why we're so upset?" Eiades, becoming relieved but also feeling wrong for lying, said, "Yes, Father, I understand and I never meant anything by it." The father got up and placed his hand on Eiades's shoulder. "Well, it's late and we both have a lot of work to do tomorrow, so I think we both need a good night's sleep."

Back in Olma, another conversation was taking place. Puri sat like a mirror image of Eiades in his cottage. Audia paced in front of Puri. "Why must you defy me? Are you trying to hurt me?" Puri watched as her mother walked in front of her. "I can't stay in one spot all day long. I want to see the world and all the beauty you bestowed upon it." Ewar appeared from nowhere. "What's going on here?" Audia crossed her arms. "I come home to find our daughter just coming back from Vianna." Ewar, with a look of disappointment, said, "How many times must we tell you, young lady? You are not allowed out of Olma until you reach adulthood. Until you shed the title of *Keta-spirit* and become a full *spirit*, then and only then shall you go out to explore." Puri shook her head. "I don't know what the big deal is!" Audia kneeled before Puri with her hands upon Puri's knees. "Hear me, daughter, and listen. I don't want you harmed, and that world can be cruel for someone such as you. Your father and I can go out because nothing will happen to us, but you are different. Until you mature, I'm afraid you'll just have to bear the fact that Vianna will have to wait." Without another word, Puri got up and ran off to be alone in the prison she calls home.

Chapter 2

$\mathcal{T}$ he days would come and go, and Eiades and Puri kept their well-hidden secret from the likes of both their parents. Eiades's parents still think he was spending time in the woods, practicing, and Puri's parents were none the wiser of her coming in right before they were to arrive. Their time spent together kept both Eiades and Puri on a high, making them feel things they never had before. Eiades stared into Puri's eyes. "I want to feel like this forever!" Puri, with a smile on her face, said, "Before we take this any further, I need to tell you something, something you may not want to hear." Eiades grabbed Puri's hand. "Nothing you tell me will change the way I feel for you." Puri let go of Eiades's hand. "Don't say things like that until you know exactly what I'm going to say. Things can change in the blink of an eye." Eiades's heart began to beat rapidly as he waited for the words to spill from Puri's lips. Puri noticed the nervousness of Eiades. "I can tell you another time. Let us go walk. I grow tired of staying around this garden all the time." Eiades agreed, then got up from his seat to follow Puri.

The evening was filled with smiles and laughter; Eiades and Puri stayed close together as if they had known each other their whole life. Puri stopped Eiades in the middle of their walking. "If I show you something, will you promise not to freak out?" Looking into Puri's eyes, he said, "There is nothing you can say or do that will change the way I feel about you." Puri, with a smile, walked over toward Eiades, kneeled down to the ground, and with a single finger, pressed to the soil where a rose grew from nothing. Eiades, with a semishocked look on his face, said, "This is what you thought I would get upset about? So what? You're really good with the Art of Knowledge. Let me guess, you're a Tormed?" Puri shook her head. "Not exactly. I'm not like you.

I can do a lot more than you because of who my parents are." Confusion was setting in on Eiades's face. "The Art of Knowledge has nothing to do with your parents." Puri, with a chuckle, said, "It does if both your parents are *spirits*." Eiades gave off a look of disbelief. "No, *spirits* can't have children! Everyone knows that." Puri thought of what she could do to convince Eiades into believing her. "Can you or anyone you know control the weather? *spirits* are well-known for their connections with weather and emotions, right? Well, have you noticed that every day has been sunny and beautiful?" Eiades was thinking of every day he has been with Puri and how she was right; every day they have spent together had been clear sunny skies. Eiades stopped in his tracks to sit down in a meadow while Puri did not realize he had stopped. Within a few feet, she noticed that she was walking alone; she then turned around to witness the frown upon Eiades's face. "What's wrong, Eiades? Should I have not told you?" Eiades played with some blades of grass. "It's not that. I don't care if you're a *spirit*, but I don't know how we will be together." Puri placed her hand on Eiades's chin, pulling his face toward hers. "We will find a way, even if I have to denounce my position as *spirit*!"

The young Eiades, now curious as to what his Puri was capable of, said, "So tell me everything within the life of a *spirit*." Puri, without so much as a thought of what she was going to say, replied, "Well, I'm not really sure because I'm not a *spirit* yet. As of now I'm only a *Keta-spirit*. I am a *spirit* that hasn't fully matured yet, and the only reason why we're kept as a secret is the simple fact that we can die by any means. Even you could kill me. So instead of letting us live our life, they keep us within the realm of Olma until we reach that age." Eiades sat very intently while Puri talked more about her life. "What's Olma like?" "Olma is basically the place where Rezorin looks after all of you. There's a portal on the floor where he can actually watch you live your daily life, but he can only watch one person at a time, and he isn't watching all the time. The entire place is complete white with no walls anywhere. Each *spirit* can create their own portal to watch certain people, mainly the ones they deem worthy to move up in rank, like you." Eiades, with all his concentration, focused entirely on Puri. "I thought I knew everything about the Art of Knowledge, and here I am face-to-face with a child *spirit*." Puri stared into the clouds. "I guess we aren't told things because of what they might mean if we were to find out the truth. As if certain aspects of the truth could change what we think, feel, or even believe." Eiades's attention set on the sun filtering its light through Puri's hair. "I'm sure there is good reason to keep all of us in the dark on certain things. Some people just don't know how to live with change." Puri and Eiades continued talking of all sorts involving *spirits*, Rezorin, and the mysterious place of Olma; Eiades listened as everything he ever wanted to know was being revealed to him through word of mouth.

When talking seemed not interesting, Puri lay down upon Eiades while he lay breached up against a stone, both staring up into the sky and trying to make out what cloud looked like what. "Words can't describe exactly the way I feel for you, Puri. It's almost as if this weren't real." Puri stretched her neck to become face-to-face with Eiades. "I felt the same way when I first saw you within Rezorin's portal. I remember it like it were yesterday. I asked Rezorin who you were and the only thing he said was that you were the most promising student he had ever seen. You know, he watched you quite a lot in the last few months. Every day he would watch you do spells or make potions, and each day he made a comment about how pleased he was with you. He said he sees the dedication in you and how, if you were to become a *spirit*, then he would want you working beside him." Eiades, face turning red, replied, "You mean to tell me that I'm destined to work right besides the almighty Rezorin? So there is a way for us to stay together! This is truly the best time in my life!" Eiades was now resting his head on the stone to just stare up at the sky while Puri began to fall asleep.

Puri stood in a field with large stones lined in perfect unison from one another, each with a different writing. Not knowing exactly where she was, Puri began walking through the massive garden of rock to read a few to gain more insight as to where she might be. The first stone read, "Loving Father who gave his life to protect what he thought was right." The next read something similar; in fact, they all seemed to say more or less that a person resided, buried in front of each stone. Puri now realized she was standing in the middle of a massive graveyard—alone. Each side of her filled with miles upon miles of tombstones, making her feel somewhat isolated. She thought to herself, What could have done this? Where is everyone, and could I possibly be the only one still alive? Puri was now beginning to become nervous, trying to figure out the best way to leave this place; each side seemed impossible. "I can't stay here! There has to be a way out!" A strange voice within the

distance called out in a whisper, "You can't save them! They have to die!"
Puri looked around, trying to find where the voice originated from, but with
no luck, the voice just echoed all around. "Who said that?" Puri was now
walking through the stones, in hopes of finding a way out, until the voice
called out again, "Your death will begin the birth of me. It shall be painful,
and I shall rejoice, for on this day, a monster will be born to destroy all that
you hold dear." Puri's heart was now beating heavily; the talk of her own
demise put fear into her soul, and with no hesitation, she began to run in one
direction. The tombstones, now but a runway guiding her, kept her on track,
but with no end in sight, it seemed useless.

     Puri woke in a cold sweat. Eiades, with a concerned look on his face, said, "Are you all right? You kept shaking." Puri looked all around in a confused state. "It was like I was in another place, like I stayed here with you but my mind was in a field surrounded by tombstones." Eiades embraced Puri. "Think nothing of it, was just a bad dream." With a look of confusion, Puri turned around to face Eiades. "Dream? What is a dream?" "You mean to tell me you have never had a dream? I thought everyone dreamed." Puri, still with the look of confusion, said, "*spirits* don't have to sleep like you do, but for some reason, this place makes me more human. It was an interesting experience. I was just resting on you when I felt a deep calm come over me. I had a hard time keeping my eyelids open, and then out of nowhere, I was in a different place." With a chuckle and a smile Eiades, tried to explain to Puri that sometimes people of this world like to take naps during the day, that sometimes it refreshes them; and she had just did the same, but unfortunately, hers wasn't a pleasant nap. Eiades held his dear Puri. "So what did you dream about?" Puri, with a most unusual look on her face, replied, "That's the weirdest thing. When I awoke, I remembered everything, but as time went by, pieces kept slipping through my memories. I can't remember anything that happened, but I have a feeling it had to deal with something important." Eiades began to laugh. "I'm sure it was nothing, and forgetting dreams is nothing out of the ordinary. Some dreams I can remember every little detail, but others are more difficult. I have no doubt that the dream you had was just a compilation of all the things going on in your life."

     The two sat around in the woods just taking in the scenery as they have done all week, each content on enjoying the other's company. Resting on Eiades,

Puri now turned to face him. "I grow terribly thirsty. Let us walk to the creek so I may get a drink." Eiades agreed, and they both climbed to their feet and began the journey to the nearest creek. The two, hand in hand, walked through the woods, hearing the sound of water trickling in the distance. Finally, they arrived at the source of water as both kneeled and scooped their hands into the creek. Eiades stared at Puri scooping her hands into the water to spread the cool liquid across her face, each water droplet gathering light from the sun, giving off a glistening effect. Puri looked up to see Eiades's stares and, with a smile, said, "Why are you looking at me like that?" Eiades stared into her eyes. "I just can't help thinking that you are the most beautiful being I've ever laid eyes upon. I wonder what I must have done to deserve you!" Puri grabbed Eiades's hand. "I want to show you something!" And with the two hand in hand, a light began to grow. Particles of light appeared from nothing and began to swirl around the two lovers, the wind picking up speed, pushing their clothes in all directions. The two began to lift off the ground while the light particles danced around them like a beautiful display of stars. Eiades looked all around and then into Puri's eyes. "You really are a *spirit*!"

In the distance, a group of hunters were searching the land for their next kill to barter at the market and maybe a little leftover for family supper. The group searched the soil, trying to make out tracks left by a deer or other such animals. A man down on his knees rubbed the ground, finding nothing but disappointment, when all of a sudden, a surprise awaited his glance up. The man witnessed a strange sight, a young man and female floating in midair, kissing. Each member of the group looked at one another in mere shock of the sight they were witnessing. One man looked toward another. "I can't believe this. Rezorin spoke of the Andemous, but I never assumed it would happen within my lifetime! What shall we do?" Each person in the group shrugged, giving no response to the question at hand, until finally, one of the men brought to the table an idea that could make them all heroes. "I say we kill her ourselves! Rezorin will surely be pleased." Each person within the group nodded their heads in agreement as each one of them readied their weapons of knives and clubs, and one person with a rope net.

Eiades stared into her eyes while also feeling the warmth and glow of the specks of light surrounding them, taking in every moment of the dance they were sharing. Remembering all the glitter that spun around shining in the light, the way the sun hit her was like something magical. Eiades, in such a trance, hadn't noticed the several men who were surrounding them. The sunlight was still gleaming, capturing every movement within their dance, and without warning, a weird object from behind Puri interrupted her show. Eiades tried to see the figures that came from nowhere, but the light was still shining until a loud thud echoed through the woods. Eiades dropped like a stone mere feet from Puri who lay on the ground with blood coming from her head. Eiades tried to reach out to his love, but before his fingers could touch her very skin, a sharp pain struck his forehead.

Standing before a cloaked figure, Eiades searched the landscape for anyone or anything. but nothing in sight besides a dead tree and this one figure. The cloaked figure hid his face, but making it seem as if it was staring directly at Eiades. "Don't fight this, she must die! Let your precious Puri go. Let them end her life, and all will be revealed to you in due time." Confusion set in. "What are you talking about? My Puri is going to die?" The cloaked figure moved closer toward Eiades. "It's something that must take place, my dear boy. You will understand when the time is right." With a shocked look upon his face, Eiades began to pace with his thoughts scrambling inside his head. "I don't believe you! I don't know you, and everything you say brings no sense."

Shouting mixed all around, Eiades looked around to see a large group of thirty- maybe forty—people standing around something on the ground. Trying to push the massive amount of pain, he was enduring from the hit to his head. Eiades tried to stand; his knees buckled, and he hit the ground. A voice in the background announced that the boy has awakened from his deep slumber, with several people from the group looking over at Eiades crawling on the ground, trying to regain stance. Three large men walked over to stand above Eiades, one spoke while the other just stood in silence. "What were you doing with her?" Eiades glanced up at the man speaking. "What do you mean? We were just enjoying a peaceful day until you hit both of us and dragged us here!" The man that spoke before reached out his foot to kick Eiades in the stomach. Eiades curled up in pain. "I grow tired of this boy. Now tell me what you two were up to? Don't make me ask you again!" Eiades held his stomach while getting on one knee. "I already told you, we were just enjoying a day together!" The men standing above Eiades grew impatient. "Fine, then tell me exactly how was she floating in the air like that? Could it be because she was the Andemous?" With a chuckle, Eiades stood to his feet, still holding his stomach. "Out of all the Enuck things I've ever heard, that surely is the best!" The two men standing silent grabbed a hold of Eiades's arms while the man in front punched Eiades in the face, blood spewing from Eiades's lip. "I grow tired of you! If she's not the Andemous, then educate me on who she is and how did she gain those powers." Eiades turned his head to face the man. "She's a child *spirit*." The men start laughing. "You must think of us as stupid, do you? *spirits* can't have children, and if they could, we would have known about it through Rezorin." Blood ran down Eiades's lips and onto his clothes. "I know it's hard to believe because I didn't at first either, but what I say is the truth. She told me the only reason we aren't aware of this fact is because they can die by our hands, and so child *spirits* are kept in Olma until they mature into true *spirits*." The two men tightened their grip on Eiades as the man in front shook his head. "Since you aren't willing to come clean, then maybe torturing her in front of you might loosen your tongue." Eiades fought the two men holding him back; the large group of people in the background began to split down the middle. The man speaking with Eiades, with club in hand, began walking over to the thing lying in the middle of the group, which now resembled Puri still within the net. Eiades screamed as the man gently hit his own hand with the club, staring down upon Puri. "No, please stop! What I've told you is the truth, please believe me!" From behind, a voice that Eiades recognized spoke into his ear, "I'm sorry, my son, this has to be done. She put a spell on you so that you would follow her. We are doing Rezorin's work!" Eiades tried to look at the face that spoke those words. "Father, please don't let this happen! She really is what I say she is. I love her, Father. Please stop this!" A tear rolled down Eiades's face, mixing with the blood from both his head and lip. "I'm sorry, my son! She obviously mixed up your thoughts. There is no other explanation for you lying to us."

Eiades fought with every bit of energy he could muster; the man cut the net that held Puri while people from the back tied her hands and hung her to a post, making sure her feet could not touch the ground. The man stood before her with club in hand as Puri was still unconscious from the blow to the head. "Telling me the truth will make this quick, but if you can't seem to tell me what I need to hear, then this could go on for a very long time. So what will it be, young Eiades? You want your so-called love to have a quick death?" Eiades began to grow tired. "Please, if it's killing you're after, then take my life and spare hers please!" His father put his hand on Eiades's shoulder. "She has really messed up your mind, hasn't she, boy? This will be hard for you to witness, but it must be done. Place your faith in Rezorin, and all will be well." Eiades watched as his beautiful Puri awoke from her coma. "What? What is going on? Where am I?" The man with club in hand placed his hand against the post that Puri hang from. "Your boyfriend over there won't tell us the truth, but you will, won't you? Tell me who you are and I will spare his life." Puri looked over at Eiades. "Why are they doing this, Eiades?" The man moved Puri's face so that they can see eye to eye. "I don't like my patients tried. Now tell me who you are and I promise not to hurt Eiades." Tears rolled down Puri's face. "I'm a *Keta-spirit*. Now please let Eiades and I go!" The man shook his head. "I'm guessing a *Keta-spirit* is a child *spirit*, right? Why can't you just admit you're the Andemous?" The face of Puri was now covered with tears, each one dropping to the ground, soaking into the soil. "I've told you the truth! I don't know what else you want from me." The clouds began to grow darker as thunder began to crack and pop while the smell of rain grew stronger. Anger filled the man's face; he lifted the club into the air and bashed the kneecap of Puri. Eiades's screaming could be heard for miles, each person watching in terror as the young Puri's leg was now bloody and bruised with a disfigured look. Nothing but pure pain spilled upon Puri's face while Eiades's cries go unheard. "You bring this upon yourself, young one. Now tell me who you are." Puri gave no answer except screams of pain; the man growing tiresome lifted the club once again, this time hitting the other knee. The club hit with such force that you could see the kneecap shattered within her skin. The group's silence was deafening as Eiades watched the horrors of his true love being butchered little by little, knowing the man would never hear what he truly wanted to hear. "What can I say to you? We've already told you what you want to know, but if you won't believe us, then what else is there? Please if you must kill someone, then let it be me! I don't want to watch her get hurt. Just let her go and take me instead!" The man still standing in front of Puri looked over at Eiades. "This one is for you, young Eiades!" With a massive burst of energy, the man swung the club and hit Puri directly in the head. Eiades screamed as his once-beautiful lover now swung lifeless from her post. The man was now wiping the blood from his club. Eiades's screams became louder and louder. The two men holding Eiades was now letting him go. Eiades dropped to his knees while covering his face. The father kneeled down toward Eiades, placing his hands upon his son's shoulders only to have them brushed away. "Don't touch me!"

The crowd gathered around Eiades with the man still bearing the club standing over him. "Now what shall we do with you?" His father stepped in. "You'll do nothing! He was just under her spell. It will wear off shortly. You'll see." Eiades pushed everyone to the side, making his way toward Puri, who still hang from the post; with all the strength he had left, he lifted the rope that held Puri's hands together off the post. Puri's body was now lying in Eiades's lap; he wiped the blood from her forehead while still crying. He looked up at the silent crowd. "Are you happy now? Do you really think she deserved this?" Eiades, without hesitation, picked up his dear Puri and began carrying her off, thinking that maybe Rezorin could revive her. The crowd would soon disperse to the town so that they may pray to the *spirits* and Rezorin of their good deed.

Eiades, walking toward the garden that he and Puri shared so many precious memories in, looked down upon her face. "Why did this have to happen? I had no idea my people were capable of anything of this nature. The way they just stared, watching you get murdered with nothing to say. How can something like this happen? Why would something like this happen?" Walking through the woods, his energy ran thin as Puri's weight began to become a problem, but Eiades's determination to reach the garden was the only thing keeping him going until, finally, he had reached his destination. He placed her body upon the stone that they had layed upon several times before; Eiades walked over to the middle of the garden to shout into the sky, "If any of you can hear me, please grace me with your presence!" His voice echoed throughout the land but no one around to hear it. "Please, Audia, hear my plea. Help me!"

The group now returned to the town, each one with their own story to tell the *spirits*, each story sounding more heroic than the next, for they helped slay the Andemous all on their own. The Adalum of the town saw the gathering and decided to check and see what was going on. The man who had murdered Puri walked over to the Adalum. "Master Oxidus, we have amazing news for you." Oxidus awaited the news that apparently needed to be shared by half the town. "Yes, my child, what is it?" The man waited for the rest of his group to join in full mass. "We have slain the Andemous!" Oxidus gained a smile upon his face. "This is good news indeed! I shall call to Rezorin so that he may hear this good news."

Oxidus walked toward the altar of Knowledge, inside the Lage, kneeling before it. "Oh, mighty and powerful Rezorin, hear my call. Your followers need your company. Please grace us with a visit!" A bright light began to take shape near the altar, shining bright enough to blind anyone near. Within a blink of an eye, the almighty Rezorin stood before the people of the town. "You have called upon me, and I have graced you with my presence!" Oxidus kneeled before the mighty Rezorin. "Oh, graceful lord, I bring you news of the Andemous! The good people of this town have slain her. She is no more!" Rezorin looked down upon his followers. "I think you must be mistaken. No one of Vianna can kill the Andemous, for only I can vanquish this person. I think someone needs to explain to me what happened in the early hours of today." With everyone silent, the room filled with awkwardness that no one dared break. Rezorin grew impatient. "You, tell me what happened!" Eiades's father lifted his head to face his lord. "Well, my lord, we believed a little girl to be the Andemous because of the things she was doing. I'm terribly sorry, my lord. We had no idea." Rezorin vanished back into the light while the townspeople silently left the school, each and every one of them knowing something went horribly wrong that day but not one of them knew exactly what.

Back in Olma, Rezorin called back everyone of his *spirits*, trying to figure out who, if anyone, was missing. One by one, each *spirit* made their way back into Olma with Rezorin waiting on their arrival. "I need each of you to search all of Olma. I need to know if any of the *Keta-spirits* are missing." Audia and Ewar gave the look of worry, both calling out to Puri but getting no response back; as a last resort, Audia created a portal on the ground to see if Puri might have made a visit to Vianna. The portal opening revealed Eiades holding Puri in his arms in the rain, crying out for someone to save his love. Both Audia and Ewar rushed back to Vianna with Rezorin following behind.

In the garden, Eiades wept as his dead lover lie in his arms, thunder and lightning raining across the land, drawing out Eiades's cries. Audia and Ewar made their way to the garden; Audia rushed over toward Eiades. "What have you done to my baby! Take your hands off her!" Audia grabbed Puri from Eiades's hands. "What have they done to you, my poor baby!" Ewar walked over to Eiades with a pulse of energy in his hands. "You shall pay for what you have done to my child!" Rezorin grabbed Ewar's shoulder. "Killing him won't bring her back. Both you and Audia leave here and go back to Olma. I shall deal with young Eiades." Ewar and Audia walked toward a bright light to vanish back to Olma while Rezorin stood before young Eiades, who was still on his knees, still crying. Rezorin lifted his hand into the air, stopping the rain from falling and making the sun shine bright.

Eiades looked up at Rezorin. "I know why you stayed behind, so get it over with. My life is meaningless now. Without Puri, I am nothing." Rezorin kneeled down at Eiades. "Ewar wants me to kill you, and I'm sure Audia feels the same way, but I know you didn't end her life. I'm assuming you know what she was?" Eiades, with tears still in his eyes, said, "She told me everything, which I tried to explain to the others, hoping that would save her life, but it did no good. Why couldn't they have killed me instead? Her life was more important than mine!" Rezorin placed his hand on Eiades's shoulder. "No one's life is more important than the other. You are worth more than you think." Without looking up, Eiades asked, "So what now?" Rezorin stood, his back toward Eiades. "I can't allow your people to know about *Keta-spirits*, and I can't allow Audia and Ewar to know what happened to Puri. I need for you to keep this secret, Eiades. I know I ask a lot of you, but this is the only way. I will make sure no one harms you. In fact, it shall be a new law that I will enforce myself." Eiades, still staring at the ground, replied, "You know this changes everything!" Rezorin stared into the sun. "I know, my child, you won't be welcome anywhere, and I am truly sorry. For this, I will reward you in the next life." Looking up with a puzzled look on his face, Eiades asked, "Next life?" With a small amount of hesitation, Rezorin began to speak, "I haven't spoken to any of my *spirits* about this, but I'm creating a new world in which all your kind will live after death. I'm calling it Earth, and when you die, I shall give you all your heart's desire." Eiades got up from the ground to walk toward Rezorin. "All I want is Puri!" Rezorin placed his head down. "As much as I want to bring her back to life, I can't, not here. I'm sorry, young Eiades, but that's the one thing I can't grant you." Within a flash of light, Rezorin vanished back to Olma, with Eiades standing in the garden that was now isolated from the entire world.

In a portal opening on the floor of Olma, Rezorin stared down at Eiades from the same place he had left him mere minutes before. "Oh, my dear

Eiades! How I wish to tell you your love will return by your side, but I must keep you away from the rest. I dare not allow the people of this world to know of our ways. For if one question becomes answered, how long until another is asked until my true identity is discovered? These people, with all their innocence, cannot fathom everything I am. In death, you shall know true love as infinite." Rezorin's speech spoke to no one while the portal followed young Eiades into his dark depression.

Chapter 3

$\mathcal{W}$eeks would pass, and Eiades stayed within the confines of the flower garden where he and Puri spent so much time together. Everything that once was beautiful and full of life was now decayed and dying, as if the very spirit of Puri kept everything alive. Eiades stared deeply into the sky; only thoughts kept him company until he finally decided that enough time had passed and he could return to the world of the living. Anger still filled his emotions, but no good comes from hatred and it certainly wasn't going to bring her back, so he had nothing left but this. Thoughts of staying dry also lingered in the back of his mind; for the weeks passed since Puri's death, Eiades seemed to have his own personal rain cloud hovering above. Surely the *spirits* had something to do with this, Eiades thought.

Eiades traveled through the woods until reaching the cabin that he once called home, smoke coming from the chimney with the glow of a fire gleaming from the rain-soaked windows. The sounds of laughter covered what Eiades thought would have been cries of concern for their missing son. He walked up to the door and slowly turned the knob, expecting a long tedious talk about being gone so long and hanging out with the wrong people, but again, Eiades was wrong. His mother and father sat around the table, eating dinner and laughing at some story his father had just told. He walked ever so slowly until his presence was known. "Why are you here?" shrieked Eiades's father. "GET OUT!" screamed his mother. Eiades, extremely confused, stood there in shock from hearing the words he never imagined would come from the two people that should understand. "Well, don't just stand there. Get out!" And with a swift push from his mother, Eiades was thrown out of the house. Standing there alone, staring at the front door, the warming light was still shining from the windows, and laughter now filled the cabin again. Thoughts scrambled through his head. *What's happening? How could those be the same people that raised and loved me from birth until now?*

The rest of the town wasn't much better; Eiades walked up to the Lage, hoping for some comforting words from his mentor. Looking through the window, he saw his teacher, the one who helped him through the years be the successful Torment he so longed to be, going over the Art of Knowledge that he had learned over the years. In Eiades's head, he imagined going into the Lage and being welcomed with open arms and telling his mentor, his friend, of what happened at home and all the horrible things that were burdening him over the last few weeks. In his head, his mentor gave him a hug and offered to take him in as an assistant. That was not how things would happen. As much as he hoped and dreamed, Eiades's own friends and family had turned against him. He walked through the door; the teacher up front gave examples on why different emotions give different effects to certain spells and how being angry made happy spells weak and vice versa. Eiades walked through the middle of the room, which was covered with fifty or so tables and stools lined up evenly to accommodate students. No one seemed to notice him until the teacher stopped his lecture and stared at Eiades. Each student surrounding the classroom kept all eyes on the new coming stranger; many knew of him from their parents, but still, a few had no idea who Eiades was until the teacher began to speak. "Eiades, you're not welcome here." Not believing the words he was hearing, Eiades, standing still, wanted to speak, but no words came from his mouth. "Eiades, did you not hear me? I said you need to leave. You're not welcome here or in this town. Get out!"

Cold, wet, and alone, Eiades set out into the woods, away from everything and anything that he once called familiar. Months would pass and sunlight being nothing but a distant memory, Eiades even forgot what being dry felt like, and the rain still showed no signs of stopping.

The portal in Olma opened upon the sight of Eiades and his now-miserable life. Audia, with hatred in her eyes, stared down at him with a look of disgust. Ewar placed his hand upon her shoulder. "This won't bring her back." Idivant, behind Ewar, said, "Everyone knows that, but this makes her feel better. Let her have this. Not everyone can grieve quietly like you." Ewar wrapped his arms around her, trying to show her that love is more powerful than anger, but nothing sank in; her determination and stare were unrelenting, and nothing would turn her attention away from making Eiades pay for what she thought he had done to her precious Puri. Rezorin sat at his throne that overlooked what was going on in Olma. Audia finally took her eyes off Eiades but glanced toward Rezorin. "You know what he did! Why do you insist on keeping him alive? Others have done things far less severe and have been punished ten times what I'm putting him through." Rezorin said nothing, for he knew this to be true but couldn't bear to tell the truth; if Audia truly knew what had happened that day within the woods, she would want a little more than bloodshed, and Rezorin knew he couldn't lose her to something as trivial as revenge.

The death of Puri would bear more onto Eiades's soul than he might like to admit each day, the wish, the plea, the prayer that it was his life, not hers, that was taken. Walking the land in constant disarray, unable to cope with what he had to witness and with the knowledge that nothing could or ever would be the same. Depression set in until anger and then finally rage filled his soul, which would affect the way Eiades viewed the very life he had lived in the past.

Living within the confines of the forest, the animals were the only thing that could resemble a family or a friend, and no matter where he lie his head, rain would pour as if a never-ending reminder that the *spirits* still blamed him for the loss of Puri. Eiades knew that every town was filled with people who hated the very sight of him, which was the reason he avoided going into a populated area unless it was the only means of getting to where he needed to go. When Eiades were close enough, he would visit his parents' house if only to view them one last time. Each visit would be the same as before; he would sneak up toward a window, and every conversation that focused on him was met with the same outcome. Eiades's father would mention of the son they once had, and his mother would act as if she had no idea of what was being said, like Eiades never existed.

Each night, Eiades dreamed of either his sweet Puri or revenge against the ones who would cause his life to be this way. So each night would be a gamble of either sweet dreams or a night of killing and murder, which would echo in the back of his mind. And even though they were only dreams, Eiades never could shake the feeling they would stir up.

Three years would pass and only a handful of people knew and welcomed Eiades into their home, making the sweet comfort of a bed to sleep in ever so inviting. And even though Eiades knew the only reason he was welcome in only a few homes was because he brought with him rain; he would never let that fact turn down a warm dry bed to sleep in even if it meant being used. He could always hear them speak of him while he tried to sleep. Always the same comments just worded a little differently—"Well, let him sleep for the night, but tell him to leave in the morning. We should have enough rain to last until harvest that way." He would try and let the words not bother him, but sometimes, he couldn't help but feel unloved and alone.

Things had changed so much in his life that Eiades couldn't help but reminisce over some of the things that used to bring him joy—the nights he would stare into the stars and watch the many multitudes of color that show themselves along the ring of the planet, thinking in the back of his mind about how that awesome ring was a symbol of Rezorin's love toward his followers and how lucky he was to live in this time. Then somehow, his life changed within the blink of an eye. How he could go from having everything to having nothing left him a little confused and mainly bitter on the fact that he knew Rezorin basically bribed him with a better afterlife, like this was supposed to make him keep his mouth shut. Eiades knew it didn't truly matter; no one spoke with him, so telling the truth would do little good regardless if anyone would listen. The only real thought on his mind was whether or not Puri would be there waiting for him since he hadn't known that *spirits* could even have children. Would she be there, or was she gone forever? He thought of asking Rezorin, but every call was left with no answer. Eiades was utterly alone to live a miserable existence, only to be used as a tool.

He never stayed in one place for very long, knowing that any linger of time would be met with a dangerous mob pushing him out of the area; no one ever wanted him around for more than a certain length of time. He learned to cope with the feelings of others; but still, every moment, he knew, would be filled with loneliness and solitude; even the animals to which he used to speak with now ran from him.

To Eiades's surprise, one morning, Rezorin decided to grace him with his presence. "What do you want? Come to see for yourself how far I've fallen?" Eiades said in a very angry tone. He stood up to begin his journey to another local, wanting nothing to do with his once-beloved god until he noticed something strange; the rain had stopped, and for once, he could feel the sun's blazing rays hitting his face. "I've come here to see you. I know what I'm asking of you seems daunting, and I'm sorry for the way you must live now." Eiades stood in an open field with his eyes closed, taking in as much of the sun as he possibly could. With his eyes still closed, he turned to face Rezorin. "Out of all the times I called for you, yet you couldn't acknowledge me?" "I heard your call, but so did my *spirits*. I am the only thing keeping you alive right now." Eiades shook his head. "My life doesn't matter anymore. No one will accept me. I'm no longer welcome with my family, and your *spirits* want me dead! I was one of the most promising students in the Art of Knowledge, now look at me! Just looking at the sun is a privilege. I have to move from location to location, and I am used by others that need rain for their crops! Death becomes more inviting with each passing day!" Clouds began to block the sun from sight. Eiades opened his eyes to see rain falling once again with Rezorin nowhere to be seen. "You couldn't even stay to hear me speak? To think I used to look up to you! I have nothing. Just allow your precious *spirits* the satisfaction of my death!" Eiades screamed into the sky.

After ranting to no one, Eiades gathered his thoughts and started walking to a cave he once used to visit as a child, but instead of using the town that lie near the outskirts of the forest, he decided to take the long route, hoping that with no prying eyes to see him that he could stay longer out of the rain.

Moving past the meadow and into a large thicket of thorn bushes and undergrowth, knowing that being dry for more than a week would be well worth pushing his way through this horrendous path. Thorns and needles scraped and poked into his skin, blood dripping and flowing in a diluted state with the rain. He walked through this nightmare for hours until, finally, he looked up to see a clearing within the distance, only a feet from where he stood, and he would be free.

Finally past the worst, he went into a small clearing he had never seen before. The forest stretched in a circle with a hill in the center. On top of the hill was once a large healthy tree, but now it stood as nothing more than a small helpless stump—black, ugly, and dead with most of its limbs either gone or about to wither away. There was something extremely suspicious about this tree; the only thing Eiades had ever seen that was dead had been the garden he and Puri visited frequently, but the garden had laid dead for a reason. *So what could the reason be for this dead tree?* Eiades thought.

Back in Olma, Rezorin stood before his *spirits*. "I will be leaving again, this time I won't be back for sometime. My time is needed elsewhere, but I am in need of one of you. Audia, I need your company with my task. I will eventually call upon each one of you when the time is right, and then and only then will you be allowed to know what I've been working on. I leave you all to your duties." Rezorin grabbed Audia's hand, and in a flash of light, they were gone.

With the darkness of space surrounding them, only light from the blue sphere they were floating above gave off any light. "So this is what you've been working on all this time? Why another planet, Rezorin?" "I needed to create a place for life after death, but I need to keep this quiet, for I don't want to scare the people of Vianna about death, which is why I'm taking each one of you one by one to help me with the final touches. Here will be the place that the few chosen will come to live forever, for Vianna has become overcrowded, and I have decided to place an age limit on everyone except *spirits*, and only I can make the decision on whether someone lives or dies but, more importantly, who comes to this new land." Audia, glaring down upon the new world, said, "May I ask you a question, my lord?" Looking toward her as if he knew exactly what to be on her mind, he replied, "Yes, my child." "Why the favoritism toward the monster who killed Puri? I only ask for justice and yet you allow him to live! Every moment rips me apart knowing Eiades still lives." Rezorin sighed. "There are things you are not meant to understand, but this new world will set things in order and you will be reunited again with your Puri. Now this is the last I shall hear of this. Just trust in me and all will be revealed." With no further spoken words to exchange, Audia set toward the planet to bring beauty and the most glorious sounds known to mankind.

Eiades stood upon the hill, staring directly toward the dead tree stump. "I don't think I'm supposed to be here. I should leave." He turned his back to walk away, but before he could get out of ear distance, Eiades thought he heard a whisper of a voice, *"Please help me!"* He stood, still not knowing if he had just heard what he heard or maybe his mind was playing tricks on him. Turning around to see if maybe there was a person behind the tree or if he were just hearing voices, he said, "Is anybody there?" Nothing more than silence, thinking that the *spirits* must be behind this while walking away toward the cave. *"No, don't leave . . . Please help me!"* Eiades, now becoming confused and, more importantly, irritated, said, "Look, stop playing games and come out where I can see you." *"I'm in the tree!"* Eiades walked toward the dead remains of the tree to see no one, nothing nearby. Thinking of this as nothing but a joke, he started walking off. *"I can grant you your heart's desires . . . I only ask of one thing in return."* Eiades, not listening, kept on walking. *"So you don't wish to make the ones who killed your lovely Puri suffer?"* Now standing still, he thought to himself, *Could this be a trap? Could this be the work of the spirits?* With heavy feet, Eiades reluctantly turned around and started walking toward the dead tree. *"I'm from Rezorin's home world and have been forced to leech of the living to stay alive.* "Wait, Rezorin's home world? Explain yourself!" *"Very well. Rezorin and myself, for many centuries, lived within the same world. We were part of a great war that had gone on since before we were born until something horrible happened and our planet was destroyed. Only Rezorin and I made it out alive. We decided to create another world free from pain and anguish, where every living soul would live in harmony. Everything was going beautifully until Rezorin's greed got the better of him. He wanted me out of the picture, and well, here I am. I have survived off the living, but I am growing weak. I can grant you the powers of Rezorin. I only ask of one thing in return."* With a look of disbelief upon his face, he said, "How can I trust you?" *"I've seen the misery they are putting you through, and I want to help. But I can no longer sustain myself by simply living off plants and animals. I need a soul to share. You share with me your soul, and I will grant all my many powers in return."* Eiades considered the proposition but needed to be sure this wasn't a trick. "How am I to tell if you're telling me the truth and not just a *spirit* in disguise?" *"To be perfectly honest, what do you have to lose? I've seen inside your mind, and far as I can tell your life can get no worse, except in death."* As much as he hated to admit, the voice was right; there was nothing more for him in this world except death, and even that didn't seem too inviting if Puri wasn't a part of the afterlife. But almost as if out of thin air, a thought occurred, which, from his mind, spoke into words from the lip, "Wait, aren't you the one Rezorin warned us all about in the beginning of creation?" *"So he knew I may have still been alive. I'm not at all surprised that he may have foreseen this, and even though I should seek out revenge, all I want to do is talk to him and try to reason with him. All I want is to be friends again since we are the last of our kind."*

Rezorin watched as Audia finished up her work upon the new planet. "As always, my child, your work never seizes to amaze me!" "You grace me with your gratitude, my lord. Is there anything else you need of me?" "No, but I may call upon you at a later date. Please send Ewar my way. I have a few tasks for him as well." "Yes, my lord." And with a swift flash of light, Audia vanished to head back to Olma.

A very paranoid Eiades, still standing before the dead tree, thought to himself, *I have no reason to listen or believe anything this voice is telling me.* Then the thought occurred to him. *I'm listening to a voice. I think I'm going crazy!* The voice was still making its presence known. *"You may have no reason to believe me, but I've been watching you for quite sometime, and I know you have nothing to lose. We both have something the other can give, and I'm willing and able to help you. All I ask for is a little trust."* As much as Eiades didn't want to admit what the voice said, he couldn't help but feel that it was correct; he did have nothing left to lose. He lost his future and his partner to the few people who were supposed to be understanding, and yet they no longer accept his own existence. If he were to take this offer, he could be more powerful than any *spirit* known to him and, quite possibly, an equal match to Rezorin, whom he wanted to teach a lesson to.

Thoughts of revenge now clouded his common sense of this being a trick; not even death lingered in the back of his mind so to detour him from making what could be a horrible decision. He could feel a sense of pressure taking control, a small nudge in the back of his mind like something nagging him to accept. With much thought and consideration, Eiades finally made up his mind and accepted the deal, but not before asking of a few conditions in return. "I will agree, but I need a few promises from you first. One, I want to know what you and Rezorin are, like what world did you two come from and are both of you really considered gods. Two, I need to know that I will have full control over my body and mind, and if I so choose, I want the right to deny you from my body at any time. And last but not least, I need to know what kind of a match I will be against the *spirits* and Rezorin. I just want to know that I won't be bullied by them anymore. *"We come from a distant land that had been destroyed by war and greed. The person you know as Rezorin is no more a god than I. We can be destroyed, which makes us mortal, but only a select few are capable of doing such an act. I give you my word that if you deem it necessary to relinquish me from your soul, I will accept this decision, but I ask that you allow me to find another suitor. And the power I am willing to give is more than enough for any and can be considered equal to that of Rezorin. You will understand more fully when we merge together, for all the knowledge I have will become yours and vice versa."*

Audia was standing over Ewar, a small portal on the floor showed the view of a young male in an attempt to steal goods from a store. The view from the floor followed the young male with each movement; everywhere the character moves, the view moves with them. Then when the moment was to finally arise, the young man looked all around the area, making sure no eyes were to be pinpointed in his direction, his hand slowly reaching out to grab the prize he so very much wanted but didn't have the means to purchase or barter. A tiny voice spoke out softly within the back of the young man's thoughts, "Is this really worth it to steal something you know to not be yours?" Audia, with a smile upon her face, said, "I love how you try to speak sense into some of them. You don't tell them no, but you let them see what they fail to see." The young man's hand stopped before hitting the prize and slowly went back into his pocket. The shopkeeper, seeing everything, walked toward the young man and said, "I'll make you a deal, son. I need some work done with my harvest, and if you can do all the things I need done, I will start you off with a tap here." Audia began to shed a tear. "But more importantly, I love the compassion and love that each of them has the ability to show."

The portal was now closing while Audia spoke to Ewar on the place Rezorin asked for him to attend. Without question or comment, Ewar took a step back and vanished within a flash of light to go speak with Rezorin on his new project. Rezorin walked among the new planet he had created as a haven for the dead. Ewar walked up behind him. "You called upon me, my lord?" "Ah yes, very good! I called upon you and soon the rest of my fellow *spirits* to help me finish this place of rest." Ewar, taking a knee, said, "Anything you ask of me I shall do." Rezorin placed a hand upon Ewar's shoulder. "I don't really need anything of you besides an ear to listen. I know you and Audia are having a difficult time with the loss of your beloved Puri, and I assure you all will be revealed in due time, but as for now, I need you and the rest of the *spirits* to go easy on Eiades. When the time comes, I will allow her to explain everything, but for now, I just need you all to do this for me." Ewar lifted his head to stare into Rezorin. "When she explains, my lord? I do not understand." Lifting Ewar up from him kneeling, Rezorin said, "You shall be reunited with Puri, but only when this place of rest has been completed." And with a giant leap and a hug, Ewar grasped his lord into his arms until finally realizing what he had done. "My lord, please forgive me. My emotions had gotten the better of me." "Fear not, my child, for your emotions are what make us all unique. Now go and remember what I have asked of you."

Eiades approached the dead tree, slowly walking toward the stump and waiting to see what would happen. Would there be pain? Would he feel anything at all? Finally, a light branched out from the tree, slowly wrapping around Eiades, engulfing itself around him. He was being lifted off the ground, a mere feet from where he once stood. All the warmth and comfort he had so missed within the last few years were rushing into him, making the feeling ever so inviting. The light danced around him in a playful fashion until finally all the light that had surrounded him merged into his very being, making the light and him one. It rushed into him with such a force that Eiades began to scream until finally the light glowed its brightest. Before too long, the light reached its end from the tree, and all that showed was a dancing display of light surrounding Eiades, still rushing into him. Finally, all the light and glow that had accompanied him now rested inside, and Eiades was slowly lowered to the ground in the fetal position to sleep and recover from the tremendous force of what just occurred.

Chapter 4

Eiades woke up next to the dead tree, feeling dazed and confused to what exactly had just happened. "I feel so weird. What, what just happened to me?" And as if someone else was talking from Eiades, a two-toned voice emerged, *"Your body is trying to coup with the powers I'm giving you. Since we now share bodies there are several things you must get used to."* Eiades thought of all the things he could now do with his new friend. "Maybe I should cast the gray clouds and let the sunshine through." *"Before you give away your hand, try doing nothing so you can catch your enemies off guard. No one knows what you're capable of, and this will give you such an advantage."* Having a conversation with what seemed like no one, Eiades had his ordinary regular voice, and while the other soul spoke with Eiades's voice, he also spoke with his own, giving a two-toned sound that resembled two different people talking at the same time. "I will resort to doing nothing, but I need to know how people really feel about me. I need to know if anyone out there cares for me." *"I know the perfect way to find out!"*

Audia stared down within a portal on the floor in Olma while Ewar stood behind her, wondering what exactly she was doing. "Why must you stare into the dead gardens? Eiades hasn't gone there in several months. I doubt he's coming back. You probably can regrow everything by now. Matter of fact, you could probably have Nephia and Neuw help you since they both have reached the age of maturity and can now go out into the world." Silence was overtaking the room in Olma, Ewar waiting for a response but was met with nothing—no word, no response to anything he had said. What little did he know was Audia's thoughts scrambled over what Rezorin had spoke about at the new planet. Could Puri really be reunited with her? If so, how long would it take for her to be able to wrap her arms around her precious daughter again? The thoughts of what Ewar spoke of was also molding the idea of her other son and daughter helping her regrow the gardens in which Puri loved so much. Then, as if a shocking revelation dawned on her, where was Eiades? She waved her hand across the portal to show the location of the one person she hated so much, but nothing happened. "Ewar, come look at this. I keep trying to find Eiades, but the portal isn't showing anything." And sure enough, Ewar waved his hand across the same portal, and again, nothing happened; the same view stayed in place. "Should we get Rezorin?" Audia asked Ewar. Scratching his head with a puzzled look upon his face, he said, "He should know about this unless this is something he is a part of. When he comes back from his project, we shall ask him, but for now, we will leave him be. After all, that's what Rezorin wants."

Eiades stood on top of a hill, staring down at his home town, gazing at the townsfolk going about their daily duties, thinking of all the ways of making all of them pay while Hanuse's, the entity within Eiades's body, plans were already underway. "The *spirits* can no longer save you! I will strike in the morning, once I've had a good night's sleep." Waving his hand in midair over the ground, a thick cover of grass grew, covering a bed-shaped area. The rain was still falling, but before the flow could reach out to Eiades, it split over him, leaving everything around within a foot of him dry and everything around that soaking wet. He lay his head down, looking up to see the rainfall until his dream took him.

He found himself looking over the town in the dead of night; everything straight in view was clear but a hazy cloud haloed the outer view. Everything was becoming a blur; one minute he was on top of the hill, the next he was standing in front of a door—the large wooden door that looked somewhat familiar—until finally, the door struck his memory. This would be the place that housed his parents. Everything seemed quiet and calm. His unwilling hand reached out to open the creaking door, pushing it ever so slowly until, finally, there would be enough room to enter. The outline of the furniture and other household items were the only things to be seen within the darkened house. Eiades watched through the eyes of the figure that would lurk in his old home. The figure casually walked around, searching and spying at every little thing until finally coming to the room that held the sleeping parents.

The hand, with palm open, reached out and placed itself on the door, gently pushing the door ajar to reveal a single bed with two individuals fast asleep. The view would fast-forward again from the front of the door to the edge of the bed. The figure leaned over, just watching, gazing upon the people who would slumber ever so innocently. Thoughts would scramble of all the nasty and horrible things Eiades's mind ever conjured up over the years; thoughts that only helped him feel better but would never act upon.

The hand rose upward, making simple motions in the air. It seemed as if something was happening, but nothing could be seen or heard. Finally, the father's eyes opened, and as if their minds were linked, the mother also came to consciousness. Before the two parents could say a single word, the figure placed his finger upon his lips to keep them quiet . . . and for some reason, it was working; no sound at all was coming from anything around. Walking over toward the father who seemed to sleep carefree within his own dream world. The hand reached over to grab the father by the neck, lifting him out of bed and into the air, while the mother remained speechless, confined in her bed. The mother tried to speak, but no words escaped her lips, and even though no words were spoken, a voice echoed within the figure's mind, "What is he doing here? Wait until we speak to Audia. He will surely pay for this!" *Could that voice really be the thoughts of my own mother?* Eiades thought. The figure never spoke a single word, just a small chuckle or two to show the true enjoyment he was having. A strange thought appeared of two sharp objects, and then as if out of thin air, two knives flew through the air and pierced the father in both his shoulders to pin him against the wall. Thunder and lightning began to roll in as if to set the mood; something or someone must know a tragedy was about to take place. The mother, now with a shocked facial expression, was all the while trying to set herself free, with tears rolling down her face, and the same voice of hers screamed within the figure's thoughts. The father strung to the wall *toward the ground* with blood flowing behind him with pain in his eyes. The two, still unable to speak, could do nothing except deal with the fact that this day could very well be their last.

Thunder crashed, lightning struck; the outside violence of nature brought down the fury of emotions of anger and revenge being displayed in front of the helpless victims. Wind picked up speed as the cabin creaked with ever blow from outside. The mother, still silently crying, twisted and turned to set herself free from the confines of her own bed while the father helplessly bled from the wall. Eiades stood and stared as he watched the people who brought him into this world suffered by what seemed like his own hands. He heard the father's pleading thoughts, begging to allow his wife to be set free of no harm, and the mother's thoughts remained to be nothing but screams.

The figure walked toward the mother until a small set of footsteps came into earshot. He turned around to witness a set of small children standing at the foot of the door, each holding some form of stuffed animal while staring with a look of horror upon the man against the wall. The figure raised his hand toward the children, and with a swift motion, the little ones formed a circle while their stuffed animals surrounded them, keeping them in place. All their thoughts rained down upon Eiades, all the screamings and begging all mixed together. The figure, who seemed to have no concern over who or what was in the room, looked down upon the mother who still remained in the bed with her face soaked in tears. He looked over toward his left at the window, staring at the storm, watching as the chaos unfolded out there and then back into the chaos that he was causing within the confines of these walls. Finally, he lifted both hands toward the wall, and as if in sync with the storm, the entire wall cracked and shattered out toward the world as a large sound of thunder hid any noise coming from this small cabin.

A wild chaotic wind blew into the room, the victims covering their faces in a desperate attempt to escape the attack toward their faces. The newly found opening let the storm cause havoc on the inside of the cabin. The figure glanced over toward the mother; with his hand up in the air, the mother was thrust out into the wild. Rain poured down, making the once-dry woman now soaked. The figure stepped out toward her as she crawled backward in the wet mud. The look of horror instilled upon her face. Silence still overtook the atmosphere while the screaming thoughts still echoed for the figure to hear. The son listened to the begging and pleading from his mother while his father was still fighting a losing battle against the wall. The figure set out his hand, palm facing the ground. A set of four rose vines shot up from the soil, each one wrapping itself around the wrist and ankles of the mother, wrapping itself around the flesh. The vines cut and dug into the skin, blood flowing out and blending in with the rain. With the veins fully fastened and secured, it began to lift her up into the air. Rain fell, and hopes began to fail;

her thoughts no longer asked for mercy but instead were replaced by a quick death to end this nightmare.

Stepping back into the cabin to face the father, the figure stared into his eyes, glancing into every painful expression. *"Look into me! The last thing you see will be my face in time of death."* The father's eyes met the figures, and slowly, his life diminished into nothing. He had thoughts of prayer for the *spirits* to come to his wife's rescue and to be forgiven but nothing to reconcile over the pain he placed upon his son.

Tiny little hearts beat across the room. The children looked with fear as they still confined to the floor. He stared as Eiades could see every thought, every small little action that the figure was thinking of doing to the helpless witnesses. "They're only children. How can you think of doing such a thing? Please I beg you! Don't do this!" *"Fear not my little ones, for you have chosen your fate when you followed your god!"* And with a swift motion of his hand, the figure reached out to the knives holding up the father. The sharp projectiles loosened themselves from the wall and into the figure's hand. Standing above them and with one quick and fast motion, the figure swiped both weapons, one in each hand, across the children. At first nothing, but as time passed, the damage could be seen—their necks, which were once clean, now were flowing red of a waterfall of blood. No screams, only silence as the mother watched. Her tears mixed with rain, her mouth gaping open as the lifeless little ones now fall to the ground in a heap on the floor.

She tried to set herself free, but with every tug, every forceful movement, the thrones of the vein dug deeper into her skin. The figure walked toward her with the blades still in his hands, bringing them closer toward his face until his tongue and their blood were one and the same. An evil smile reached out upon his face, showing that all this was merely a game. Thoughts of anger now spread from the mother and into the figure's mind, thoughts of her god and the *spirits* and how her son would pay for everything he had done this night. Eiades's confusion set in. "She said her son." His thoughts scrambled to decipher what all this could mean until, finally, the mirror on the wall told the truth. The reflection standing before him was his own; he was responsible for everything. The blood dripped from his hands, and his father saw his own son before he had died, and his mother was being tortured by him.

Eiades woke up in the same spot he remembered falling asleep. His head throbbed as the sun, which he hadn't seen in years, bared down upon him. Walking down to the nearest creek to spread some water upon his face, he noticed a large hue of red coming from his hands, and with a look down, the sight of a crumbling red substance fell to pieces from his palms and fingers. At first this sight seemed unnatural, and the thought of what it could be escaped all he knew until the flashes of what he thought was a dream from last night instilled into the back of his mind. *It can't be true,* he thought. *It was only a dream!* A panic began to spread until Eiades drew short breaths. A faint whisper called out from the back of his mind, the same voice of his new friend and the figure from his dream. *"Calm yourself!"* "What have you done to me? You killed all those innocent children and my parents. How could you do that to my mother and father?" *"You speak of innocence like it's a real concept. How amusing. You should know better than most that no one is innocent, not children, not your family, not even the one in which you called god!"* "You've made me into a murderer. I never wanted this. I never wanted to become a monster." *I made you into a monster? Everything I did last night came from your very thoughts. You thought of it before I ever acted. All of you speak of things as if the world is so unfair, yet you have no basis of comparison. I've given you everything your little mind wanted—power, revenge, and control—yet the first time you see what your wishes bring, it's suddenly not right and I'm the one you blame. Where would you be without me? Still stuck in the darkness of days, talking to yourself about how horribly unfair life can be and about how no one cares if you lived or die. I've given you the world, and you repay me with talk of me making you into a monster. If I only acted upon from your thoughts, then what does that make you?*

A loud cry came from the town nearby. Eiades ran toward the screams, hoping to help fix the mess he had help cause. He ran up the hill to see a sight that would haunt him until the end of time—the town stood in ruins, piles of ash and debris were all that remained. Burned figures littered the landscape. The only true standing structure happened to be Eiades's parents' cabin. Only this time, a wall was missing from the side of the home. The screams had been coming from here, where a young couple who happened to be passing through started investigating the surroundings when they stumbled upon the murderous scene. Eiades's father lay on the floor, stuck in his own blood. His mother lay against the bed, her wrist and ankles cut open. Her arms rested with three lifeless children wrapped in her arms, their necks cut. Blood marked on everything, flaking with just the slightest touch.

People now appeared from the forest; one by one, they reached the town only to stare in awe as the once-beautiful town lay in ruins. While the majority just stood and stared, a small few ran to dig through the remains that maybe their loved ones would be the lucky few, but nothing could be salvaged, no one could be saved. After much weeping, the people who gathered to mourn would eventually turn to Eiades as he still stood before his parents' cabin, staring down at his blood-encrusted hands. The crowd gathered behind him, each with anger in their eyes, each with violence in their hearts.

Eiades could feel something happening, something he couldn't explain. It felt as if the world was slipping from sight, the same tunnel vision as the dream from last night. He could feel his arms and legs going numb until he couldn't feel them at all. He could still see and hear, but it felt as if he was looking through someone else's eyes. Eiades no longer had control of his own body. *"Your thoughts of suicide will ruin us both. I've decided that to better both our life's that I will take over indefinitely!"* The people around him took a step back for everything that was said was spoken aloud with a two-toned voice. The figure that once claimed the name Eiades stood up. Facing the crowd, he drew a smile, and with hands raised high, a large group of vines grew from the ground behind them, blocking their path. A sinister laugh could be heard for miles as the caged group of people would soon meet the one Rezorin warned them about so many years ago and how their foolish and careless ignorance brought them to this point by the death of a small *spirit* child named Puri.

Chapter 5

*R*ezorin was still concentrating on the fine details of his new heaven, the intense work bearing down upon him until suddenly he was finished. Floating down to inspect every little thing, he noticed something in the distance. A few feet ahead, in a bush, something had made its way into hiding. Going in for a closer inspection until three small children jumped out to grab hold of Rezorin's waist, all three soaked with their own tears. "My children, how have you come to be here?" All three were sniffling, wiping the tears from their wet faces. "We don't know. All we remember is a storm with a man standing in front of us with a knife and then we were here." Rezorin stood with a surprised look until a thought crossed his mind. "Do you remember nothing else besides the man with the knife?" One of the little ones stopped crying long enough to talk about a sharp pain on his neck and then a bright light. This sharp pain followed by a bright light could only mean one thing to Rezorin—these young children had fallen to death and were now part of the new world in which all who were deemed worthy would go. Chance would have it that Rezorin had decided to allow all children who would die before the age of ten immediate passage.

Perplexed at the thought of anyone on his world committing such an act, he decided to take a few precautions before heading back to Vianna. He first made shelter for the three children; a hot meal and fire awaited them inside, and as the three began to head toward the new structure, Rezorin grabbed the last of the three. "Can you keep a secret?" said Rezorin as he kneeled down to face the child. The child stared up, his wet face drying as the wind began to blow. "I need to share a very special secret with you, but you have to close your eyes." With both eyes closed, a bright light began to emit from

Rezorin's mouth. The light spread all around, turning and twisting around the young child, covering him from head to toe. The child still waited, but no words would ever leave Rezorin's mouth until, finally, the child opened his eyes only to discover the blinding light. All the light that had come from his mouth now came to a stop; he stepped back to witness the child being lifted from the ground while the light began to sweep faster and faster around him. Scared and confused, the child began to panic, his heart racing. Wind picked up speed, blowing everything in all directions except the child and his light. Rezorin was still standing down below just watching, waiting, until suddenly, the blinding light took over and began rushing into the child. As the light passed into the child, all that could be seen was the look of agony, but as soon as the light came, it suddenly vanished. The seemingly lifeless child was now slowly being lowered back to the ground. "I know you can't possibly understand this right now, but you are their last hope. May the *spirits* be with you and your offspring to guide and train all that must be taught." And with nothing else left to say, Rezorin opened a portal to return back to Vianna while leaving the child lying on the ground to recover from what had just happened.

Before Rezorin would have a chance to make his way back to Vianna, the *spirits* had their hands full with the uncontrollable Eiades. Bodies would litter the ground while blood soaked into puddles scattered about. One brave *spirit* named Neuw, who just became mature enough to join the ranks of full *spirit*, walked up to Eiades while he was in the middle of murdering an innocent victim. He had the poor female held high off the ground, his nails digging into her throat until her blood covered his entire arm. Neuw screamed for Eiades to let her go, but it was already too late; her life had already left, and all that remained was her lifeless body dangling helplessly in Eiades's hand. As he requested, he simply dropped her dead body to the ground and faced the now-alone *spirit*. Eiades stepped slowly, each step grew him closer to the *spirit* that dared interfere with his good time. Neuw grew nervous as he watched Eiades take a long lick from his blood-soaked arm, *"Oh, how I love the taste of innocence!"* "That's close enough. Take not another step forward, or I'll be forced to act!" A sinister laugh overtook Eiades as he began to step even closer. "I warned you!" Neuw's hands now extended with a giant pulse of light coming from his whole arm; it reached out and struck Eiades in the chest, knocking him to the ground. People who were in hiding began to come out to clap and cheer while in Olma, the *spirits* stood above a portal, watching and cheering as well. Neuw now let all the applause sink in and, with his confidence boosted, began to walk toward the fallen Eiades, keeping one hand out to make sure some form of weapon had its hold on this murderer while a flash of light from the sky brought all the *spirits* away from Olma to make sure they had a great seat for the live punishment about to take place. Audia, floating overhead, shouted words of encouragement while Ewar reminded everyone that even though Rezorin was away, he still made it clear that Eiades was to not be harmed. Ewar's words made Audia grit her teeth, but everyone knew he was right, Eiades was to remain in the land of the living until Rezorin returned, and of course, Audia thought that he would certainly change his mind about this monster after hearing what he had done now.

The crowd formed a circle around the two, each chanting and shouting words of encouragement toward Neuw while Eiades slowly brought himself to his feet. A small amount of blood dripped from his mouth while a shadow overcast above him. Neuw now stood above him. At his ready to finish the task, Ewar tried to yell above the crowd, making certain that Rezorin's laws were absolute. Seconds felt like minutes as Neuw delivered the final blow; Eiades now lay lifeless on the ground as a sudden burst of energy pulsed from Neuw's body and into Eiades. From Ewar's prospective, everything grew silent; everything around him was slowing down as if time itself stood still. He slowly walked toward his son, trying to think of what he could possibly tell Rezorin to spare his son's life and make everything all right; nothing came to mind. He almost reached his son when the lifeless Eiades rose from the ground. Ewar, witnessing this new sight, tried to warn his son, but it was already too late. Ewar's arms waved his son, still accepting cheers from the crowd, all the while Eiades standing on his own two feet. Neuw's back toward him gave the perfect advantage. The crowd began to notice, and no one said a word; silence was now the only thing being heard except Ewar who was still screaming for his son to turn around. Confusion settled in as Neuw slowly turned himself around to look down upon Eiades; only what he thought and what he saw were two completely different things. Ewar would watch in horror as his son was lifted off the ground by his own neck. Eiades, with the same sinister smile as before, said, *"Do you really believe that a weak little thing such as this could possibly end me!"* Everyone around heard the tone of his voice, but all gave the look of confusion to everyone around them. Audia made her way toward the tragic scene, but it would make no difference for as soon as she would make her way to save her son, Eiades had already ripped her son's head from his body. Panic would ensue as everyone began to scatter about. Audia, in a fit of rage, ran toward Eiades, but Ewar grabbed her to bring her back to Olma.

Rezorin, now back in Olma, witnessed his remaining *spirits* gathering around a single portal, viewing the man who had killed one of their fellow kin. He pushed his way toward the center of the crowd, no one saying a word to their lord, only speechlessly watching. In the portal, Eiades stood in the middle of a town, sparing no one. Men tried to fight as best they could, but nothing prepared them for this onslaught as each man who stood in front of Eiades was ripped limb from limb. Some women held their infant children by their bosom with children old enough to run traveled beside them, all trying to find a safe place to hide; few got away, but the rest were met with death. The blood began to gather in puddles in the soil, and the only thing to be heard were men crawling on the ground in agony, trying to call out to their god. If you listen closely, you can hear the helpless women praying and the children silently crying in the confines of their hiding spots.

Rezorin stepped back with the look of horror upon his face, each *spirit* looking over at him, not knowing what to say. Audia made her way toward him. "Rezorin, please you have to do something. Our people are being slaughtered by the hundreds!" But before Rezorin could speak, one of the *spirits* yelled out something, "My lord, what is young Eiades doing?" Everyone near the portal watched Eiades walking up a hill and beginning to chant an odd language toward the sky. The clouds turned dark and began forming overhead; the winds picked up in a chaotic fashion, blowing debris all around. Audia looked up toward Rezorin. "But, Rezorin, he isn't strong enough with the Knowledge to know how to control the weather! What's happening?" "Something I wish no one had to bear witness." And as Rezorin spoke those words, something was happening down on Vianna. The trees all around began to grow dead and fall apart under their own weight; the grass, which was once green and alive, turned brown until it showed no more. Everything around the area changed from living to dead within a matter of a few seconds. Mounds of soil began to shift to the surface in different areas around the hill at which Eiades stood. Something started making its way toward the surface, first hands and then arms. This scene began happening all around, and all the *spirits* could do was watch as these new creatures emerged from the ground.

The wind picked up even more speed as more creatures found their way into the living; thunder cracked the sky while lightning struck every few seconds. Eiades, with his arms held high, kept on with his chanting, his voice growing louder, which echoed throughout the land for all to hear. Everyone in Olma was still staring, hoping Rezorin had an answer on what to do, but their lord just as speechless as the rest. "My lord, why are you not striking Eiades down with your mighty powers?" said Ewar. Rezorin placed his head within the palms of his hands. "I suppose I need to explain what Eiades is now." Each *spirit* was standing attentive, staring at Rezorin, while, at the same time, gazing upon each other in a confused state; no one could understand how their lord could allow this to happen. "The person you see as Eiades is no longer the same person. He has most likely been replaced with someone I used to know in a different life. I had warned you about this person when I created you, and I asked of the first four to warn the people of this planet. But there are a few things I haven't spoken of. This new person is my brother." A small amount of whispering began to spread throughout the *spirits* as Rezorin now stood with his back away from his loyal followers. "We come from another world that had learned like many of you on how to use the Knowledge but were so far advanced that our power equaled that of a god. A great war called the Omatta War, which was waged on my planet for many a millennia, left most of my world in ruin until my people had made peace with the majority of the other fractions. The only group left was that of my brother's. Everyone except him had decided to surrender. He had always been stubborn in his ways. To him, death was more inviting than losing. Everything was set up for the Peaceful Age to begin, but we didn't know that my brother had other plans. He created a weapon that had the destructive power that would destroy an entire solar system." The whispering had now stopped as every *spirit*'s attention was now focused on the story coming from Rezorin. "I had left to make my way toward the ceremony, but as I was walking, I saw my brother carrying a weird-looking device in his arms, making his way toward our Sun. At the time, I had no idea what he had, but I did know I needed to stop him. I knew him all too well, and whatever he had, I knew, wasn't going to be good. So I followed him. I tried to sneak up on him, but he saw me coming and threw the object toward our moon instead. The explosion was so massive that no one had time to escape. The blast that blew me farther into space passed our solar system, also carried my brother. We both floated around space, unconscious until I awoke to find him above me trying to throw me into the nearest star. We fought for what seemed like forever until I finally had enough. I mustered up every little amount of energy I had left and called upon a very powerful energy and then . . ." One of the many *spirits* called out, "And then?" Rezorin then looked up. "And then nothing. I had killed my own brother!" The crowd gasped and then silence.

Eiades was still standing upon the hill while the new army began gathering around him; the wind, thunder, and lightning were still littering the landscape with a massive storm. He lifted his head toward the sky to finish the chant he had begun several minutes before until, finally, he was done and the sky brightened a little to allow a small amount of gray to break through the black skies. *"My children, the time has come! With this new plane,t we shall shed no mercy, allow no one to survive! There is no such thing as innocence, and we shall practice this through our actions. Now go out into the world, sniff out the remainder and add to your brothers!"* The speech had come to an end and the army went out into the world to make sure their master's orders were followed.

In Olma, the *spirits* were still standing in front of Rezorin. "So you've been lying to us this entire time? You never were god!" "Whether or not he lied is beside the point at this time. We have other problems at hand. We need to find a way to handle Eiades!" called out Ewar. Each *spirit* looked at one another. "How do you suppose we do that? He killed one of us already. He is much too powerful for any one *spirit* to handle." Rezorin turned to face his *spirits* to push his way toward the middle of the conversation. "With my help, we may be able to cripple him long enough for me to think of a way to fully destroy him. Although I don't know what else there is, I had already used the most powerful thing I knew and even that wasn't enough." "We must try or everything we know to be will come to an end!"

Women and children hiding in the bushes were eventually found; these new creatures seemed to have a certain sick way about them. They could smell fear, and they seemed to feed off pain and agony. They eat flesh, but they seemed to act as if they didn't have to, anything to cause pain to their victims. Many tried to run, but it made no difference, for this new army could run and track anyone that could feel fear. Hours would pass and very few people were left alive, for the beauty of the planet was now replaced with the scattered remains of all who had lived here. And with each corpse that lay on the ground, another creature would join the ranks of the army.

"My brother will not stop until everything that I've created has either been turned over to him or destroyed." The *spirits* looked down through a portal to watch as the army, which had grown massive, ran around the planet to kill and destroy everything within their path. As they all stared in awe, watching as the innocent were torn apart, they watched as men with farming tools tried with all their might but ended up being a bloody pile of nothing on the ground. Evony broke away from the group. "Please, Rezorin, there must be something that can be done?" Rezorin placed his hand upon her shoulder. "I'm sorry, my child. He has called upon an ancient form of magic. He has called upon the Evower Army." "The Evower Army? Is that anything like the magic you tried to destroy him with?" Rezorin was still staring into the portal, watching as the army destroyed everything he held so dear. "Yes, it is, but the only people to learn that form of art are the ones with darkness clouding their souls." All the *spirits* turned away from the portal to face Rezorin. "So what can we do?" Rezorin took his eyes away from the portal to look into the eyes of all the desperate souls within the room. "With this army at hand, he has become too powerful for any of us to take on one on one, but if we stick together and try to work as a team, we may have a chance, but I'm going to need the help of all of you, especially the first four." But with a simple look around, they found that Audia had already left Olma.

Ewar approached Rezorin. "You have to help her. She is still bent on revenge." Rezorin then opened a portal to see exactly where Audia had headed. It was then that they realized that Audia had been gone much longer than they had originally thought. She lay motionless within an artificial bubble on Vianna, Eiades standing above her with the worst intentions.

Chapter 6

*A*s the many *spirits* discussed with Rezorin what should and what needed to happen in order to keep their planet from the likes of the person who was once known as Eiades, Audia walked a few feet away from the crowd and opened a portal where no one could see to make her way to inflict revenge on the one person responsible for taking her child.

She had made her way down to Vianna without causing any attention toward herself, and sure enough, Eiades was still standing upon the hill with the many creatures branching out to secure the people of this world. She slowly made her way toward him, hoping to catch him off guard. While he turned around to walk down the hill and over toward the next town and as he passed through a valley, she made her move. As he walked through the valley, he suddenly hit his face into an invisible barrier. Audia created a temporary bubble that would sustain the both of them. At first Eiades was a little confused, but eventually, he knew what was going on, and with a swift turn, he now faced Audia. *"I knew it was only a matter of time before you finally faced me."* "You will pay for what you have done to my child regardless of who you are You being Eiades means nothing to me. I will still call you a murderer." *"It amuses me how ignorant you can truly be. The truth was and is staring you in the face and yet you still can't face it. What if I were to tell you that Eiades wasn't the person who allowed your precious Puri to be killed? What if I told you that even though he is trapped within the prison that he calls his mind that his feelings for your daughter are still as strong as the day they met? You deal with pain with revenge and anger and that I respect, but the way you blindly follow these emotions is less desirable."* "YOU LIE!" Audia's face now withered with the painful memories of her daughter, wishing she had known to check on her so she might have been able to stop her death. "Do what you will, for I am tired of these little games of seek and revenge." "I will make your death an example for all to see!"

Audia made her walk toward Eiades, every second soaking into her mind. Every precious moment seemed to slow down as she imagined all the pain she was about to inflict. "You don't deserve mercy even if Rezorin request it for you." Eiades just stood there, without a smile, just a faint expression of nothingness, waiting as Audia made her way toward him. She finally stopped mere feet from him; she breathed slowly until finally taking in a giant breath of air. She made sure no one was around before she attacked as she knew that anyone within a few feet from the two of them would also be harmed. Audia then let out a screeching tune; birds flew from nearby trees, and small animals that had been hiding within their homes underground scattered to get away from the noise that was piercing their ears. Eiades dropped to his knees as soon as the voice came from her lips, the look of agony replacing the blank stare he had worn before. Audia kept her stand with a smile on her face as she hovered over him, trying to inflict even more pain. After a few minutes, Eiades lay lifeless on the ground. Audia stood over him with a sense of satisfaction and accomplishment.

Her job was done, and it was now time to tell the *spirits* the good news while breaking the bad to Rezorin, but something was wrong; no matter how hard she tried, she couldn't create a portal, and the barrier that held the both of them was still standing. "This doesn't make any sense. It's like all my powers have been taken away!" As much as she tried to figure out what was going on, the only thing to come to mind was Rezorin. "I bet he took my powers because I disobeyed him. Well, no matter, power or no power, this had to be done." But as Audia stared into the barrier trying to figure out a way to set herself free, she had not noticed Eiades slowly pushing himself to his feet, giving the same sinister grin as before when he had been killing all the other innocent townsfolk. He watched as Audia felt around the barrier he helped reinforce, making it impossible for her to escape. He slowly walked up behind her, keeping the element of surprise.

Without a sound, Eiades stepped up behind Audia as she still looked for signs of freedom. With a quick thrust, he grabbed her by the throat and lifted her from the ground. Her hands took hold of his arms while she gasped for air, struggling to release his hand from her neck. *"Did you seriously think you could defeat me so easily? I thought Rezorin taught all of you better than that!"* Her desperate attempts would soon not matter as Eiades threw her into the barrier with such force that blood began to come from her mouth. The impact created such a blow that the barrier swayed in and out like a raindrop hitting water. Audia held her side, which carried with it such pain; with every breath carried a new form of agony. Blood was flowing from her mouth, nose, and ears as if the very foundation of her mind had been liquefied from within her skull. Blood poured from her side as a rib stuck out from her body, piercing her white robe. Eiades made his way toward her. *"The one I share this body with has much hate toward you, and I will do what he cannot. His hatred is strong but not strong enough to do what must be done. I made an example of one of you already, yet you still attempt? Such a pity. I thought Rezorin would have taught all of you better, and now you will beg for death by the time I'm done with you!"*

She lay withered on the ground, barely holding herself up as her tormentor stood above her, calling out all the ways he would inflict pain upon her. His hand reached out to grab her by the hair while she tried to resist, but it was of no use. His strength tossed her across the area in which they were confined, and again, she crashed into the barrier but, this time, headfirst. The impact left her without movement while he continuously chuckled.

By this time, the *spirits* have arrived while watching the tragedy that had shown true within the barrier standing in front of them. Nephia and Ewar rushed over to the edge of the barrier, trying to grab Audia's attention, banging their hands on the force field while yelling. Audia was still motionless where she had landed before with no amount of yelling or commotion waking her; Eiades was standing before the crowd with an evil grin staring at Rezorin, his hand raised over Audia with a bright shining light coming from his palm. Suddenly, she would rise with a good portion of her blood flowing back into her body, her rib forcing itself back inside her with her becoming conscience once more. Ewar screamed for her to teleport out of the bubble, but no sound could enter or exit. She reached out and placed her hand upon the wall where Ewar was standing; he reached out to place his hand upon hers, and a single tear ran down her cheek. Her lips mimicked I love you, and then Ewar began to shed tears as well.

In her last stand, nothing else was left to do but try and destroy this monster once and for all. She opened her mouth and screeched as loud and as powerful as she could. The *spirits* outside all closed their ears and dropped to their knees where the only people standing were the two brothers from a distant world. No matter how loud or powerful her voice could get, nothing was having any effect on Eiades. *"Do you see, brother? This is what happens when you play God!"* She continued as Eiades grabbed her by the back of the neck and flung her across the area; this time her body crashed hard enough to break the barrier, and she continued flying until her body would be stopped by a very large tree within the distance. Without a moment's pause, Rezorin opened a portal and sent Audia back to Olma.

Rezorin stood before Audia while she tried to gather enough strength to push her way off the floor; with every push, her body would crumble back to the position in which she had previously been in. Other *spirits* appeared one after another until Ewar and Nephia made their way back. They pushed their way toward her weak body; Ewar took her hand while Nephia stayed close by, each with tears running down their faces. Rezorin looked into Ewar's eyes. "It's worse than I thought. I could hear Eiades being tormented inside his own mind." Ewar took a moment to tightly grip Audia's hand, and then he looked up at Rezorin. "And what does that mean?" "That means Eiades no longer has control over his own body. My brother, Hanuse, has taken over completely. Eiades must have been weaker than I thought, for that is the only way Hanuse is able to fully take control of any one person." All the *spirits* were talking among themselves, "Now what do we do?" "There is no way for any of us to go up against him!" "Who's to say he won't come for us here in Olma? We've got no place to hide!"

Tension filled the air as resentment filled the emotions of all remaining *spirits*; each felt betrayed that Rezorin kept what he truly was away from them. Rezorin could see their looks; he could feel their thoughts turning on him. "I know I should have let all this known, and for that, I ask for your forgiveness, but don't let this new problem change the fact that I created you. You seem to forget how all of you came to be, on how hard I have tried to keep all of you safe, how I've spent every waking moment of my life here loving all of you as my own children, my own flesh and blood." The room changed dramatically as each *spirit* now stared at their feet. Evony pushed her way toward the front.

"It's not that we don't appreciate all you've done for us, but we feel betrayed. You lied to us throughout our whole existence. We just want you to be honest with us. We can handle it." Rezorin stepped toward Evony, placing his hands upon her cheek. "My dear child, no, you wouldn't have understood for none of you are at the level yet to allow such information to truly sink in. I keep things from you just like I keep information away from the people who live on Vianna because you all are still too young."

The people on Vianna tried their best to fight, but with no proper training and only farm tools and other such simple things at their disposal, they were of no match. Eiades's teacher gathered around the remaining left to help guide them with speech. "This is our time, my fellow men and women. This is the time to show Rezorin what we are made of. This test shall weigh in our true faith, and as long as we stay true to the Art of Knowledge, we can overcome any obstacle! Let your faith guide you, show you the true path, let the Knowledge guide you toward the light of truth, for without Rezorin, we are nothing! So let us bear arms and fight until nothing remains of this new evil. Let us banish them all to the evil place from which they came!" The crowd were so into the speech that many shouted and screamed for blood and vengeance while raising their weapons of choice into the air; some wielded racks while others held axes or shovels.

Rezorin gathered his remaining *spirits* around Audia. "Listen, my children, we haven't much time before he shows himself here in Olma. I've foreseen this future, and in that wake of insight, I've planted my seed on the new world you had helped me create, but I must ask a lot of you and even more from one of you." He stopped his speech to stared down at Audia. "I never wished this to happen, but I don't know of any other way. I cannot save you all from his wrath, and it is already too late for the inhabitants of Vianna. What I must ask of you will not be easy to accept, but it's either this or death. Before any of you decide upon the idea I have to offer, I just want you to know that I truly loved every second of every day that we had spent together. I consider it a joy to have been able to watch all of you grow above and beyond my expectations and that I would never change a single moment. You all have been and always will be my children, and no matter what happens from today until the end of time, I will never be disappointed in the outcome." Each *spirit* were rendered speechless while Ewar held Audia, who still remained lifeless on the floor.

Nephia remained weeping by her side. Rezorin placed his hand upon Ewar and then leaned down toward Audia. "Please save her, Rezorin!" Ewar cried. "How can I make you understand? He has already taken so much out of here by keeping her alive this long." All hope now faded from Ewar's eyes while a small tear rolled down his cheek and dripped down to hit Audia's forehead. Within an instant, a small glimmer of life appeared in her, and she began to wake but still in a great deal of pain.

The remaining people on Vianna stood at attention while the Evower Army gathered on the opposite side, each group waiting on the moment to attack. The sun was shining above with nothing but blue skies as far as the eyes could see. A gentle breeze blew the foliage back and forth in a very calming manner; birds could still be heard chirping. Everything about this moment was calm and peaceful until a screeching voice broke the silence. Hanuse yelled for as loud and as long as he possible could; no one knew what any of the noises meant except for his faithful army, for when the noise escaped his throat, the army began to storm forward toward the opposing force. The earth shook, which made the birds leave their nest throughout the trees. A small few of the remaining men traded looks of confidence with looks of terror and confusion as when the massive number of the army approached, they knew their end was near.

Audia, with all the strength she could push out of herself, managed to lift herself to her knees, and with a little help from Nephia and Ewar, she was able to stand upon her own two feet. Rezorin ran his hand down her hair and then to cuff her cheek. "My beloved Audia, I know you've been through so much, but I need your strength right now. You are the only one that can help me in defeating this new evil brought into this world. You and I are the last remaining hope for our people." Audia was being held like a doll on strings as she raised her head. "Whatever it takes to destroy him!"

The army, with their razor-sharp nails, sliced through flesh and bone as each monster cut at the remaining survivors. The remaining few left tried with all their might to kill as many as they could, but each hit only delayed them slightly. Blood drained from Rezorin's creations, and with another death came a new member within the army, making their numbers unstoppable. Hanuse stayed behind the massacre, laughing as he watched each one of the many townspeople cry and scream for help. *"Pray for your god. Ask for his help! REZORIN! REZORIN! Come help your followers. Come save them from death!"* Each one of the soldiers from the army, with their blood-soaked hands and teeth, looked for their next victim, smelling the air to catch the scent of fear from within the bushes. Women and children with silent tears lay sitting within a ditch, waiting for the moment where it would be safe to come out, but that moment would never come as the army found their scent and would soon drag them out. The children would be among the first; the mothers and cowardly fathers could do nothing but watch as their children were torn limb from limb. Mothers reached out for the safety of their little ones, but they too would meet their end with each attempt of saving their children.

Rezorin stroked Audia's hair as Ewar and Nephia continued to hold her up. "I need you, I need all of you to understand what's about to happen. With Audia's help, we will join as one, and with this, a weapon will come forth. This weapon is unlike anything you have ever known. It will have the ability to give any of my offspring the power to kill a god. When we join, we will no longer be. I will be the weapon while Audia's *spirit* will be the only thing encasing my power. Only someone with my blood running through their veins can unleash the fury trapped inside." "But, Rezorin, you don't have any children," said Evony as the other *spirits* nodded in agreement. "While I was down upon the planet in which I have created as a place to rest, I happened to come across some children who had already died on Vianna. I only knew of one person who could be capable of such a tragic act, so I shared my soul with one of the children. The only thing that can save us now is what rests inside that small boy!" Rezorin stepped back away from Audia to face all his *spirits*. "I ask all of you to guide the last surviving children of the new world, and when our last hope grows old enough, he will need to be trained. This is a tricky magic. It calls for everyone left with the Art of Knowledge."

Mothers and fathers watched in horror from what little was left whole of their children on the ground-blood-soaked soil littering all around, limbs of each child scattered all about. A fearful mother ran past the monsters to slide across the soil to reach for her daughter who had been split completely open from side to side; her bottom half lay somewhere nearby as her entrails emptied out on the ground. Her mother reached down to forcefully stuff her daughter's inside back in, the mother's tears dripping down onto the daughter's open eye. A scream, a shout of pain rang out behind the mourning mother, and with a look back, she would see the terror of all her fellow people being slaughtered one by one.

They would run and panic, but nothing would stop the torment. One man ran past the others only to hear their agony echo through the air until all he could see behind him were the dead in pieces in a murderous heap several feet behind him; not a single monster could be seen, which gave him a small glimmer of hope, until he faced toward his front that held a single monster with his sharp claws extended out. The man would run right into the sharp claws with enough force that assisted with his own beheading.

Rezorin would try to completely reach out toward the *spirits*, but even though they all seemed to understand what was at stake, none could truly realize the future to come.

Chapter 7

*R*ezorin gathered with the remaining *spirits*. "Come stand in a circle with me. Ewar, bring Audia toward the center." Each *spirit* stepped in their own position. "I must warn all of you, what we are about to achieve will take more from you than you might have. Weakness may consume every inch of you, but you must stay focused. Everything that happens now will determine the outcome of our future." Standing at the front of the gathering, Rezorin lifted his hands while a pulse of light began to emit, which traveled from him and onto to Audia. The *spirits* all joined in with his actions, each lifting their hands, while Rezorin started chanting in a weird language with light coming from both him and all the other *spirits*. Light traveled from everyone to Audia, the light gaining strength until her lifeless body lifted off the ground to float several feet in the air. Her body stood in standing position, her legs stayed straight while her arms branched out from her body.

With innocence not enough to save the last remaining of Vianna, each monster gathered in different sections of the region to take out the last survivors just as their master had demanded. At first only men would step out to stand against the army, but such as before the women and children with the small remaining cowardly men would be found last, everyone suffered the same fate. The fighting would continue through the darkness of night.

Audia glowed with such amazing light that everything around was blinded. Rezorin still chanted his nonsense until all of Olma shined with the light of Audia. This light spread further than any light before it, such was the power of greatest sacrifice in history. The confines of Olma would not stop this light, and soon Vianna would be gifted with the bright star in the sky, bright enough to light up night as day. Both man and monster stopped long enough to stare up into the sky to gaze upon its beauty, but as quick as it came, it vanished without a trace. Some saw this light as a sign of hope, but Hanuse knew that this could only be the work of Rezorin. *"You have only delayed me, my brother! I will have this world and any other you have deemed worthy for your people!"*

The gathering stood in the midst of the light until, finally, it would vanish; both Rezorin and Audia went the way of the light. No sign would be found of either, which brought a river of tears down Ewar's face. Each *spirit* broke out of their circle, some sitting down from being extremely exhausted from such power surging from their bodies while others talking among themselves about what to do next. Ewar held on to Nephia as they both grieved over their lost loved one until a stranger showed his presence. Ewar stared into the face at which he promised to protect via Rezorin's word. "Eiades, what the hell do you think you're doing here?" *"You speak to me as if we know each other. Trust me. You know nothing of me. Rezorin only showed you the good side of himself but dare I say he never spoke of all the bloodshed that we both had such a great deal of pleasure accomplishing."* Silence took over the room, each *spirit* looking at one another in an attempt to signal for something, anything that could possibly help their situation. Each knew what Hanuse was capable of, and none wanted to end the way of Neuw.

"I should have foreseen this. How could I have been so gullible? No matter, it will just take me a little longer to accomplish my ultimate goal!" Hanuse began his walk toward the *spirits* with a sinister grin; in his mind, terrible things would accompany his actions, but the moment he reached the still-mourning *spirit*, an invisible wall stopped him. He tried with all his might to push his way through this barrier, but nothing allowed him entry. Frustrated and confused, he stood back, thinking of what to do next but every possible answer to this mystery proved to be nothing but a failure. *"I can tell he loved you all very much. The magic he used can only be performed by self-sacrifice, and that could only be the thing stopping me from killing you!"*

With nothing more to accomplish, Hanuse vanished into thin air while the *spirits* evaluated their future with no Rezorin. Tension and sadness filled the air, each *spirit* too weak and exhausted to even consider going after Hanuse.

Ewar, still holding Nephia in his arms, glanced over at the chair Rezorin had always sat down to speak with him or the others, knowing his presence would surely be missed. Breaking apart from Nephia, he grabbed a small cloth to hang over the chair, thinking to himself that if Rezorin wasn't here to fill the seat then no one should. He began placing the cloth over the chair until a small scroll lunged into the back caught his eye. He turned the scroll completely around to reveal his name written in big bold letters.

My dearest Ewar:

    If you are reading this, then the sacrifice has worked, and I am no longer among you and the others. I'm writing this mainly because I hadn't had enough time to fully warn you and the others of what must happen in the coming years. Hopefully I have fully made aware that my blood is now walking around the new planet I have dubbed Earth and will need guidance before ever coming close to destroying my brother. So I put all my faith in the last remnants of you and the others, only with all your guidance will we have any chance.

    With everything I kept from all of you, all I can say is I did it for the safety of you and the people of Vianna. So I have a small confession to make. On the day Puri was murdered, it wasn't Eiades who killed her. The people of Vianna saw her using her powers and assumed she were the Andemus. I asked Eiades to keep my secret safe about Keta-s pirit, and even though he agreed, he grew bitter and angry over the events after Puri's death. He joined my brother because of me, and I bear that burden alone. We all left him alone; we all saw him as a burden and nothing more. Before the death of Puri, I watched over the two. I saw them that day in the garden. I watched as they sat underneath the stars and yet I never spoke of this for fear that you or Audia would intervene, and for this, I'm sorry. I wonder what could have happened if the people of our planet knew the truth. I always assumed more questions would follow, and that dreadful question of whether or not me being a God would come forth, so I kept all hidden, but this time nothing but pain came from my actions of not knowing. Nothing I can say will ever make up for the secrets I've kept but know this that I only kept things of this nature to myself to protect everyone.

I write this letter to you as a guide for the next coming years that will test the very foundation of all your well-being. The magic used for sacrifice was nothing you or anyone else, not even my brother, has ever seen—so powerful that a protective force is now surrounding you and the other s as we speak. My brother will no doubt try everything in his arsenal to overcome this, but even this is beyond his understanding. The love we shared throughout the years gave me enough power and momentum to fuel the sacrifice, which is something he could never fully comprehend.

The generations to come will face something that not any of us have ever witnessed. An army of such large numbers is gathering even as you read this letter. You must show strength, for whoever goes against this army will need all the help that you can allow.

I wish I could be there to answer all the questions I know you must have, but I'm afraid that is not possible. My brother's gift is the ability to live in, or dwell if you will, into anyone of his choosing. He can control dreams, read thoughts, and with enough time and patience, can alter the very memories of the victim. So the less you know and understand, the better. The one and only thing I can truly tell you is where Audia and I went. I spoke of a weapon, something my blood can use against my brother. Well, think of me as the most powerful orb of energy and Audia as the casing that keeps me from becoming free. When unleashed gives the user the ability to destroy pretty much anything; it is very close to being the most powerful thing in existence. From what I've learned about this type of magic, it appears to be very unclear on how the user obtains this power. I memorized the scroll in hopes of fully understanding: "Only when truth is set free shall the power find its true home." I've spent centuries trying to figure the true meaning, but with no example of this type of magic being used within my lifetime, it seemed impossible.

*I hope this scroll finds you, and please tell all that still remain
that I never wanted this to happen and that I will always love them.
Our future now rest in your very capable hands.*

With Love Always,
Rezorin

Ewar rolled the scroll up and looked at this fellow *spirits*, his eyes beginning to water with a small amount of rage filling his soul. Idivant asked what the scroll had read, but with a second look upon Ewar's face, he backed away.

On Vianna remained the last casualty of what would now be known as the Great Massacre. He lay against a stone, his stomach completely cut open with his insides resting in his hands. The lower portion of his intestines wrapped around his fingers, blood mixing to create thick goo like substance that covered both his hands and lap. He stared into the sky, hoping, praying that all this could be a dream, a nightmare in which he would awaken from. These thoughts would linger until his body grew cold, and finally, his last breath left his lungs.

Everyone who once lived now have nothing but a distant memory; no hope lingered on as dark gray clouds filled the sky. The stars became covered as gray clouds moved slowly into view; the symbol that once showed Rezorin's love for the planet, Ouri, was now shown no more. The years that came after remained bleak with no sign of hope. The mountain of Ulma, later known as the Vice, where Rezorin trained only the most promising of students, began to crumble all around its sides. Ulma would remain intact at the highest levels, but all around would hallow out over time. With no sunlight, the vegetation withered and died, which killed off all the remaining animals. Within only few years, the planet became barren and dissolute. The only structure that remained intact would be the castle Hanuse himself summoned from the soil of Vianna. The rock castle stood overlooking a large hill, its gates stretched twenty feet in the air with another smaller gate fifty yards farther downhill that housed his army.

Ewar guided the rest in the final wishes of Rezorin, each given a task at hand to assure the survival and guidance of the bloodline of their lord. The following years to come would be testament of everything they believe in.

Epilogue

The Bloodline Written by Ewar

𝒯 he first generation proved to be extremely willing and able to accept their fate, but with each generation after another, the words of our lord began to thin, and more questions would be asked, questions I couldn't give the answers to.

The Art of Knowledge is nothing more than a simple myth now; only a few people still believe, but society as a whole has long forgotten, and even the true believers know not of Rezorin, but only the mere basic principles of the Art of Knowledge. To watch these people live along with no guidance from a god of any sort is both depressing and entertaining. They live in filth, knowing not of love and peace. Anger and fear dwell within most of their hearts while greed and selfishness linger through their thoughts. I've grown tired of watching them fumble around with no clue as to where they came from and why they are here; some ask but only for their own reasons. I'm lucky to see a good kind person within a handful of them.

The first of the bloodline was more than willing to be trained and be accepted as one of the few to bring down the Evower Army, but with the inability to find Audia, he soon met with his death. Hanuse took great joy in destroying the first one but we did well in hiding his offspring; needless to say he was most unhappy to find yet another within the blood line. An oversight he surely would never make again.

The second generation, though still accepting their fate, proved more difficult to train. We made the unanimous decision to allow the chosen one to procreate before training, which is a difficult option when love isn't part of the equation. Luckily, she found someone who struck her fancy and another was born, but training didn't start until a year later, which might have been the reason why she was no match for the army. This time, Hanuse allowed his creatures the satisfaction of the kill. I wish I could say it was painless and that she died with honor, but none of those would be true. They caught her off guard one afternoon while she was picking fruit to eat; they gave her no warning before ripping her to shreds. I still hear his laughing as she begged me to save her; these memories will never leave my thoughts.

Without Rezorin to provide proof that any of what I was teaching was true made convincing all the generations after the second incredibly difficult. Our religion was slowly dying, and with society losing faith at a tremendous rate, it looks as if Hanuse will win this war.

I tried to keep the faith and continue what Rezorin asked of me, but the more time went by, the more some of the other *spirits* began losing their way. Nephia continued by my side; she still hopes that one day her mother would return with Rezorin. I don't have the heart to tell her there isn't much hope, that our religion was that of a distant memory, and that the only ones to save us rest in the hands of Rezorin's bloodline, which is something I'm beginning to lose hope.

With each passing generation, Hanuse began using certain methods of temptation; most looked the other way, but the ones who gave in became his greatest students. With all the many lessons taught from our faith and with only a few minutes Hanuse had the few who would listen at his side. Maybe I should have tried harder. If only Rezorin were here, for his guidance could have saved them.

There is only one left. Hanuse made sure to completely tear apart this young man's life. After Seth's father joined Hanuse, something I have never foreseen, his mother mourned her way into a deep depression, which led to her suicide. I can still feel his soul tearing itself apart after he walked into the kitchen to witness his mother's lifeless body hanging from the rope, a single chair knocked over by her feet. I shed a single tear as he and his brother stood at her tombstone while the authorities rushed the two to an orphanage. Since then, I had lost track of Seth until now. As I had predicted, Hanuse has already invaded his dreams and has frightened him enough into running away toward the big city. He manipulated Seth's brother and foster mother into believing he never existed. Seth is truly alone.

This next generation will test the very foundation of everyone left. Nephia has already voiced her concerns, and Evony has been watching over him for the last few days with tears always running down her face. I shall make my way into his culture slowly, and with each slow step, I hope to gain his trust over time. I just hope something I say will fully reach him. From what I've seen of him, trust is not something he knows or is something he will give very easily, and with him being the last of the bloodline, I hope I can either make him strong enough or convince him to bear another.

Each day, I hope for the return of Rezorin; since his departure, I've had to bear witness to every evil action known. Only two generations of the bloodline ever came close enough to unleashing the power of the weapon in which Audia and Rezorin created so many years ago, but they have all failed to free the power that lurks within. We still are unaware of how the two actually found the device, and they seemed just as clueless when asked. It pains me to know that I can show them what they are up against but can't guide them to the means of ending this war.

Tomorrow, I shall embark on the journey. This will test everything I have left in me; if I fail to enlighten what most likely is the last of the bloodline, then both Vianna and Earth will fall to the darkest reaches of hell. The Great Massacre will happen again, and all will be lost; our faith and freedom remains on the line. This will be the end of us all if I fail. Let Rezorin's teachings guide me through these dark days and into the light.

Evower

Chapter 1

S chool had just let out a couple of hours ago, and young Seth and Stan remained playing outside until their mother came home. Every day was the same—school would let out and both brothers ran to their bikes to see who could beat the other home; and of course, the outcome was always the same. Seth was older, so Seth always won. And even though Stan never won this little race, he never paid much attention; he just felt glad to be included. Once they both made it home, the bikes got pushed to the ground and playtime would begin. Both would be laughing and giggling as they play tag until the same familiar noise of a car pulling into the drive would arise—Mom's home! They both ran up the hill to see the same blue station wagon, but this time, something new was about to show its face.

Both Seth and Stan ran up to greet their mother when, out of nowhere, a strange man got out of the passenger side door. Seth, giving away his look of confusion, stopped in his tracks and stood there motionless. "Who is this?" Seth replied. Seth's mother gave him the evil eye and said, "Don't be rude, Seth. This is Steven, and he will be staying with us for a little while, just until he gets back on his feet." Seth was still standing there a little confused; all the while, the stranger slowly got out of the car to greet Seth. The man who stood from the car looked Seth in the eye and, with an evil screeching tone, said, *"Pray for an end!"*

Seth wakes up in a cold sweat, still confused from his dream; he wanders around, trying to grasp his position. Looking around, he comes to realize that he is still standing in the alleyway he calls home, the same location he found seven months ago when he ran away from his family. Staring at the bright full moon in the sky, Seth begins to ask the same question he always asks every night when he wakes up from a cold sweat—"What's wrong with me?" Seth doesn't understand, but his dreams mean more than he could ever possibly imagine. With the new day, the young Seth stares up at the sky, the sun trying to overtake the big city, its light beaming off every building, giving an orange hue over everything. The scenery was always breathtaking, but Seth knows the importance of getting an early start, and so he begins preparing for his day.

Seth stands to see who has come back to claim their piece of alleyway; several people occupy both left and right, many starving and cold. But he can't be bothered by any of them, for he knows what it's like to be homeless—never being able to trust anyone, never knowing where you're next meal is going to come from, and most importantly, always looking out for yourself because helping someone else could get you killed. It takes a heartless bastard to survive in this city. Seth has been beaten several times to get that point across, but every beating added an extra shell to his soul, making him stronger, making him more immune to the heartlessness that he has to see every day. He still remembers every person, every child that couldn't make it in this rough terrain. Seth will always remember.

The day started out the same. Seth walked around each alleyway, looking for food in the dumpster; and if that was to fail, then he would have to try and get cleaned up enough to walk into a store and steal the food he was going to eat. He walked down several alleyways, one right after the other to find nothing, when, out of nowhere, he spotted several grown men beating an elderly gentleman. At first Seth ignored what he was witnessing, allowing only the sounds of the tormentors. "This is the last time you ask me for change, old man. Every day I walk down this street and every day I have to deal with your bullshit. How about instead of asking me for change, you go out and get a damn job, you piece of shit!" The old man, with his hands over his face, said, "I'm sorry, I didn't mean to cause any trouble. I just need some money to get something to eat is all!" The tormentor punched the old man in the stomach, and as he fell to the ground, the tormentor began to brutally kick him. Seth glanced over but does nothing except turn around to walk away. But something was different; he kept hearing a very faint voice telling him to help this victim. After a few minutes of thought, the voice began to get louder when, out of nowhere, Seth turned and started walking toward the violent scene. With no thought, Seth grabbed one of the men blocking the main tormentor and threw him across the alleyway into some trash cans, almost as if he had the strength of ten men. Next, he grabbed the main bully by his neck and lifted him off the ground. A strange feeling had come over Seth, something he couldn't explain, almost as if he was in a dream, not being able to control his actions. Seth was having trouble controlling himself, but what's worse was that he was not quite sure if he even wanted to. All the anger and depression Seth had dealt with his entire life was being released into a huge ball of rage. The struggling man stared down into Seth's eyes, the look of fear held strong upon his face. His friends were just staring, not knowing exactly what they should do or if it even would matter.

The other men stood and watched the horror that Seth was showing. Seth's hand clawed its way into the man's skin, and in one instance, Seth ripped out the man's throat. The man's body, once beaming with life, was now an empty shell, blood flowing out like a waterfall. Seth, still holding the large chunk of flesh within his hand, held it up in the air where he just ripped it from the man's body; and with a calm motion, Seth just tossed the external portion of the man back unto him. Speechless and stunned, the men just watched as their friend's dead body lay lifeless on the ground of that empty alleyway. With a smile on his face, Seth tilted his head toward the rest, as if to say, "You're next." The men wasted no time to run away.

As if he was waking up for the first time, Seth came to his senses. He looked around to see the chaos he had caused, staring at the bloody heap that lie on the floor and then at the bloody hand that caused the crime. Looking at the old man, Seth said, "What exactly happened here? Did I do this? I thought I was dreaming." The old man, bloody and beaten, stood up with a smile and said, "Thank you, young Seth. I knew this day would come. I knew we would find each other some way or somehow. I just hope it isn't too late." Seth, still standing speechless, had much of nothing to say. With blood trickling down his hand and Seth's mouth wide open, he could do nothing but turn around and walk away.

Not knowing what was going on, Seth was having a hard time dealing with all that had just taken place. He sat near the river in a lifeless gaze, talking to himself. "I couldn't have killed that man, could I? There was no way I could just lift him off the ground like that. He was three times my size. What's happening to me? I actually felt happy while I was killing. This can't be happening!"

Seth's breathing was getting faster and faster, his heart beating a mile a minute. He was having a hard time controlling himself, his thoughts racing. What should have been an everyday search for food turned into a murderous rampage where an innocent man died by the hands of Seth. His heart raced as he was unable to control the very breaths his lungs would take in until Seth crashed to the ground.

Seth and Stan sat down at the dinner table, their mother busy in the kitchen, finishing up dinner. Steven was sitting across the table, staring at Seth with a grin on his face. Stan was unusually quiet this night, almost as if he was afraid to speak. To break the tension in the room, Seth started to speak to Stan, "What's wrong, Stan? You are usually chatting up a storm about school? You didn't even mention how show-and-tell went. Did everyone like the dummy you brought in?" Stan said nothing, allowing the room to remain in silence.

Finally, the mother walked in the room with a large dish with steam coming from the lid. Seth looked around to see if their mother can brighten up Stan but still nothing; this worried him. Then out of nowhere, Seth looked across the table at Steven and still witnessed the same grin as before. Seth, speaking his mind, looked Steven in the eye and said, "WHAT! Why do you keep looking at me like that? Is there something you need to say to me?" But even with Seth's confrontational words, Steven said nothing. A little irritated Seth opened the lid to finally eat that night's dinner. At first he couldn't really seem to see anything; all the steam rushed out of the pot and into Seth's face, but as soon as all the steam floated to the top, Seth finally glanced down into the pot. The pot held the severed head of both Seth and Stan's mother. Frightened and confused, Seth dropped the lid and began to scream. Shaking and scared, Seth began to look for his mother, first within the empty kitchen he had just seen her walk into, then into the living room with the darkened silhouette of his mother sitting in the rocking chair. Still a bit shaken up, he started to rest his breathing. Slowly walking toward the figure, he began to speak, "Mom, is that you?" His mother calmly lifted her head to speak, "Yes, honey, what's wrong? Come closer. Did you have a bad dream?" Seth slowly walked closer to his mother, just enough to have the light from the moon shine down to reveal Steven behind his mother, his hand shoved through Seth's dead mother's back. Steven's hand ran through the back and neck into the head, almost as if Seth's mother were a puppet. Steven was using his own hand to make the dead puppet speak and, with his clever changing voice, mimicked Seth's mother exactly. With this scene, Seth rushed outside, not knowing what to do or where to go. He ran through the woods behind their house, thinking of nothing but getting away from the horrific scene he had just witnessed. Panicked and scared, Seth continued to run until he tripped on a stump and lost consciousness.

A large group walked past Seth's body, yelling, "Get a job!" Seth finally woke up from his deep sleep. Day had become night, and with his sleepy confusion, he looked around, trying to make sense of things, and with a simple look down at his hand, he realized that what he had done wasn't part of the dream. Seth made a mad dash to the edge of the road and down to the river to nervously clean the dry blood from his hand; the blood started to wash away, leaving his hand haloed around a dark red-stained wall of water.

In the midst of Seth's scrambling, the old man from the alley returned to speak with him. "What I am going to tell you is going to be a hard to take in, but you have to trust and believe me, for what I tell you will hopefully allow you to end this." Seth looked up with a very puzzled look on his face, but without speaking, Seth began to walk away. The old man started following Seth in a desperate attempt to make him listen; the old man began to speak again, "Look, I know you don't know me, but I know you. Your name is Seth Fairchild, your mother's name is Naomi, and Stan is your little brother. You left home a little less than a year ago because of a man named Steven. You are a part of something huge, something you could never possibly understand without my help. I am here to guide and train you. You are our last hope." With this new information, Seth stopped in his tracks and turned to face this new stranger. "How did you know all that?" Seth asked. The old man smiled and said, "There's much that I know that you must learn." Even though Seth still remained skeptic, he decided to listen. "Go ahead, old man, tell me why you must speak with me. I will listen only for the time being, but after this encounter, I will listen to you no more."

With Seth's ears open to listen, the old man began to speak, "I can't tell you everything right now, but what I can tell you is meant to help you on your path. Soon, you will face an army of epic proportions, an army so huge it may seem endless. This army isn't manned by men but of creatures of pure evil. They don't feel emotions or sleep like we do and will take advantage of the fact that you do both. They feed on fear and sorrow. Their leader will take anything and everything away from you and will use any tactic to wear you down. He also has another line of defense, twenty-five other things that resemble man but are not. This war has been waged for thousands of years, and you are now our last hope. Like I said, I know this is a lot to take in at once, but I have been watching you for quite a while, but we're running out of time and your training must start immediately."

Seth's eyes were wide open at this point; not only was he told that he was some kind of soldier, but he was also given the task to fight in an epic war. "Now that I have let you speak, what do you want me to say? Am I supposed to accept this? Just nod my head and tell you I will? I am tired of your lies, old man. I have heard you, and I will hear you no longer." And with that said, Seth turned back around and walked away.

Back at the same alleyway from this morning, Seth sat down against the brick wall to rest. Seth, feeling a little weak and hungry from not being able to eat today, began to rest his mind. He only wished for the end of this day. But before he could even shut his eyes, several grown men approached him with knives and guns. One of the men walked over to Seth, picked him up by his shirt, and dragged him into the light. "You can't be the one who killed our friend!" said one of the men. "I swear to you he is the one. He ripped Mike's throat out right in front of my eyes. I swear he is the one." And with that being said by one of the men in the back, the man holding Seth put his gun straight in his mouth. "What do you have to say for yourself, you little shit? You killed my best friend, and now I'm going to take your life just like you stole his!"

Suddenly, something happened; Seth started changing inside. The same dreamlike feeling came over him once again. He grabbed the gun's barrel and bent it to the side, grabbed the man who was holding the gun, lifted him up in the air, and in front of his crew, broke his back over his knee. Without pause, another one of the men came after Seth with a knife and unsuccessfully tried to stab him in the stomach. Seth then grabbed the man's arm and, with a swift thrust, ripped the man's arm from bone and skin. The man holding his mutilated arm began to scream, but before the man could start running, Seth picked him up by his shirt and threw him to the ground, crushing every bone in his chest and basically liquefying every internal organ. Full of panic, all the men in the group dropped their weapons and started running. A faint laugh echoed in the back of Seth's mind. Seth fell to the ground in a weakened state, his mind unable to focus on a single thought, his breathing becoming rapid once again. And with his body on the verge of a meltdown, Seth lost consciousness.

Seth awakened in a field full of tall dead grass. Nothing was around except one single tree in the middle of the field and a small pond. The sky darkened with a faint red hue, with light all around but with no sun in sight. Seth was looking through his memories, this place looking rather familiar to him, maybe he had visited this place before but his mind drawing a blank. He tried to find signs of life by yelling out, "Hello . . . Is there anyone out there?" Only the sound of his echoed voice would be heard. Then out of nowhere, a large vibration knocked Seth to the ground. Standing stunned, he got up and dust himself off just enough time to feel another weaker vibration hit. The pond that was nearby rippled with each shock wave; with Seth's anticipation growing, he looked around to see if he could find the cause of these interruptions, but nothing. Finally, a loud screeching yell cried out from over the hilltop nearby. Seth eagerly climbed to the top to see what could make such a noise when, suddenly, the sight came into view—a massive army that had to be well into the millions. Each section was organized with twenty-five soldiers, five from right to left and five from front to back. Their numbers were so massive that the end seemed to blend with the skyline, and each step would shack the very foundation of the land.

Seth nervously started walking backward to get away from their numbers, all the while tripping over his own feet, and with a loud thud, Seth fell to the ground. He quickly got back up to make sure he had not alerted the army marching toward him, and sure enough, one scout gave out a terrifying yell to alert the others of Seth's presence. What once was steady marching quickly turned into a freight train of noise heading toward Seth. The organized vibrations coming from the ground turned into a massive shock. As much as he tried, Seth couldn't outrun them; they were far too many and far too fast. Soon, Seth was rushed to the ground; the creatures clawed and scratched into his skin, leaving him with open wounds dripping with blood; he could feel their teeth sinking into his skin, hitting bone. Seth stopped fighting, knowing that the more he resisted, the more it would hurt; he had given up. He began to grow numb, and now the only sound he could hear was the sound of his own heartbeat echoing through his own body, which seemed to be growing more and more faint until the sound could be heard no more.

Waking up gasping for air, Seth wiped his forehead of sweat to notice he was no longer where he thought he was. He found himself on top of a roof somewhere in the middle of the city. Seth, a little dazed, stood up to look at his surroundings, but it did no good. He had no idea where he was. Before he could look for a door, the old man showed his face while sitting on the edge of the building. "Why do you not believe me? You see what you are capable of but you still see me as a liar?" the old man told Seth. "Look, sir, I keep seeing all these horrible things and every time it happens, you are nearby. Why do you expect me to just sit here and believe you? For all I know you could be doing this to me," Seth replied. "I know it sounds strange and you have no reason to believe me, but you must open your mind to the possibility of what I am saying." With a short pause, Seth looked at the old man and spoke, "Okay, suppose what you are saying is true, why me? I may have some form of special ability, but I can't control it. What makes you think I am capable of fighting a war? Hell, I don't even know your name." The old man spoke, "You can call me Robert. Even though that isn't my real name, it will keep both of us safe for now. And the reason why you can't control your gift yet is because you are not properly trained. Right now your powers come out during self-defense and anger. With my guidance and your will to learn, I can have you ready before it is time, but you have to listen to me without question. Your lack of trust toward me has got to stop. I know I'm asking a lot of you right now, but we have very little time as of late. So if you're willing to trust in me, then we will start training tomorrow. Now go home and rest. This is the beginning."

Walking down the stairs of the building to which he had no idea of how he got there, Seth thought to himself, *Why should I trust this crazy old man?*

I don't even know him, and of course, he can't tell me his real name. Although there are strange things happening to me, and for some reason, I think he knows something. I'll just play this by ear. I will allow myself to trust him for the time being, but if anything happens, then I'm out! Finally reaching the exit door of the building, Seth was not entirely sure where he was, but since he really didn't leave anything of importance behind, then he saw no reason why he couldn't make the alleyway nearby his new home. After all, there were probably people looking for him anyway since he would now be considered a murderer. Searching the nearest dumpster, Seth found several newspapers and a few cardboard boxes, which had been broken down flat. He took the cardboard and newspapers and hid them out of sight. Still hungry from not eating, he began his daily routine of searching for food. There was a spiritual commune nearby, so this would be Seth's best bet. The dumpster near the back proved most useful; Seth found a half-eaten sandwich and some discarded remains of what looked like baked beans and mixed vegetables. In this harsh reality, Seth knew all too well that having a weak stomach would be the very end of your survival; he knew that if you didn't eat anything and everything that you find, then you may very well starve to death. Although there were certain rules you had to go by—like if any food has mold, you cut it off—if you can't stomach the smell, then it would most likely make you sick; but when your hunger takes over, then you will eat most anything even if what you eat does make you sick.

The day would come and go, and Seth's insides were no longer speaking to him of hunger. His thoughts was still racing of what Robert had planned for him tomorrow, and still the very question that lingered in the back of his mind was why should he even trust this old man. But still Seth had gone through a lot in the last couple of days, and so he began to ready his alleyway for sleep. He took out the cardboard and placed it on top of the cold concrete ground; he then placed waded-up pieces of newspaper and shoved them in his sleeves and into his shirt. The rest of the newspaper would be used to cover up with, for the cold night could make things extremely unpleasant. He stared up at the stars, something he did on a nightly basis. The twinkle of each sun was billions of light years away, yet he was witnessing their beauty. His eyes was getting heavy until keeping them open seemed like a chore, and within seconds, he fell asleep.

Seth sat in his room, working on homework. Seth's mother burst through the door. "Seth, come quick. Your father is severely ill." Without pause, Seth tried to get out of his chair, but something seemed to be keeping him down. The scenery started to change, and now Seth was lying down in his bed, just slightly older; and again, his mother burst through the door, telling Seth that his father didn't have much time left, that if he wanted to say something to him, now would be the time. Again, Seth tried to get up, but he couldn't; he tried with all the strength he had, but he just couldn't move, but before he could do anything else, Seth's mother walked in one last time and spoke of the passing of Seth's father. A tear rolled down Seth's cheek with this news and now with the guilt of not speaking with his father during his dying days. The scene changed once more. Seth was now standing at a funeral, everyone around him crying and giving Seth the judgmental eye. Seth could hear everyone talking about him—"I heard he wouldn't even speak to his dying father," "Why is he even here? Everyone knows that it would be best if he never even showed his face, especially since he never really loved him!" "He would rather be off playing video games than to even waste one breath to speak to his loving father," "If I were him, I would just end my life now," "Yeah, save his poor mother some pain and anguish." Seth couldn't take it anymore. With his face full of tears, Seth began to run, passing hundreds of tombstones, each looking exactly the same as before. In the background, Seth didn't see, but there were dozens of creatures lurking behind the trees past the graveyard. The ground began to become softer and softer until Seth fell through the soil of the earth, falling and falling deeper into what must seem like forever of nothing. Seth began to hear voices; they began very faint at first, but within time, the voices get louder and louder until their sounds became too much for any one person to handle, and Seth had to cover his ears. He couldn't quite make it out, but it sounded very familiar, like maybe someone had spoken these words to him before. The words began to become clear, but still not clear enough to understand, but before he could even attempt, young Seth would wake from his slumber.

Seth woke up in a hysterical panic; crying and shaking, he began to come out of his dream-induced coma. Staring at the moon, Seth started to feel calm; a cool breeze blew all around him. Seth closed his eyes to see his mother's face, thinking to himself, *Who would have known my life would be like this? I only hope Stan is all right. I shouldn't have left him, but I was scared and didn't know what to do. I panicked, and the only thing I could think of doing was run away. I should have brought you with me!*

A few hours passed, and Seth climbed the stairs to head back up to the same rooftop that Robert had asked of him. The skyline filled with the early colors of morning; bright orange hue shed light around everything within sight. Seth looked around, thinking, *He asked me to come back, but he can't find it in himself to be here.* Then as if out of thin air, Robert arrived. Seth, a little confused, looked at Robert with a sign of disbelief. "You weren't up here a second ago. Where did you come from?" Robert simply looked at Seth, turned to an empty spot on the roof, and sliced a hole into what seemed like nothing. "Step through," Robert said, "for this will be the place at which you will be trained." Out of all the things Seth had seen throughout his life, this one thing puzzled him the most. "You open a hole from within air and you expect me to just walk through it? Do you play me for a fool?" Robert, standing next to the portal, said, "I've asked you to trust me, and you can't even do that. If you can't take my word, then at least go on faith. Do you have faith, Seth?" Seth, looking away from Robert, replied, "I did once. When I was a child living at home, I had faith. Until I found out that faith is useless. Faith can't stop someone from beating on you. Faith can't allow someone to see that you desperately need help. Faith won't give me back my life!" Robert, walking over toward Seth, said, "Listen, I can't give your life back. I can't really promise anything to you. But you have to trust in me. We have very little time!"

Seth, with his guard up, reluctantly went through the portal, thinking to himself that if this were a trap that he would have to think of something quick to get the upper hand, but after walking through, he only noticed a hazy gray mountaintop that seemed to be crumpling around its sides, almost as if it were an apple's core. To Seth, the mountaintop felt out of place; everything around him was fully alive and beautiful, but everything outside of the mountain was depressingly dark and dead. Robert explained that this world used to be the same world he had come from, and what little life that was surrounding Seth was all that was left. A great massacre broke out, and everything and everyone had been murdered at the hands of one man. Robert went into further detail, "This is why you must train because the person who did this to my world is planning on doing the same to your world. I know I spoke of an army to you early, but please don't take my words lightly, for the creatures he commands can't be reasoned with. They don't sleep, they feed on fear, and they are an empty shell with no soul, knowing only how to kill. We must be extremely careful, or he will sense that I am here."

"Who?" Seth asked. "Who is it that you keep referring to?" Robert's face turned into a serious tone, almost as if he was looking at death itself. "You don't need to know as of yet, but you will in due time." Seth, thinking back to some of his earlier dreams, said, "But this army you speak of, how big is it again?" "In the millions. Their march shakes the very soil if you're nearby." Seth, with a surprising look upon his face, said, "I think I've had a dream about them. I was standing on a hilltop and I saw a massive army of creatures marching in unison. Every time their feet touched the ground, it would shake the soil beneath my feet. Could this be the same army you speak of?" Robert nodded in agreement. "Yes, that very well may be the same army. You see, he is already invading your dreams, giving you a small taste of what you are up against. Now do you see why your training is so important?" Seth, just standing in one place, remarked, "This is too much to take in, Robert. In one week I have killed two people, been told that I am one of a select few who have to fight within a war, and now you are telling me that someone out there is controlling my dreams! I don't know if I can handle this!" "Sometimes life doesn't give us many options. Sometimes you're dealt a crappy hand, but you have to face facts and just deal with it. There isn't another soul on this world who can handle what I'm asking of you. I know it's a lot to take in, but the facts still remain—you are our last hope. If you don't start your training, then all this . . ."—Robert pointed to the large city in the background—"will be destroyed, and everyone in it will either die or be enslaved. So please, Seth, let us begin."

Staring into the dark abyss that surrounded him on top of that mountain, Seth could only wonder and contemplate the thoughts of why he would be the only or even the last remaining warrior, why was he so special. He was searching the landscape down below for any signs of life, but nothing would catch his eye, for everything about this world was dead and bleak. The gray clouds up above gave off a dreary cold feeling; the only sunshine came from up above what Robert would later refer to Seth's training ground as the Vice. Seth finally turned around to face Robert. "Okay, I will train. But I still don't trust you, and if for any reason I think you're using me, then I'm gone. So let us begin."

The dawning of this new day set forth a new beginning. This new land, new friend, everything surrounding him would breathe into Seth's new life that would guide and shape the future he had not foreseen for himself.

Chapter 2

$\mathcal{T}$hree years have passed and Seth was almost ready. Learning from Robert every day, he began to piece everything together, and although Robert was unable to fully tell him what he was up against, their luck began to wear thin.

Up on the same mountaintop that both Seth and Robert have been meeting every day for the past three years. Tired and covered in sweat, Seth began to stop for the day. While trying to catch their breath, Robert and Seth headed back to the rooftop before starting a conversation. "So, Seth, have you still been having those dreams?" Seth, sitting down along the rooftop, replied, "Yes, but they've been getting worse. They're more vivid than before. I can almost see the face of my tormentor in a few of them." Robert, with his hand over his chin, said, "If you would, can you tell me about one?" Seth began to get up from where he was sitting and gradually walked over toward Robert. "The one I had last night, I was standing in a hallway. The monsters that I always see were coming after me, trying to cut at me. I kept using all the techniques you showed me to fight them, and it worked for a while, but the more I kept killing, the more monsters kept attacking me. I started losing after a while. But this one dream wasn't like the rest. For some reason, you were there watching me." Robert backed away. "How long have you been having this one dream?" Seth gave a casual answer, "Not too long. A week, maybe less." Robert turned around and began walking toward the edge of the roof. "I have taken you as far as I can, Seth, and the rest of your journey is up to you." Seth, looking a little confused, said, "Wait a minute. You're done training me because of a dream I had? I'm confused. I have this dreams all the time. What makes this one so special?" Robert, standing at the edge of the building, replied, "Like I've told you before, he's watching you, picking through your mind to see what he can use against you and to find out who is helping you. He will use me against you, and I can't allow that to happen. I need you to continue, but I can't help you any longer. Please, Seth, you have to promise me to stay on track, don't lose your faith, and remember I will always be watching you." "You can't leave me, Robert. You still have much to teach me. I can't do this on my own, and you know this! And with this news of knowing my dreams are no longer mine, I need you more than ever." Robert turned toward Seth. "What do you mean new? I told you all this over by the riverside!" "No, we've spoken in the alleyway, when I was leaving to go home and on this very rooftop." Seth turned around again. "This is exactly the reason why we have to stop. He is messing with your own memories. And now that he knows I've been helping you, he can and will use me against you. It's best if you continue on without me."

Before Seth could get out a single word, Robert walked to the edge of the rooftop turning to Seth. "I know this is a tall order, but you have to remember to never give up. Remember what I have taught you. Keep training. And, Seth, never forget, I will always be with you." As Roberts leaped off the building, Seth tried to run after him, but it was too late. Robert would be no more. Seth stood speechless, looking at the heap of death lying on the sidewalk; dropping to his knees, Seth began to cry, "How could you! I can't do this alone!"

Seth, with what little compassion was left in him, decided to bury his good friend, Robert. So with the small amount of light left in the sky, Seth grabbed a shovel, picked Robert over his shoulder, and headed for the landfill; surely no one would be there to disturb him. This feeling was very well-known to Seth. With everything in his life lost, it was hard for him to even think of a world that doesn't involve death or losing someone in one form or another. Finally, after a long and tiresome two hours, Seth finished the hole, and it was now time for it to be filled. Seth simply dropped Robert within the hole and started the last bit of this project. After the grave was filled, Seth decided to say a few words, "It's hard to know that I've lost someone like you, Robert. You've guided me and looked after me for so long, yet the time feels so short. I can't promise to be the man you want me to be, but I will give it my best. It's funny. I thought you were just a crazy old man. Who would have thought you'd end up being my best friend? I wish I could have found a better spot for you, and I hope you're doing well wherever it is you might be. I'll never forget you!"

Tired and fatigued, Seth started his journey back to the alleyway in which he first arrived in this city when all of a sudden, he saw a small amount of movement coming from within the trash heap. Moving closer to get a better look, Seth began to push and pull all that appeared to be in his way. Almost there, Seth started to see something. Not sure what it was, he grabbed a sharp object, expecting the worst, when out of nowhere, a bright light that, at first, was a small spec began to grow larger and larger. And then finally, a large pulse surged out and knocked Seth off his feet, making Seth lose consciousness.

Seth appeared on top of a hill in front of an empty valley. Something that looked like mist began to float down toward him; finally reaching Seth, the mist began to take shape. This strange mist took the shape of a human's body, everything visible except the face, which was covered in a thick black foglike substance. The strange person began to speak in an echoed-tone voice, "I am here to give you a choice. Join me and forget about this silly war or turn me down and I will show you pain like you've never seen before." Seth, staring at the emptiness of the field, replied, "So you're the one Robert spoke to me about." Laughter began to engulf the strange figure. "You mean Ewar? Yes, it was difficult to figure out who was helping you, but I eventually saw through him. Because of him, you aren't ready to face me, so you should be thanking me for this offer." With an evil eye and anger in his voice, Seth replied, "What makes you think I am not ready to face you? I was ready even before Robert found me! I am much stronger than you realize, with or without the man you so-called Ewar." The stranger began to laugh. "Oh, how I love you and your fellow brothers' attempt at humor. I will return when you've had more time to think about my generous offer. But believe me when I say that you will change your mind or perish."

Waking up, Seth stood to try and find that same glow that had attracted him before but found nothing. "Could that have been real? If so, then I wonder if that was the same person Robert or Ewar spoke to me about. He didn't seem so tough. Maybe I can take him."

Seth began to walk back to the one place he could still call home when he realized he would have to go back to all the loneliness and despair as before. Robert gave him something besides his training, and Seth hadn't figured that out until it was too late; Robert gave him hope and, most importantly, friendship. "I will never forget you, Robert, and I promise that I will never give up, even if it kills me. I will kill this stranger just for ending our time together. He will pay. This much I promise you."

By the time Seth got back to the alley where he, for the last few years, had called home, he ran into a young petite female being harassed by a large burly man. Staring deeply into the whole situation, Seth noticed something beginning to grow inside, much like the same feeling as before in his training ground. "I will make Robert proud," Seth said to himself.

Seth walked up to the man, grabbing his arm before he had the chance to lay another hand on the female. Seth held the man back, called out to the young female, "I will hold him, you run!" The young woman ran for safety. The man turned his head to face Seth. "This is none of your damn business, boy." Seth, still holding the man's arm, stared into the face of the tormentor. Seth stood there, provoking the man. "So you think beating on someone smaller than you makes you more of a man? Well, I am smaller than you, so let's go!" The man, with a smile on his face, took one swing at Seth, and with Seth's other hand caught the man's hand and began to squeeze harder and harder until you could start to hear each and every bone in the man's hand break and shatter. Seth, with a violent stare, began to speak, "You see, not everything is as it seems, and I will make sure you understand that what went on right here will never happen again, even if it kills you!" And with that being said, Seth let go of the man's arm and, with the other hand, grabbed his neck and lifted him the ground and, with Seth staring into the man's eyes, began to tell him, "If I ever see you or even think that you are still doing this, I will find you. If I hear someone mention to me that a man such as yourself did anything similar to this, I will find you. I will be the last thing you see! Now get the hell out of here before I really lose control." Without hesitation, Seth removed his grip from the man's neck and with no pause the man ran out of the alleyway while holding his hand in agony.

Seth fell to his knees and began to shake. "Even though I kept control, why do I feel so weak and helpless? Does it take a lot out of me to keep control? Robert, why can't you be here to help me through this? Why do I have to be the last hope? It just isn't fair. I don't want this power. I don't want this life!"

A faint voice called out from the distance, "Seth, remember what I taught you. Don't allow this to break you. I have watched you grow stronger with each passing day, and I know you can handle this. Out of all the others I have witnessed, you seem to be the strongest out of them all. I haven't left you. Just remember I am always with you, watching you, guiding you. Make me proud!" With a tear rolling down his cheek, Seth looked up at the sky and, with a faint voice, whispered, "I miss you."

Dark clouds began to roll in; what once was bright blue skies turned into dark black violent storms. As if Seth's emotions controlled the weather, with every tear rolling down his cheek, the more rain would fall; with every crying outburst, thunder would shatter the sky. Seth was running and running until the very thought of home became nothing but a distant memory, and with a gunshot heard overhead, Seth realized where he was. "How in the hell did I make it to the bad part of town!"

"Excuse me! Excuse me! Did you not hear me calling you?" said the young woman Seth had saved moments ago. "I have been following you for quite sometime. I wanted to thank you for saving my life." Seth, with a blank stare, just eyed the young woman. "You don't speak much, do you? Is there any way I can repay you?" Seth, still staring, began to speak, "Yeah, you can leave me alone. I don't need your thanks, and I certainly don't need to be repaid." With a look of disgust, she said, "Why do you have to be like that? I was only trying to thank you and maybe do something nice for you. Has anyone ever been nice to you before?" "There hasn't been a need, apparently until now," Seth replied. "Now leave me. You have no business being in a place like this." Without another word, the young woman just turned around and walked away.

Depression set in, and Seth had no one there to tell him that everything would be okay. Sitting against the wall, contemplating his very existence, he asked the same question over and over, "Why does everything I touch turn to shit?" No answers were ever given. Around these dark times, suicide thoughts would always seep in, taking control of your very being, making every second of life seem like a never-ending hell. First his family, now his mentor. Seth could only think that if he was to shut himself off, then he could never feel like this again or maybe even end his own life, but even though that thought occurred more times than Seth was willing to admit, he never indulged in the act. Seth wasn't sure what happens to you if you take your own life, but he assumed it wasn't a very good place to end up, or so he was brought up to believe.

The dreams were beginning to get worse until it was best to just not sleep and walk the world in a zombielike state. Seth would average around five to six hours a week of sleep, and to any normal person, that would be extremely unhealthy, but it was the only way to keep the monsters at bay inside his own head. And even though Seth was extremely careful about how and when and for how long he would sleep, being careful just isn't enough. The dreams were becoming more vivid and detailed, and no matter how intense the dreams would become, Seth could never wake up until whatever he was meant to see was seen. Some nights were worse than others, and Seth would have no other options than to fall into a level of deep sleep no matter how hard he tried to fight temptation.

Seth was standing within an empty hallway. Faces on the right that seemed to be melted within the wall shifted and swayed while moaning for help, and on the left, written words. It was dark and damp with only enough light to see the faces and all the writing on the wall. The lettering appeared to be written in a dark slimy substance that resembles blood; the majority of the writing couldn't be read, but a small few were in large text—"Hand over your soul," "It's always a good time to die," "This war will consume you!" "You can wash your hands, but your soul shall never be clean!" "You left him with that monster!" Everything written wouldn't be clear to anyone else but to Seth, and after reading most of what was written, Seth fell to his knees and began to weep. An extreme fear consumed him, which led him to crawl into the corner to cry. "How could I leave my own brother with that monster? I'm a horrible person!" Where in the real world Seth's soul was like a guarded fortress, but within his mind, the littlest of things could break him. Just the very thought of his brother would make him break down and weep.

The room began to get even darker until his very hand couldn't be seen mere inches in front of his face. A loud screeching noise began to shriek across the room, getting louder and louder until the very sound threatened to burst Seth's eardrums. Suddenly, a voice began to call out, "Don't worry, this will all be over soon!"

Waking up in a cold sweat, Seth began to grasp for air. The very thought of suicide was now thick within his thoughts. Every notion kept signaling him to end his life, a voice in the back of his mind, a cool breeze calling to him, telling him how easy it would be and how quick he could make it. The thought was so overpowering that Seth picked up a sharp piece of glass and cut his wrist deep enough to hit bone. The blood flowed from his arms like a river that just had a dam break upstream. The daylight began to become dim until darkness overtook his sight. The feeling of cold was taking shape; a small tinkling feeling consumed his arms until numbness was all that was left. The numbing gave Seth a moment of peace until a deep state of cold consumed his entire body. Seth, alone in the alleyway, propped up against the wall. His eyes shut and his arms stretched out by his sides with blood still flowing out, his skin turning pale.

A faint gleam of light shone down into Seth's closed eyelids. Light fixture, sweeping faster and faster, passed his vision. A pulse whispered its way back to show the life Seth had so desperately wanted to give away. Seth, with a weak voice, begged to be left alone, "Please, just let me die! My life means nothing. You're only postponing the inevitable." Everyone was responding to one another as if Seth wasn't even in the room; no one would listen. Panic took shape as the doctors fought Seth with every step as he pulled every cord and tube from his body. Finally, the doctors inserted a strong sedative, and Seth slowly fell into unconsciousness.

The same hallway stood before Seth. Dark and dim, a small light illuminated from the written letters that were beginning to show more visible. Glaring almost blindingly, the door at the end of the hallway called out to be opened, a voice whispering, channeling communications to the one person meant to hear it. The walls moving with the shapes of faces moved fluidly in all directions, a thick bloodlike substance flowing freely from the ceiling. The door called with an echoed deep voice, "Your life is not your own. Make pain and suffering a weapon, and we shall rule all. Only by my hand will you ever know what true power can become. I can give you everything! Follow me through the passage and I will show you everything!"

Seth walked ever so nervously to the door, turning the knob in an almost frightful way, not knowing what to expect on the other side. Finally, the door unlatched with a slow creaking with every inch being pulled back. The light began to turn dark, and an empty plain began to show—the empty terrain, dusty white, with nothing as far as the eye can see. Bright blue sphere hung in the sky. A tall dark figure stood in the distance, waiting for Seth. The stranger began to speak with the same voice as the door, "So we meet again I see. You know why I called you here, and so now I will make you the last offer. Join me or everything you know and care about will be destroyed." With a longing stare and a look of confusion, Seth began to speak, "I already tried to kill myself. I don't know what more you want from me. I will not join you, but I also won't fight in this war, so you have nothing to worry about." The stranger, with a disappointed look, rose from his stance, floating off the ground toward Seth, a glow of red shining from his eyes. "That is not an option. You either choose me or nothing! I see I will have to show you the power I would have given you, the power that will now destroy you ALL!" The stranger flew above Seth, lifted his arms to the sky as if he trying to grab something out of reach. Finally, something began to take shape, a large chunk of rock glided across the sky. Guided by the strangers hands, the rock picked up pace; the stranger slowly turned toward Seth with a smile on his face. The rock ripped through the deep blue sphere, which now resembled Earth. Crushing and ripping through the inner layer, the rock crashed directly onto a continental island sending ripples through the entire planet. A dark cloud of dust begins to cover the world; the island the rock crushed into was now nothing more than water. The planet began to shift farther away as if the balance of gravity had been altered. "Your oceans will boil, the plants will die, the ozone will slowly disappear, and everyone will burn to death or die from lack of air. The very planet you hold so dear is now on a collision course to the Sun. You see, Seth, I have just ended everything you care about. The power I have shown could have been yours, but you have chosen to be difficult and everyone else will have to pay for this decision. You really should have chosen ME!"

A swift grasp of air, Seth woke up in what looked like a hospital. "These dreams just won't stop. Robert, why can't you be here to help me through this?" Seth, feeling the signs of depression, looked down and noticed the restraints the nurses must have placed on him to keep himself from trying to commit suicide again, but no matter what, he figured he could always play the role of being healthy and then try again when they finally released him. Seth thought that no one would get in his way of ending his own life; death was the only thing on his mind that could possibly end this nightmare that he called life.

Several weeks would go by with no visitors, like anyone knew where Seth was anyway. Boredom would set into discomfort of being placed within the same position day in and day out. Seth would get a visit from a nurse or doctor once every day or two but only to make sure he was still in the same room and not trying to escape or to bring him his food every other day. Seth finally figured out what had happened; someone found him in a puddle of his own blood, someone who actually cared for him and brought him to the hospital. After the hospital, the doctors, on Seth's behavior, decided that he was too much of a risk to be let back out, so they sent him to the asylum so the proper people could keep an eye on him; and with no money being spent from Seth, then he gets the worse treatment. Taxpayers' money doesn't afford the luxuries of everyday meals or letting you out of the bed to walk around or even go to the bathroom, so the only options you have is to shrink your stomach and hold your bodily functions. Seth figured out that if you use the restroom on yourself, then the nurses would have to attend to you due to the smell that gave you a few minutes out of bed; well, that is if you can handle all the bitching you will most likely hear. But he could care less about how he was treated within the confines of this institution. Even though he was trapped into a bed, he figured that anything was better than living on the cold streets, which at least the asylum kept the temperature at a steady degree to satisfy their workers, even though the patients were the last on the list to get any form of special treatment.

The weeks would come and go, but nothing ever changed. Even though Seth didn't mind being confined, there is only so much the human body can handle until it begins to snap and the only thing that creeps up in the back of your mind is how to get free, but Seth had other reasons to want to be free. Feeling that enough time had already passed, Seth took it upon himself to try and escape; with each passing day, he would try as hard as humanly possible to loosen the constraints. When this proved to be useless, he tried to steal something sharp away from one of the doctors or nurses; when this failed, Seth felt hopelessly lost within the confines of the asylum, which he now referred to as the Beast. Seth, almost giving up, heard a voice within the room; looking around frantically, Seth could see no one. The voice would get louder and louder until Seth could finally make out what was being said. An echoed soft voice of a man said, "Use what I taught you. This is nothing compared to what you can really do. Use the inner power I taught you how to control." As if forgetting everything that had been taught to him, Seth finally realized that he had the power to escape all along. After a short few days, he learned how to concentrate long enough to control the power that lurked inside, and with a violent thrust, Seth ripped the arm constraints from the bed and tore the leather leg constraints. Thinking he could just walk out, Seth started heading toward the door. No one paid him much mind until he reached the front door. Mere inches away from freedom, Seth grabbed the door handle to pull it forward when a hand reached over and stopped the door in its tracks. The strong deep voice called out into Seth's ear, "Where the hell do you think you're going, sir? If you think you're leaving, then I got some bad news for ya." Seth turned toward the tall muscular man; the sight of this gentleman was enough to make anyone stop in their tracks. Seth, with a blank stare, just looked into the man's eyes and said, "If you don't take your hand off me, I will make sure you never use it again." The same voice Seth heard in his room spoke again, "Seth, keep control. Don't hurt him but remove him as an obstacle." Seth grabbed the man by the shirt and simply threw the 310-pound man through the front door. Shattering the glass, the man flew 15 feet before hitting his head against a metal fence. Seth casually walked through, not looking at the man he just sent flying but to just get away from the Beast.

Walking a few blocks, he noticed the sidewalks were empty, which was a little strange since lunchtime was almost approaching. The noise was almost unnerving when Seth first heard it, and then a glance in front would show the confrontation that awaited him. A wall of policemen guarding each sides of the street made sure no one, not even Seth, could escape; waiting for Seth to get closer before trying to take him out would with some tranquilizer darts.

Any scene of this nature would scare any living person but Seth just thought, finally an end, but before he could react the voice called out again, "This will never be a battle that can be won by fighting." Seth had learned a long time ago that more than likely the voices he kept hearing were almost always right. So he simply lay down on his stomach with his arms stretched across his back; all the while, the police officers screaming for him to do the same. The only thing Seth was hearing were footsteps and yelling; most of the yelling were directed at Seth or about Seth. In the back of his mind, he wondered why the voices kept telling him to do things and then, out of nowhere, telling him to give up. "Robert, if that's you calling out to me, why tell me to break free when at the end I am to give up?" But before anyone could get close enough, Seth felt a dart strike him in the neck, and sleep followed.

Seth found himself within a dark twisted building, the walls lined with a thick dark slimelike substance. Seth seemed to be invisible. A dark shrouded character stood in front of the room with another male figure kneeling. Seth stood by several creatures that resembled men but were not, their skin gray and deformed, all of them having claws and sharp teeth. The dark shrouded figure spoke, "You have done well siding with me, and between the both of us, we will turn the rest or destroy them all." Seth, too curious, started walking toward the front just to see if he could see the man's face that was kneeling. The closer Seth got, the farther away the two would become. A walk turned into a run, but it still wasn't enough; this moment wouldn't allow Seth to look at the face that would later betray him. Beginning to become out of breath, Seth was about to stop until the floor gave out and Seth dropped within what must have been a bottomless pit. Falling and farther and farther, it seemed to never end. Through the darkness, nothing but silence, and the nothingness began to engulf Seth's inner soul.

Two voices talked between each other. "Hanuse, why do you continue showing him these dreams?" *"Because, my child, I want to tease him, to provoke his curiosity. I want to keep him in the game so that I may have a challenge for once!"* "But with each passing day, he grows stronger and his control becomes greater. Are you sure you want to continue provoking him?" *"So you think his power is greater than mine? Out of all the destruction we caused and all the mayhem that has been witnessed by you, you still doubt me? You must not forget that the more control he gains, the weaker his power becomes. In order for him to be as powerful as me, he must give in to complete chaos."* "I'm sorry I doubted you, Hanuse. This shall be the greatest challenge yet!"

Delilah

Sitting within the classroom, Delilah stared up at the clock, waiting for three-thirty to hit so this day, and more importantly this whole school experience, would end. Tonight would mark the last remaining ritual she would have to endure at this school or within this small town, for tonight marked her graduation. Each minute passed as if to tease and taunt her; each second was becoming longer and longer until Delilah was beginning to give up and turn her head away from the daunting symbol that mocked her so. Staring at everything, she soaked in all the sights and sounds that she would never hear again—watching the teacher sit at his desk, seemingly waiting for the exact moment she was. Each student was anxious and excited, tension growing ever stronger until the final sound, the final draw that would release them from this day, the final sound of the bell that granted everlasting escape.

The crowds rushed as if the school was about to collapse, pushing and shoving through the door that would lead them all to the sweet scent of freedom. Summer vacation, the only thing on anyone's mind, all the parties and get-togethers that would follow until the next school year, came to claim all the students' spare time. Delilah finally reached the door to smell the fresh air; knowing this scent would never smell so sweet, she savored every moment, every second until the time to savor comes and goes.

The buses all lined up to take the nondriving students back home until next year. Delilah walked toward the parking lot, finding her car that her daddy bought her for her sweet-sixteen birthday party. The car, gleaming within the sunlight, still looked as new as the day her father placed the keys within her hand and said, "Happy birthday, honey!" She walked up toward the driver's side door, took out her key, and unlocked the door. She even savored the sound the car makes when the lock turns, making every sound a record within her memories, knowing that the sounds she heard today would never be repeated; they would never sound the same on any other day. Delilah lifted the door handle, letting the window of her escape swing open, allowing all the heat to rush out so that maybe the car would be manageable enough for her to start the car and turn on the air conditioner. Even the drive home would linger in her mind, for this was the last time she would ever drive off this parking lot. She waved bye to all her fellow students and then began the drive home.

Every other day, Delilah met her house with the same scene as before—the gardener working in the front yard, her mother tanning by the pool in the side of the backyard, and her father more than likely still at work or on a business trip—but today was not a normal day. When she reached her destination of home, she was greeted with a new car in the driveway with a large ribbon on the hood. Delilah rolled her eyes, knowing exactly whose gift this would be. "Here we go again, someone trying to buy my love!" She rolled into the driveway and parked her car right behind the new gift; she unbuckled the seatbelt and got out of her car to meet with the parents. Just like clockwork, as soon as Delilah shut her car door, the parents came rolling out the front door. The father, with a smile on his face, walked over to his only daughter. "There's my favorite high school grad!" The mother, with a glass of wine in her hand, said, "I'm so proud of you, dear!" Delilah walked over to hug both of them but feeling only a small sliver of love, as if love in this family could only be represented within the confines of material objects. The father, crossing his arms, said, "So what do you think of the car? It was the most expensive on the lot. And no daughter of mine is going to be caught dead in anything but the best while she attends the best school in the country!" Delilah, trying her best to not break his heart, replied, "Thanks, Father, but I'm not sure your old college is the right school for me. I think I need a little more time off to decide what I want to do and I just want to have a little fun for once, you know to clear my mind of responsibilities." The father, glancing at his daughter, said, "That's nonsense. When I was your age, I just jumped right into college. The best four years of my life, you'll see!" Delilah, knowing this conversation wasn't going anywhere, decided to try and stick with her guns. "I don't know, Father. I think I might want to live in the big city for a while. I need to get away from this small town and see what life is like in a different setting." And of course, the father fired back with, "No daughter of mine is ever going to live within the city. It's too dangerous on your own. You're going to my old school, and that's final!" The mother, trying to get between the two, said, "All right now you two. This is supposed to be a special occasion and you're ruining it! Delilah, thank your father for the beautiful car!" Delilah, with nothing more to say, stormed off to her room in a hurry.

A knock on Delilah's door was met with an extremely upset young lady lying on her bed, clutching her pillow between her arms. The mother walked in. "Delilah, what's a matter, honey?" Delilah sat up. "When do I make my own life choices? Am I asking for too much when I ask to wait on college? Daddy's school will always be there. I just want to have a little fun before I have to hit the books again for another few years!" The mother walked over to sit next to Delilah. "Listen, your father is just worried about your safety. He knows what it's like in the city and just doesn't want you going alone." Delilah looked up toward her mother. "Maybe, but I already kind of made plans with a school friend that we were going to move into an apartment together. We already found a place, and the rent is very manageable, and it sits in a very respectable part of the city." The mother put her arm around Delilah. "Give your father a little more time. I'll try and talk to him, see if I can get him to settle on a compromise. Plus aren't you going to a concert tonight in the big city?" Delilah, with a smile but still a disappointed tone, said, "Yeah, we're seeing Alma." The mother put her head on Delilah's shoulder. "Then why are you pouting? Enjoy the show tonight and worry about the rest later. Cross that bridge when you come to it." Delilah looked over at her mother. "Yeah, I guess you're right." Delilah's mother left the room, and she grabbed her diary from underneath her bed.

June 8

My attempts at leaving this town can never seem to agree with my father. He just doesn't understand the caged in feeling that I have. I need to be set free from his control, and I can't take it anymore! He wants me to go to a school that he's an alumnus to, but it's nowhere near the big city. All I want is a little freedom. I want to live in the big city for a year or two to let my wings out and then I will do whatever he wants. I just don't want to feel trapped by his life anymore.

It seems like all I ever get from anyone are materialistic things. Why is life all about what you have and not about whom you share everything with? All I ever wanted from anyone was to feel that I'm more important than a new car or anything that's expensive to them in their eyes. I want what I don't have and I have what I don't need.

She put the diary away so that it may lend its ear for another day, back down under her mattress. She set everything up for the concert, but with a few hours before she had to start getting ready, she decided to take a little nap to make sure she's fully awake to see one of her favorite bands.

Delilah was standing upon a mountain; everything surrounding her was lush and full of life, but the outer world around the mountain seemed desolate and barren. At first Delilah couldn't understand what she was standing on; the edges seemed to drop off as if the land she stood upon was floating in midair, but what she didn't realize was this mountain had been eaten away and corroded from its sides, leaving only the top untouched. Delilah stared at all the scenery, brushing her hands across the flowers, gazing upon her reflection within the small pond next to the tall tree in the center of the mountain, feeling the wind blow through her hair. All these things made her completely relaxed and calm, making her feel euphoric.

A figure, standing in the distance, masked by shade and speaking in a very distinctive voice, said, "This life you lead will guide you to a man, a man that needs to be led to the light." Delilah walked closer and closer to the darkened figure, trying to get a good view of the person speaking to her. "What man and how will I know?" Delilah was trying to get closer, but the more she walked toward him. the farther he seemed to be. "Something inside you will make you aware. You won't understand this feeling, but you will accept this as fact." Delilah gave up on getting closer, sitting down on a rock next to her, "Why am I guiding this man? Of what importance is he?" "He is our last hope. Without him, our worlds will surely die. Guide him and help him see the light. The light is the only thing that can save him and us." Delilah stared off into the abyss. "What do you mean save us? Save us from what?" The shrouded figure suddenly turned into mist and blew away in a breeze.

Delilah woke up in a state of confusion. "What was that all about?" But as quickly as she thought of the dream, she soon realized she needed to get ready, pushing the dream out of her thoughts.

After getting a shower and rushing out of her room, Delilah ran downstairs in just enough time to greet her friend that arrived mere seconds before. Without saying much, Delilah grabbed her friend's hand, waved good-bye to the parents and headed out the door. The two rush into the car as if they were escaping from something sinister and sped out of the driveway.

The ride to the big city was always Delilah's favorite thing; she normally only did this with one of her friends, meaning only conversations that interested her and her friend would come up. Delilah's friend, Jennifer, was a little different from her; she wanted all the things Delilah wanted but none of the barriers that blocked her way, which came to no surprise to Delilah when she learned that Jennifer already had an apartment in the city, that she would be moving into tomorrow. Jennifer, with a smile on her face, stared at Delilah. "You know, I'm going to need a roommate for this apartment of mine." Delilah, looking back at her, said, "I know what you're thinking, but I can't. My father is content on me living at home to go to his college. I really want to, but I can't." Jennifer, with a little smirk on her face, said, "But what if, somehow your dad could be convinced to let you move here for a little while, what then?" Delilah, with a frustrated look on her face, replied, "That will never happen!" The smile on Jennifer's face was getting bigger and bigger. "Well, I have some awesome news for you. Me and your mom convinced your dad to let you live in the city for a few weeks, and if all goes well, then you can stay for the year or until the lease is up!" Delilah's face lit up as if a whole new world was presented to her. "Are you joking with me? He really is letting me stay here with you!" Jennifer was still smiling. "Yeah, but on one condition." Delilah's face was getting serious once more. "All right, what's the catch?" Jennifer, without pause, said, "Oh, it's nothing much but if something were to happen here, like you get hurt or anything dangerous, then you have to move back without question and do what your father says. Basically, that was the only way to let you stay here." Delilah's face lit up once more. "I can't believe you did this for me. Thank you so much! I can't wait for the city life!"

Delilah remained happy, but she really knew why Jennifer wanted her up there; her father was rich, so if Delilah wanted anything, she would get it, which meant if Jennifer wanted anything and could convince Delilah that it was a good idea, then she would also get what she wanted. No matter, though, she was willing to be used in order to live the life she so desperately wanted.

Delilah finally arrived at the one spot that could make this moment even better. The bridge to the city gave off a view that mesmerized Delilah with every visit. The way the city twinkled and glowed within the night was simply breathtaking. Delilah would stare at this sight, saying nothing, trying to soak in every second so she may play it back in her mind back home. But the thought occurred to her; she could now see this sight every night if she so wanted to, that this moment wasn't confined to just a single visit every other month.

Jennifer, breaking Delilah's concentration, said, "Oh, I almost forgot. Your dad is having your new car sent over to the apartment. It should be there by the time the concert is over. And your things will be gathered up and sent over within a day. I have something for you to wear in the meantime, so don't worry about that." Delilah wondered if she actually woke up from her nap or if this was some sort of glorious dream that she would be waking from.

The car finally arrived at the parking structure, and both girls got out to head toward the arena where Alma would feel the night with good times. This area was the clean part of the city; everything was nice and perfect as if it had just been built a few weeks ago. There wasn't a single road where you couldn't find a police officer, and every shop or bar was filled with men in suits or the intellectual type with nice clothes. Everything within this area screamed rich snob, and if you happen to be anything otherwise, then more than likely you'd be arrested for something meaningless, just to throw you out of the limits of this area.

The two friends arrived at the doors to begin the adventure that would echo in the back of their minds all night. "Wow, I've never seen this many people here before!" said Delilah to Jennifer. "Yeah, I know. I mean, I didn't know they were this popular around here. I guess great minds think alike." And before another word could come from either of the two, Alma took the stage with fireworks going off in the background. The stage was incredible;

the big cubed screen up above showed the band in case you got seated at the top of the arena; fireworks would go off after every big moment within a song, and whoever was doing the lighting effects made the show feel surreal. The night was filled with euphoric moments that no one could describe, and when the show was over, the girls headed back to the place they would now call home.

The apartment sat in a gated community, with large fences surrounding the entire area. When they passed the gate, Delilah noticed this community was pretty self-contained; there was a gym and pool area when you first came in, then beyond that, there was a grocery store, followed by a movie complex and gas station. Delilah couldn't understand any of this. "Why would you build a town within a city if the only people you're getting money from are the people who live within this gated community?" Jennifer, while still driving, replied, "Well, it's easy when all your prices are extremely high. People don't seem to mind, though. I think they would rather pay the prices than have to go out into the city to find what they need. Kind of a convenience issue, I guess." Delilah nodded her head in agreement. "I can't believe how nice this place is. I saw the brochure but that doesn't prepare you for this sight."

They finally arrived at the structure that held their new home, a big white building with many apartments connecting each other, ever home with their own balcony. In the middle of the structure, stairs wrapped around. "Come on, Delilah, our apartment is on the top floor. You're going to love the view. You can see almost the entire city from there!" Without haste, Delilah and Jennifer ran up the stairs to the top floor. Jennifer tried to hurry and get the key out of her pocket, finally pushing the metal key in to unlock the door. They both push themselves within the apartment, Jennifer running to the couch to fling her body on the cushions in a fashion of excitement. Delilah's only concern was the view she heard her friend speak about; she opened the sliding door to the balcony, and sure enough, the view stood right in front of her. Delilah gazed upon the lights and sounds of the big city; it was almost as good as the bridge view and certainly worth many looks in the future. Jennifer, getting up off the couch, said, "Delilah, why are you always looking at the city in that way, almost like you've never seen it before?" Delilah never took her eyes off the gleaming views of the city. "Because this always gets me! It doesn't matter how bad of a day I have or how crappy my life is. I can always look at this view or think of this view, and all my pains just go away. Like someone put this here for me, just for me!"

That night filled Jennifer with sweet dreams of the concert while Delilah couldn't sleep knowing that her dreams had just come true. Delilah was thinking, *Why waste time sleeping when my dreams can never get better than this?* So she stepped out of the apartment, walking along the sidewalk of the gated community, knowing she was safe from any danger that may veer its ugly head. The night breezes blew in her face, cooling her very soul to the core.

The weeks would go by Delilah and Jennifer as they lived in sweet harmony. Nothing drastic would ever show its head, and nothing happened that would make Delilah have to move back to her parents' house. A phone call would reveal Delilah's father's disapproval of the entire situation, making comments such as the fact that he would feel more comfortable knowing that Delilah was safe and sound within the confines of her true home. Delilah was not caring what her father spoke of; she was happy exactly where she was, and nothing would detour her from living the life she dreamed of having for so long.

One day, after Jennifer came home from her daily job, she went to Delilah to have a small talk. "Delilah, as you know our lease is up in four months, and I know you love it here, but I can't see myself living in the city anymore. I did everything I wanted to do, and now I want to move back home." Delilah was sitting with a shocked look on her face. "But I thought you loved it here?" Jennifer got closer to Delilah. "I know you love it here, but I hate the hassle I have to go through every morning just to get to work. I thought living here would be easy and carefree, but I constantly have to go through the bad part of town in order to get to my job, and I can't do it anymore. I have asked my parent and they will pay for the rest of my rent, but next week I am moving back home. I don't want to do this to you, but as of right now, I can't deal with this life anymore." Delilah looked at Jennifer. "I don't want you to go, but I also don't want you to go through anything you don't want to do. I just don't understand. How bad can where you work be? It can't be any worse than any of the bad neighborhoods back home." Jennifer looked at Delilah with a sheer outlandish look of disgust. "How would you know? You're up here all day. Have you even left the gated community? No, you're up here standing out on the balcony or walking through the gated town, so you don't know!"

"I bet it's not as bad as you make it seem, Jennifer. You're just being selfish like you always are, using me to get what you want from my father like you've done with almost everything in this apartment." Without another word spoken to Delilah, Jennifer got up and dialed a number on her cell phone. "Daddy, I want to leave now. Screw that job I want out right now, so I'm heading back home today once I get everything packed up!" Still talking on the phone, Jennifer ran into her room and slammed the door, knocking several pictures off the wall.

Later that day, Jennifer packed all her things into her midsized car and drove off, leaving Delilah by herself in complete loneliness. Delilah sat alone on the couch, thinking to herself, *It can't be that bad. Maybe I should check it out for myself. She was just being the same old Jennifer that I've known since high school, always thinking of herself and no one else. Tonight I will go to where she used to work.* But before Delilah could think anything further, her cell phone rang. "Delilah, I heard Jennifer left the apartment. Now you know our deal, which means you have to come home." "No, Father, our deal was if anything was to happen while I were up here, then I would come home, and so far, the only thing to happen is Jennifer left. I haven't been in danger, so our deal hasn't been broken." "Delilah! I don't want you up in the city by yourself. It is far too dangerous for a young female such as you!" "Father, my mind is made up. I am staying. Our deal is still standing, and it hasn't been broken. So I'm staying, and when the moment arises that I get into some form of trouble, then I will come back home and won't say another word about living in the city." And without warning, Delilah hung up on her father.

That evening when Delilah was waiting for the lights to come on, she remembered her decision to go into the heart of the big city. She packed water and started heading out the door to get into her car. Out of the community was easy enough; now it was time to turn down the road she thought Jennifer always took. Then the thought dawned upon her; she really hadn't been out of the gated community, that Jennifer might have been right. But feeling confident that it couldn't be as bad as what her friend had said, she continued out to the heart of the big city. Each turn was lead down a one-way street; the traffic wasn't terrible, but Delilah wasn't the only one on the road, which was met with several irritated motorist behind her. Delilah was beginning to panic; she turned down a street without looking, each road looking like the last until finally she was lost. Each building looking the same; each street name was remembered and forgotten. Delilah searched for someone, anyone that could possibly help at getting her back on track, but hardly anyone was out and about.

Delilah, about to give up hope, finally had seen a bunch of men step out of a bar of some kind. She parked the car as close as she could get and began running to the large gentlemen. "Excuse me! Excuse me! Can you help me? I can't seem to find my way back home. Can someone give me directions?" The men all looked up at once, laughing at each other while one, who seemed to be the leader of the pack, said, "Well, look what we have here! Little miss is all alone and needs help! Well, I got some help for you!" He then proceeded to grab Delilah and began rubbing her crotch. Delilah, fighting with every bit of strength she could muster, hit him anywhere she could and tried to knee the man in the groin, but the chance never came. After a few minutes of struggle, she finally became free from her tormentor and started running toward her car. The men, taking off after her, got just a mere few inches within reach; they managed to make Delilah head down a darkened alley. A hand stretched out, and Delilah was eventually caught for more sexual abuse. The same man, the leader, started yet again, rubbing and feeling all over Delilah while the others stood there to help keep her contained and to watch; she was still struggling and thinking within her own thoughts, *How did I get myself into this mess? I should've listened to Jennifer. Why did I not listen!* Her screams were getting louder and louder with no one listening; she could smell the alcohol on their breath, which was enough to make her gag a few times. The tears ran down her face, smearing her makeup into a runny mess. "STOP! Someone please help me! PLEASE STOP!" The friends of the leader decided to sit this one out after slowly sobering up but allowed their friend to continue while they left.

Without warning, a young man came up behind the leader, grabbing his arm. "I will hold him, you run!" Without haste, Delilah ran out of the alleyway but decided to stick around if only to see the face of her rescuer. The darkness was still covering any light she could use to view the young man. Finally, the man that caused so much abuse on Delilah ran past her while holding his own arm. Delilah rushed back to witness the young man on his knees talking to himself, the light shining just enough to give her a view of the young man. She took it all in, remembering every curve of his body, every detail of his face; Delilah was about to thank the man that saved her life, but the thoughts of what kind of person this might be lingered around in her mind, leaving her with too much doubt to engage in confronting him. Delilah simply turned around to head back to her car. She put the keys into the ignition and was about to turn the key when a huge storm began to roll in, bringing with it rain and lightning. Out of nowhere, she saw the young man leave the alleyway, running toward the very place she had went for help earlier. Delilah, sitting in the driver's seat of her car, thought, *I should at least thank him if nothing else. I mean, I do owe him that. It's not every day someone saves your life.* The young man had already made a large amount of distance between him and Delilah, so she was going to have to drive some of the distance just to try and catch up. It finally seemed like she was farther enough to try and catch him, so she parked the car and leaped out as soon as he ran by. The rain washing away the remainder of the makeup was still left on her face. Delilah was now running after the young man, trying her best to catch up to him while calling out, "Excuse me! Excuse me!" Then out of nowhere, a gunshot echoed all around the area with a loud paralyzing shock wave, which made the young man stop within his tracks.

Delilah finally caught up toward the young man; all the while, the rain stopped and the thunder within the clouds began to halt. Delilah began to thank the man who just saved her life moments before. Delilah would try and explain to him that she was following him and how she wanted to thank him for saving her life but was met with only negative remarks, which left her sour, so she just turned around and walked back to the car.

Once again sitting in the driver's seat of her car, she was thinking, *How can anyone be like that to someone who's just trying to say thank you? Can someone be that rude and thoughtless? Well, he did save my life, so maybe it's not really him but maybe what he's been through.* Her thoughts were still rambling on and on, but a feeling was taking control of her very emotions, something inside her was telling her to help this young man. Then out of the blue, Delilah looked up to a sign that showed an arrow pointing to the gated community that she called home. Before any other thought could find its way to her head, Delilah put the car into drive and started heading home.

Finally feeling safe and secure within her own world at the gated community, Delilah drove past the pool and gym that she thought she would never see again, staring at the grocery store with a smile and then finally parking in her spot in front of her home. Opening the door with the key, she walked inside, feeling somewhat safe, but the strange feeling that her personal space had just been violated still lingered on. She took a shower and got ready to sleep, completely ignoring the lights of the city to just head for bed, but before sleep would take her, she grabbed the diary from within the mattress and began to write.

July 14

Tonight will live in the back of my mind forever. I got lost within the city and tried to find help but was met with several men trying to take advantage of me; only one succeeded. I thought I was going to die and my body will never feel the same again; nothing can ever be the same as it once was. Just when things were looking their worst, a young man saved me from being raped and possibly murdered. I'm not entirely sure what the young man did to my tormentor, but from the way he ran out of the alleyway, I can tell he was in a lot of pain.

I tried to thank him, but he told me to go away and to leave him alone. Something is telling me to pursue him, to help him or at least repay him for his kindness, but I wouldn't even know where to start. The first thing I need to do is learn this city and how to navigate through it.

I can't explain it, or maybe I shouldn't; maybe I should just roll with it, but I feel something special inside when I was around this young man. I don't even know his name, but I feel so strongly for him. This has never happened to me before, meeting someone for the first time and immediately falling for them just doesn't happen, so how can I explain this to myself? Or should I even try? I don't know much, but what I do know is that I certainly need to find out who he is, even if it's just to repay him.

Chapter 3

"*W*ake up! Wake up! How much sedative did you give him? Listen, I don't know if you can hear me, but I am getting you out of here, this much I owe you."

A half-asleep Seth began to awaken from a deep sleep. Dazed and confused, he looked around to a different surrounding. "Where the hell am I?" Seth asked. A young female who looked awfully familiar stepped into the light. "You might not remember me, but I will never forget your face. I was the one you saved that night in the alleyway. I have been watching you for the last few weeks and couldn't watch any more abuse that they were dealing on you." Still trying to focus, his eyes began to see a little more clearly, just enough to make out the face that was speaking with him. "Yes, I do remember you. You're that helpless cunt I watched get beat before I stopped him. I don't owe you anything, so leave me alone. Let me die within these walls." Stunned and silent, the young female took a step forward. "If anything, I owe you my life, so that's why I am helping you. My name is Delilah, and if there's anything you need, just let me know." Seth rolled his eyes. "Yeah, there is something you can do. Get the fuck out of here."

Days would pass in which Seth prayed for death, hoping one day would grant him the wish of an end. What he didn't realize was Ewar was watching over him with each step, trying his best to keep Seth safe, but when self-destruction was the only thing on one's mind, that task can be rather difficult. Seth would try cutting his wrist, saving as many pills as possible so he could take them all at once; he even tried stealing a gun, but every attempt was met in disaster. At least at the other location, he could get away with a lot since no one really seemed to care.

A week would pass when young Delilah returned to just sit and talk; a sedated Seth could do nothing but listen. "You know, I have asked the doctors to keep you off medication, but it seems every time they do, you try and kill yourself. I can't change who you are, and I can't say I know what you have been through, but I do know death is not the answer. We live our lives just doing the best we can, and sometimes life throws us things we can't fully handle. That is why we have to ask for help no matter how strong we are. I want to help you, but you have to let me in. I will do my best to make you see the light, but you have to trust in me. You saved my life. Now it's time for me to save yours. I will check in from time to time and make sure they are treating you right, but think about what I said."

On top of a mountain, the sky glazed with a light hue of orange and red. A calm breeze was blowing against Seth's face, relaxing every muscle in his body. The wind picked up pace while leaves and debris flew all around him. Slowly, he lifted off the ground, floating while spinning slowly in place mere feet from where he once stood. An inner light floated all around Seth's body, filling him with warmth and comfort. A soft low-toned voice called out, "We live our lives just doing the best we can, and sometimes life throws us things we can't fully handle. That is why we have to ask for help no matter how strong we are. I want to help you, but you have to let me in. I will do my best to make you see the light, but you have to trust in me. You saved my life. Now it's time for me to save yours. I will help you see the light!"

Waking to a weak groggy feeling, Seth was so full of drugs he couldn't remember what reality felt like. With his sight beginning to come back into view, Seth saw only one thing—a young petite female with long brown, almost black, hair. "Yes, I asked them to take you off medication a few days ago. It's just taking some time for them to wear off, but if you promise not to commit suicide, I will make sure they keep you off." The young Delilah walked slowly near Seth to take his hand. "I pray for you every night. I pray that you could see the same thing I see in you every time I lay my eyes upon you. If only you could see the potential I see in you. I have only known you for a short time, but you have grown within me. It's almost as if something is telling me to be near you. Please speak to me." And with a glaze in his eyes, he said, "I can't understand why you are still here with me. You don't know me, and you can't know what I have done to be here, so why are you persistent on seeing me?" Delilah stood with only a smile. "And exactly who do you think put you here, who do you think saved you in the alleyway, who do you think didn't want you to commit suicide? I had been watching you, so I may properly thank you for saving me, and I find you sitting alone bleeding out around you. With someone capable of compassion like you, I couldn't allow death to take you, so I checked you into the nearest hospital." Expecting a warmth heartfelt thank you, Delilah stood there still holding Seth's hand until Seth broke contact. "I didn't ask to be saved. You couldn't possible understand what you have done. I don't need your help. You basically doomed me. Leave me. I am not someone you need to be around." "I wish you didn't feel that way, Seth. I will leave, but I am not giving up on you." Seth with a long stare, replied, "I said leave me!"

Seth, alone with his thoughts, was thinking of the female that kept bugging him, thinking of Robert, Stan, and certainly his mother. Seth never used to think of life or how shitty his had been, but since he had so much time on his hands, it seemed like those thoughts would always linger around. Seth would contemplate if anyone had a life shittier than his, or if he were doomed to be the only one to suffer this much, but he had no idea what plans awaited him. But as promised, Seth refrained from killing himself or so he figured he could always fake being well enough to leave and then continue in a secluded area; all Seth had was time, and that was all he needed. But still, this female was a mystery to him; every thought would reflect who this woman was and what she wanted with him. "She says she knows me, but how can that be since we haven't spent any time together? Is she looking for some attention, like I'm some kind of wounded animal in need of rescuing? In any case, she won't be around for much longer. When her life turns to shit because of me, she'll just leave without question."

The next day, the young Delilah returned, this time bearing gifts of kindness. "Hi. How are you doing today, Seth? Hopefully today is a much better than the others you have had in the past." Seth, with a look of annoyance, replied, "Look, I have nothing to give. There is nothing you can take from me. If you think you owe me something because you think I saved your life, think nothing more about it. I hate assholes, and so even if it weren't you in the alleyway, I still would have dealt with him." With a cute little laugh, she said, "I think it's funny how you haven't learned by now that I am not going to leave you alone, so you might as well get used to the fact that I'm here and I'm not going anywhere, and technically, I saved your life, so I believe we're even. You seem tense, Seth, so I have asked the doctors to give you something to help you relax. It's a new drug that's supposed to work wonders. You talk about having nightmares, well, this drug will help suppress them." Within minutes, a doctor walked in Seth's room. "Don't worry, Seth, this will help you relax." The doctor took the drug in hand and slowly added it to Seth's IV. The doctor left the room to attend to other patients. Delilah was sitting at Seth's side, holding his hand until the drug kicked in. And with the drug slowly entering Seth's bloodstream, he began to lose consciousness.

Seth stood before the same hallway as before, except there was now more writing on the wall, this time more visible. The room felt dark and damp; you could feel depression thick within the air. There was a little more light surrounding everything this time, and the dark thick fluid running from the wall now appeared to be free-flowing blood. Seth didn't dare look at the writing; he already knew most of it was addressed to him. Slowly walking down the hallway, Seth noticed that this time the door was brighter than the last time. He wondered whether or not to even open it; he remembered the sight that was so vivid and didn't think he could take another image such as that again. Nonetheless, Seth continued walking, making sure not to get too close to the walls. Finally at the door, Seth paused, his thoughts racing out of control of what could await him on the other side. Each bad dream within Seth's mind was still remembered, still etched in the back of his brain like he had seen them yesterday. And with a turn of the handle, he swung the door completely open.

It took some time for Seth's eyes to fully adjust, but when it finally happened, he saw nothing in sight except dark gray skies. With dust rolling within the wind, the cracked dry ground crumbled from underneath Seth's feet. Seth turned around to find the door from which he came was now gone, vanished as if it never existed. The temperature rose hotter and hotter until Seth couldn't help but wipe the sweat from his forehead. Finally, the temperature got to be too much, and Seth collapsed to his knees. Within seconds, a great shock wave came from the ground; the floor began to break up and split down in the middle. The ground continued to break apart until a large canyon revealed itself in front of him; a bright orange light shone from the bottom of the canyon. The heat was almost unbearable, but Seth couldn't resist looking down the pit to see what lay beneath. One hand was covering his face from the blistering vapors that rose up from the canyon, trying to keep covered from the heat without much success. Seth's eyes squinted to take a glimpse of what could possibly be giving off so much light when he accidentally pushed a large piece of rock off the ledge; the object fell until it finally reached the bottom and, within a flash, caught fire and vanished. What Seth was looking at was a large river of molten lava flowing mere feet below him. Seth, still on his knees, feverishly crawled backward from the sight that could very well end his life in an instant; with each step, another small chunk of ground dropped down below to be one with the river.

In the distance, the voices of small children playing echoed throughout the land. In front of the children, Seth's little brother, Stan, stood staring into his eyes. With a light red glaze within Stan's eyes, he spoke with a two-toned voice—one of a little child, the other as if something evil lived inside. "I thought you loved me, big brother! But you left me with that monster. You killed our mother, and you allowed him to overtake me. I was only a little child and you abandoned me to save yourself." Seth's mouth moved, but no words could escape. A small tear rolled down his cheek. Seth could do nothing but listen. The pain, so overwhelming, brought Seth back down to his knees. "How does it feel to have saved yourself and left everyone that loved you to die? I have made it so you can't speak because I have no time for your excuses! I want to see you plead, I want to see you beg, I want to see you cry in misery, and most importantly, I want to watch you die!" And with a point of a finger, the horde of children started transforming into something else, something evil. Their nails and teeth began to grow into long sharp points, and their eyes started to emit a glowing red. Seth began to panic, slowly backing up inch after inch until Stan began to lift off the ground and began to float toward Seth. "I see you don't like it when the tables have turned. Well, that's too damn bad. You will sleep in the bed you have created for yourself. I will enjoy watching you DIE!" Seth then turned around to run, but the ground around him gave way, leaving a mere three feet in all directions. Stan was still floating in front of Seth. "He showed me the way, and he wants to show you the way, but I told him you *would decline. Such a foolish waste. If I can't turn you, then my wish shall be granted in destroying you. Poor Seth and his miserable life. You're weak and could never possibly understand the power at hand, so give your soul to him or allow me my wish. You may now speak." Seth's breaths were coming back. "Stan, please listen to me. I never meant for any of this to happen. You have to believe me. I am your brother. He is using you to get to me. I love you! Don't allow him to consume you. You're nothing but a puppet to him!" "You will make your decision, or I will make it for you!" "Then my answer is no. I will never allow someone to have control over me. To live a life that isn't my own is no way to live at all, so kill me if you must, but my answer is no!" "I was so hoping you would say that, my brother. This shall be the day to remember, the day I destroyed the monster that gave me this hell!"*

Stan, with the deformed children behind him, stood ever so confidently in front of Seth. "Kill him my siblings and bring me his head!" And with the last sentence, the children, in one giant horde, started running and leaping for him. Like a pack of wild animals, they jumped and attacked every inch of young Seth's body, tearing skin from bone. Seth tried to fight them off but found every attempt useless, for every child he threw into the pit of burning lava, another came to take its place. Each claw mark dug deeper into Seth's skin, blood dripping from his forearms, draining him ever so deeper. Bone began to show as their claws dug deeper until flesh just dangled in place. The fight was pointless; nothing could stop the mound of bodies attacking. The pain grew to the point of exhaustion and then on to brink of death. But before death could take shape, Seth looked up for a split second to see Stan eagerly smiling at the pain being inflicted. A voice called out from Stan. "In the end, we all die, my brother, but it's up to you on what type of mark you make in life. You will always be a traitor, the weak link in the chain. You will always be remembered as the one who destroyed our family, which is why it gives me great joy to savor this moment."

Awakened with a deep breath, Seth opened his eyes from panic. The room was completely trashed from top to bottom, and Delilah was standing at the foot of the front door with her mouth opened in shock. Deep claw marks were embedded into Seth's forearms, blood dripped and soaked into his hospital bed and covered all into the floor. His restraints, ripped to shreds, lay on the floor and into several different pieces. Four guards were knocked unconscious in the middle of the room. Seth, with a puzzled look, asked the faithful question of, "What happened?" But before anyone could answer him Seth, was given an extremely large sedative.

Delilah was staring at the large heap of Seth lying on the floor; the doctors standing behind her each baffled at how such a small teen could do so much damage and wondered where the marks on his arms came from. Each consulted another. There wasn't a single sharp object in the room; how in the hell did he cut himself with such precision? Seth was placed in another room while they stopped the bleeding and dressed the wounds and then set him up on an IV to transfer blood back into his body, with his old room being studied for clues as to what happened, for the only person who had seen everything, Delilah, wasn't talking. Still at his bedside, Delilah held Seth's hand, trying to comfort him. "No matter what it takes, I will never leave or give up on you. You need me now more than ever."

Seth was awakened from a deep dreamless sleep. "What happened? Where am I?" Delilah, still at his bedside, said, "You were resting, just lying there peaceful and calm and then, out of nowhere, you went wild. You began jumping up and down frantically. I have no idea how you cut yourself. There wasn't anyone near you, and like the doctors have said, there weren't any sharp objects within the room." Seth, with a puzzled look on his face, said, "My dreams are bleeding into my reality. Now do you see why I can't continue to live? I am dangerous. I could have killed you and yet you're still here. I don't understand why you continue to be at my side." Delilah, with a smile on her face, replied, "I just see something in you that I guess you don't see. You are meant for so much more, and yet I can't really explain it. It's like someone is telling me to stay with you and guide you on your way. Through thick and thin, I will always be here, that much I promise you."

Delilah talked among the doctors in the hallway outside of Seth's room; after her conversation, she walked back to Seth. "I have made plans for you to be released from here, but you have to do a few things first. I guess conditions, if you want to call them that. First, these episodes of harming yourself and suicidal crusades have to stop. Second, you have to see a psychiatrist. I don't care how much you fight me on this one, but it is a must. Third, you have to find a place to stay—no more living on the street. After all that is settled and done with, then and only then will you be released. Trust me, they wanted to keep you in here for good. I had to talk them into this, and those were the only conditions that I couldn't argue out of." Seth shook his head. "What if I don't want out of here? Maybe everyone is much safer with me in here rather than walking the streets?" Delilah placed her hand on Seth's hand. "I hope you really don't believe that. You're not as dangerous as you might think. This world needs someone like you." Seth quickly released his hand from hers. "Your world has forsaken me for something horrible. I am nothing more than a bastard child destined to kill and suffer. I am not the type of person you want to be known with, so do yourself a favor and leave me before something terrible happens to you." Delilah got up from the chair. "I wish you wouldn't speak of yourself in that way. I will be back tomorrow. Hopefully you'll be in a better mood then."

Seth was alone with only his thoughts to keep him company. *What have I done? How could I leave my brother with that monster? I am no better than the monster that killed our mother, and now he hates me. My own little brother hates me and wants me dead. But why did he say I killed her?* Seth was beginning to become angry. "That monster tricked my brother into thinking I killed our mother. Maybe I should live if only to kill him! I will make my own anger my weapon. I shall learn to control myself, if not for Robert, and to make sure that piece of shit knows what it's like to be on my bad side."

Months passed, and Seth began training once again. Delilah was in constant contact with Seth and would keep him company just to talk. Day in and day out, he grew stronger and more in depth with his strengths; he slowly learned to control the power that lurked within, but still not enough to control the anger that hid inside. A strange thing occurred while Seth trained—the more Seth tuned in to his strength, the weaker the power became. So in an essence, the more he controlled, the weaker he was, and the less he controlled, the more dangerous he would become.

Each day, Delilah came to visit, sharing herself with Seth. Even though Delilah was a bit of a wild child and had always seen the positive, she too felt alone in the world just like Seth. She constantly told him stories of her childhood. Seth would just listen and take in the memories he so wished were his. She would ask every day for some stories from his side of the world, but every day he sat silently with a look of deep dark misery on his face. Delilah told Seth, "I was given everything in the world except for the one thing I truly wanted. Money and gifts are only a short fix for happiness. I see you and I know you have nothing to give, all I want is you." Seth would never say much; he just kindly let Delilah do all the talking, which she was more than happy to do.

Days would turn into months, and soon Seth had been at this hospital for a year, with not a single suicide attempt. What once was an ill-mannered, ill-tempered young man now stood this strong, seemingly confident and a quiet gentleman. The days were approaching that Seth would be released, yet the only person that seemed to be excited was Delilah. "I just can't wait for the day to come that I can take you away from this place. I already have you an apartment. I hope you don't mind living with me. And my father has a job lined up for you. He doesn't know a lot about you besides you saved my life, so please don't mention anything to him." Shortly after this conversation, a doctor walked through the door to give Seth some good news. "Hello, Seth. How are we feeling today?" With a whispering voice, Seth replied, "Good." "Well, I have some good news there, champ. I'm glad the medication is still helping to suppress your dreams, and since we haven't had a single incident from you in almost a year, we will be releasing you in just a couple of weeks. How does that sound, Seth? Do you want to be released?" Still with the same voice, Seth said, "Yes, sir," but this time, Seth gave a small nod as well. The doctor was writing notes down as he spoke simply giving a smile, and continued to say, "Good, good." Delilah, with a huge smile on her face, could barely keep her excitement to herself. "So when do you think I can take him home, Doctor?" The doctor, still writing within his folder, simply stood there to finish his last sentence before looking up and saying, "We'll give him another two weeks, so fourteen days from now, but that's only if there aren't any situations before then." Delilah, almost jumping for joy, moved swiftly toward the doctor to give an uncontrollable hug and to thank him almost half a dozen times. The doctor shut the folder, tucked the pen within the pocket of his jacket, and then started walking out the door. Delilah ran to Seth and wrapped her arms around him. "I am so happy. I thought this day would never come." Seth was reluctant at first but slowly moved his arms around Delilah. There was only one thing running through his mind. *I haven't felt like this in a long time. I almost forgot what it feels like to actually have someone there who loves and cares for me. I wonder how long this will last.* The inner shell that was Seth's soul was still holding strong, knowing that he couldn't let down his guard again. He may be strong physically, but mentally he's about to fall apart. Another hit would just destroy everything that was Seth; the emptiness, like a black hole, was ready to devour him completely. Delilah and the thought of his brother were the only thing holding him together.

Still, the thought of what would happen if he lost control outside of this institution would most likely prove unwanting for him and for everyone around him. God forbid, he might do anything to harm Delilah. Seth wanted to ask for an extension but knew the very comment might break her heart, plus this would be a perfect opportunity to see how strong he really was; this would prove useful in determining if he really had the power to control the monster within. And the medication did seem to work; he hadn't had a dream in almost a year, so there was also that.

Each day, Seth sat in the chair next to the window, staring out above the people doing their daily routine while Delilah went on and on about his new home and how she had fixed it up to make him feel more comfortable. To Seth, anything was better than the streets from where he came; even the hospital was more inviting than the alleyway he used to share with the local residents. But to sleep in a bed where someone wasn't constantly watching you was also a plus. Although Seth wasn't out of the woods yet, he still had to contain himself long enough to be set free, and he knew all too well how badly his luck screwed him over. Each thought was never of him getting better but more of, *I wonder when my life goes back to the way it was. When do the dreams start up again? When will Delilah drop him and leave him stranded with no one?* Each question ran through his mind, yet no answer in sight; then the thought occurred, *Maybe I should just enjoy this while it last. Seems how I know it won't last and will be back to the way it was.* So each day, Seth just enjoyed the simple things that everyone takes for granted.

Two weeks would come and go, and when it was finally the day for Seth to be released, Delilah was at the front and center for the big event. "This is the day I have been looking forward to, almost as if I'm a little kid again and this is my first birthday." With a nervous look on his face, he started walking out the door. "Don't worry, Seth. I know it feels weird to leave this place behind. Being in one place for a certain link of time makes you grow roots, and sometimes uprooting yourself can be very difficult, but trust me, I will make sure your transition is as comfortable as possible." Seth, still walking, kept thinking to himself, *I should tell her I'm not nervous about my transition but more of me not being able to control my abilities. I want so much to live a normal life, and yet my life has been anything but normal.*

Slowly walking down the hallway, Seth took in every aspect of the place he was leaving behind. The wait of leaving left him little time to prepare for the outside world, nervously walking down each halfway, staring through each windowed door to the people he would probably never see again. Sweat began to drip from Seth's forehead; his heart was beating rapidly, the shakes began to take control. The doctors asked Seth if he were all right with Delilah, confirming that he was just a little nervous of leaving the hospital and that he would be fine; what little she knew of the fear Seth really felt. They were finally outside with what looked like a new car awaiting them at the curb. The doctors escorted Seth to the passenger side of the car while Delilah got in through the driver's side. "Take one last look at this place, Seth. This will be the last you'll see it," Delilah said in an excited tone. And with one last look, the car pulled away.

The traffic within the city was almost unbearable; car piled up left and right, car horns could be heard several blocks away, which made for a very frustrating time to be a driver. The car ride should have taken only thirty minutes but instead took an hour and ten. Seth was half asleep when Delilah said, "Well, Seth, welcome home. You now live within the gated community of Alegra Haven." Seth looked out the window of the moving car—large white apartment buildings stretching eight blocks, each apartment had a balcony with clear sliding doors leading to them. Seth had never seen anything like this, almost as if he was dreaming. The only thing Seth could think, *What did I do to deserve this?*

Chapter 4

*D*elilah got out of the car to show off the new apartment to Seth. "I hope you don't mind, but they ran out of rooms with more than one bed, so we will have to make do with one. I hope that's not a problem." Seth, still a little dazed, just gazed at Delilah with a look of, "I don't care." "Oh, and before I forget, your first appointment with the psychiatrist is tomorrow." Seth rolled his eyes with a look of disgust. Delilah crossed her arms. "I don't want to hear how you don't want to go, and you know you have to. It's part of your rehabilitation." Seth said nothing while Delilah continued to give the look of disappointment.

The move to the new apartment was easy enough for Seth, only because he had nothing more but the clothes on his back; he owned nothing else. And so they began walking up the stairs to the third floor of the apartment complex, which was where their new apartment sat. Seth walked through the door of apartment 31; a fresh new sight was to be seen. He had never seen a place so nice; everything looked clean and well kept. Nothing was out of place, almost as if this place wasn't real like a picture in a catalog. Delilah, with a smile on her face, said, "Yes, Seth, this is your new home. I hope you like it!" It seemed. for once. he was in a place in his life that he felt somewhat happy; he had a place he could call home, a person who actually seemed to care about him, and the dreams were gone; but he didn't allow this feeling to last for long. He knew this wouldn't last because it never does and it never will. Still, he took everything in with greed—the nice comfortable bed with no shackles, and the refrigerator that held real food instead of having to be served food from the hospital, even the view, which overlooked the city, was breathtaking. Seth took nothing for granted. "Oh, and before I forget, I got this for you." Delilah then handed over a box with a gold heart symbol on the top. "It's so we will always remember each other, forever." Seth opened the box to reveal half a heart gold necklace with the word *ever* etched into the facing. Delilah lifted the other half of the necklace from within her shirt; hers showed the rest of the meaning that read *For*. Seth was not saying too much; happy emotions were never something he used often, but in his head, the feelings were becoming apparent that he might actually love this girl.

Seth's appointments to the psychiatrist came and went, and they all seemed like the same visit—he would sit in the doctor's office, sitting in the chair and not making a sound. The doctor tried to get him to talk, but nothing made him speak his mind. Finally, within the third visit, the doctor had a small talk with Delilah. "Listen, I don't want to alarm you, but if he continues this, then I will have no choice but to diagnose him incompetent, which means that he will have to have someone with him at all times. I am trying to get him to open up, but all he ever does is sit there and stare at the paintings on my wall, and by the agreement you signed, I must give the okay before allowing Seth to be fully integrated into society." Delilah, with a concerned look on her face, replied, "I understand, Doctor. I will talk to him and try to make him grasp the importance of these meetings. I promise the next time you two meet, it will be a better visit."

Back at the apartment, Seth was sitting on the couch, watching whatever was on at that very moment, with Delilah sitting at the bar and staring at the back of Seth's head with a concerned look on her face. "Listen, Seth, we have to talk. These sessions where you aren't speaking need to stop. The only way for you to stay out of the hospital is if you make progress. They want you to start being normal, and I can't take seeing you back in that hospital, so please, will you do this for me? Will you at least try with the doctor?" Seth was still sitting in the same spot, gazing at the rug down at his feet, staring at the patterns within the rug's many shapes. Delilah, now becoming irritated, remarked, "You aren't going to speak?" And before Delilah could leave in a fit of disgust, Seth began talking, "I know you're trying, and I know I can be difficult, but some things I can't help. You have been with me not only to see me at my best but also at my worst, and I thank you for that, but I need time. I can't just switch to something I'm clearly not. All my life is one bad dream after another, and for once, I have something good, something I can smile about, and I want to smile, but I just need more time. I am trying, and

I will try harder, but I can't and I won't trust anyone except you." Delilah was standing within the door of their bedroom, with her head propped up against the frame. The look of disgust was gone, traded for a concerned sincere look. Before any more words could be exchanged, Delilah walked to the couch and sat next to Seth. Softly grasping his hand to hers, she leaned over to gently place her head on his shoulder. "I'm sorry for what you have been through, and I know me pressuring you isn't helping, but this decision isn't up to me. If it were, I would have signed those papers weeks ago. You have shown real promise, but it's just not enough for some people. I didn't want to bring this up, but I have an idea that I want to run by you. It will most likely deal in great with your privacy, but it's the only way to truly get you to talk without several sessions, to which we don't have the luxury. I don't think we have much of a choice, which is why I am going to ask the doctor if he could perform hypnosis." Seth pushed Delilah away. "You want me to let someone in my mind involuntarily? I can't allow anyone within my walls. I've seen things, and for anyone to know, for anyone to open that box, I just don't know if I can. I . . . I need some time alone." Seth got up the couch and awkwardly left the apartment.

Walking along the street, Seth's thoughts rambled on and on; his shadowy silhouette was the only thing keeping him company. The homeless were nowhere to be found; things change so much when you no longer live within the confines of lower society. It's weird no longer being able to hear gunfire or the sounds of cars that should have been looked at by a mechanic ages ago. All the sounds and sights changed to children playing in the park and mothers gossiping to one another on park benches. If you've seen a car, you didn't hear it. This area was so clean and respectful. Seth felt out of place, and it appeared everyone thought the same for all the angry stares. He would walk along the sidewalk of the park, his thoughts to himself as he walked past middle-aged women giving him the evil eye, as if he didn't belong within their society. He could feel the stares, one by one, each with their own notion on why Seth should leave their well-renowned neighborhood. These looks and thoughts didn't bother him; this was a normal feeling for him; love and kindness were the feelings he feared and didn't understand.

The past few weeks, Seth learned of all the hidden places he could be alone; the janitors shed with a hidden basement underneath, the roof that overlooked the city, but Seth's favorite spot was a pond with rocks scattered all about. He would sit upon the largest rock and stared at the pond's rippled water; thoughts would race with each visit. Usually, the thoughts remained the same, but this moment was different. "How can they expect me to allow someone to know my inner demons? I don't like knowing what I've seen much less want anyone else to know. Still, this is for Delilah, and right now, if I can't do this for her, I can't do anything. She is the only one I have." Seth fondled the necklace Delilah gave to him, rubbing his fingers across the letters with every stroke a memory of Delilah. With many hours of thought and contemplation, Seth decided to go along with Delilah's plans of hypnosis, thinking to himself that she had sacrificed so much to be with him that if this one thing could bring them closer together, then he should at least try.

Back at the apartment, Seth walked up to Delilah, grabbed her gently by the shoulders, and said, "I can't promise anything, but I will do the hypnosis, but I must ask that you do something for me. Give me one more session with the doctor. I will try to open up, and if it doesn't work, I will do the hypnosis, but if the doctor can't fix me through hypnosis, then you have to let me do whatever I feel is necessary." Delilah rejoiced with a hug but then suddenly pushed away as if a revelation had just brought itself into light. "I hope you're not talking about suicide because you know how much I hate you talking this way." Seth brought Delilah back into his arms. "Trust in me. Whatever I decide will be best for all, but you must have faith in me." Delilah held him tighter than she had ever before. "I just don't want to lose you. I love you too much." Seth stroked the back of Delilah's hair while kissing her forehead. "I will always be with you. No matter what happens, we can never be apart as long as we have moments like this."

A week would pass and Seth's appointment just mere hours away. Delilah talked with the doctor in private. "I'm not sure if you are trained for this, but I have an idea that could possibly open Seth up without lengthy sessions." The doctor stared into Seth's file. "You must be talking about hypnosis. I must warn you, though, hypnosis is a very dangerous practice with this form of background. You must be 100 percent on this." Delilah, with a confident look on her face, said, "We talked it over, and both me and Seth agree that this is the best way, but he wants to try a normal session before we commit into doing something drastic." Still staring into Seth's file, the doctor looked up at Delilah. "Very well. We will have a normal session, and we will play the hypnosis by ear if or when we get to that road."

Seth still in the waiting room until the receptionist called the faithful words, "Seth, the doctor will see you now." He felt as if this was the first time he walked down the hallway he had done many times before; sweat started to run down his forehead, thoughts scrambling, racing, and screaming. Seth was talking to himself, "I know this will end badly. I just know it." The doctor was standing in front of the door. "What will end badly, Seth?" Seth, with just a nervous stare, said nothing more. "Well, Seth, if you're ready, we can begin today's session, I talked to Delilah, and even though I believe hypnosis to be very dangerous, I believe she may have a point in suggesting it, but before you say anything, no, we won't be practicing that unless this session is a failure." Seth found the nearest chair and sat down to begin what hopefully would be one of the last visits he would have to make. The doctor, standing in front of a filing cabinet, put away folders of the previous session. "Okay, Seth, let's get comfortable." The doctor finished and took a sit. "So what should we talk about first?" Seth, with a monotone stare, just sat there. "Delilah said you would be more cooperative. Are you trying to make her out to be a liar?" Seth simply raised his head up and shook with a no. "Very well then, Seth. Let's start with the suicide attempts." Seth, with a very low voice, said, "It's just better if I'm not around people. It's much safer, and I don't want to hurt anyone." The doctor, a little puzzled that words actually formed from this patients lips, began with more questions. "And why do you think you *hurt* people?" The doctor was completely oblivious to the word hurt that had just escaped from Seth's lips seconds ago. Still a bit silent, Seth added, "I don't want to hurt anyone. It just happens sometimes, like I can't control it." The doctor was writing notes with every answer and statement given by Seth. "So you're saying you have no control on when or who you hurt?" Seth, now looking up to face the doctor, replied, "Most of the time, it lashes out when I'm angry." The doctor, still writing, continued, "Can you tell me about your parents, Seth?" Seth, with a very profound and confused look on his face, said, "I can only remember bits and pieces." Seth was thinking, *Why can't I remember anything from my childhood? All I can think of are the dreams I used to have and my days on the street.* The doctor shook his head. "You mean to tell me you don't remember anything from when you were young? Did you know your mother and father? Did you have any siblings?" Seth put his head within his hands, pushing his hands through his hair. "I don't know why I can't remember. I know I had a mother and a brother, but it feels like something is blocking my own memories from me." He started to panic, for the very thought of his own mind playing tricks on him was beginning to drive him insane. A disappointing look came over the doctor. "You mean you can't remember or you don't want us to talk about it? Because I can't help you if you don't help me, so please, Seth, try and remember." Seth shook his head. "I want to remember, but it's like those memories are now gone, like someone stole them from me." The doctor was writing notes within Seth's folder. "I think this session is over. We will start the hypnosis next week."

Seth walked out of the office to a concerned-looking Delilah. The doctor got up out of his chair, walked to the doorway, and said, "Ms. Delilah, may I speak with you?" Delilah was breathing heavier than normal, for what she expected to hear wasn't what she wanted to hear. The doctor sat down at his desk. "Please have a seat. This session was a little bit of an improvement, but I think I'm still getting nowhere. He is either playing with me or his telling the truth in the fact that he can't open up his own memories. I'm afraid we have no choice but to start with hypnosis next week." Delilah, sitting in her chair, was unable to control her nervous shakes. "Please, Doctor, just do your best to help him. I know he is very troubled, but this is his last option." The doctor got up to place Seth's file back within the filing cabinet. "Look, Ms. Delilah, this is the fourth session we have had, and the only thing I am doing is wasting your father's money. I will do my very best, but if next week's session isn't a success, then I will have to refer him to the psych ward, and I doubt your father will miss those charges on his credit card."

Back at the apartment, Delilah asked Seth to sit at the table for a very important talk. "Listen to me very carefully, Seth. I don't know what you said to that doctor, but he seemed a little upset. Now our only option is hypnosis, and then after that, I won't have the funds to help you any longer. My dad knows of you and that you saved my life, but what he doesn't know is that I have been using one of his credit cards to pay the psychiatrist, but his fees are too small for my father to notice. But if next week doesn't work, the doctor is going to send you to a specialty hospital designed to take care of people like you, and the bad news is I can't pay for it, and my father will notice those charges, so it isn't an option. My father thinks that I have already repaid you for saving my life by paying the hospital from which you came. He doesn't know we are in love." Seth grasped Delilah's hand, stroking it ever so gently. "Don't worry. If next week's session doesn't work, I will figure something out that doesn't involve a hospital. You have already done so much for me that I need to start doing certain things on my own. This will no longer be your burden."

The time seemed to fly by so quickly, and Delilah used every bit she could to spend time with Seth. They would walk the park holding hands in the morning, go down to the deli around the corner from their apartment for a bite to eat in the afternoon, and then a walk along the pier at night to stare at the stars and listen to the gentle waves breaking along the shore. Some nights they stayed up all hours in the park, lying on the ground, and all felt safe and secure with each other by their side. But time is no one's friend, and six days had passed and Seth had one more day before his fate would be decided. And on the sixth day, Delilah woke up next to an empty spot next to her in bed. With a concerned feeling, Delilah jumped out of bed to run into the other rooms, screaming Seth's name. Upon entering the kitchen, Delilah found him sitting at the table perfectly calm and quiet. Delilah put her hand on her chest while trying to slow her breathing. "What are you doing in here alone, Seth?" He looked up slowly to face Delilah. "I'm trying to find a way to tell you something, something I do not wish to burden you with, but I feel as if you should know. You may not believe me and that's okay, but I wish for you to at least hear me and know why I've chosen another path if tomorrow is a complete failure. But I must warn you, you may think I'm crazy, but everything I'm about to tell you is the truth." Delilah grabbed a chair and placed it directly to the left of where Seth was sitting. "You can tell me anything. I want to be in your world. You just have to let me in." And with a gentle sigh, Seth began to let her into the very world he so sought to avoid. "Five years ago, I came to this city with nothing but the clothes on my back. I had run away from home because of my stepfather. I left my family behind, and like I told the doctor, I can't remember much about them, like something is blocking my memories from me. Within that year of being homeless, I have knowingly killed two people, but I have a feeling that number is much worse. I just can't remember the others if there were any. But I met a man named Robert, who taught me not only to control myself but also told me of a story, a story involving me and a series of horrible acts that I am destined to perform. You see, I'm apparently one of several within a bloodline that have been chosen to kill someone of great importance. This is the same being that was invading my dreams. I have seen things that would turn your stomach, things that can break your very soul. Maybe I shouldn't have said anything to you, but I felt like I owed you the truth about me, and I wanted you to know before the doctor, that is if he succeeds." Delilah sat in the same spot, speechless and her mouth wide open. "Are you trying to push me away, Seth?" Seth got up out of his chair. "This was a bad idea. I don't know why I wanted to tell you. Just forget all that I have said." But before she could get any words out, Seth stepped toward the door, turned to Delilah, and said, "Today, I want to be alone. I will find my way to the doctor's office." And with those words spoken, the door closed shut and Delilah still sitting at the table speechless.

Walking along the sidewalk in the park, Seth looked around, making sure no one witnesses him entering the one spot he could go to be alone, the one spot no one knows about. Sitting on the rock near the pond, Seth curled up with only his thoughts. *I should have known she wouldn't believe me. I'm such a fool for thinking she could handle my world.* And within that spot Seth would remain, he thought not of food or water but of a life without Delilah, a thought so horrible it brought him to tears. *I can't believe I made myself vulnerable. I have built my shell so that nothing and no one could hurt me, yet I let my guard down with the first hint of love, and this is what I get—a large dose of heartache and pain. Maybe I should just run, run away and see where life takes me.* But the very thought of breaking his promise made Seth feel ill. *No, I must keep my appointment and try to get better, if not for me but for Delilah. She may think I'm crazy, but I still love her.* And there Seth remained upon that rock, staring silently at the sparkles that glittered on top of the water, gently stroking the necklace.

The next day, Seth arrived at the psychiatrist's office with Delilah awaiting his presence in the parking lot. With a huge leap, Delilah ran toward Seth and wrapped her arms around him. "Don't ever leave me like that again. I was so worried you wouldn't show." Seth let go of Delilah's hug. "I promised you I would show, and I was hoping to see you again. I wanted to tell you how much I appreciate everything you've done for me and for all the love you've shown me. No matter what happens, I will always love you and I will always be with you." Delilah was beginning to shed tears. "Please don't say these things, Seth. Everything will be fine, you'll see." The tears were now coming down like a waterfall. Delilah began hugging Seth once again. Seth, holding his dear Delilah once more before his session begins, said, "Just remember that I love you!" Delilah, still crying and holding on to him as if this was the last moment between them, simply said within a soft whisper into his ear, "I know and I love you too."

In the front of the office, Seth's name was being called from a loud voice, "Seth, the doctor will see you now." The doctor, with the same white coat as in previous sessions, a pencil in one hand, and Seth's folder in the other, said, "So how are you feeling today, Seth?" Seth nervously awaited for the doctor to tell him to lie down, assuming that was how all doctors put their patients under. And with a soft mumble, he said, "Fine, Dr. Ian. Not to be rude but I would much rather get this over with." The doctor, writing the last little bit into the folder, agreed and asked Seth to sit in the very same chair he had done in every other session as before. This confused him a little, but he did what the doctor asked and sat in the chair. The doctor pulled up a chair directly in front of Seth. "If you're ready, we will begin. Now first I want you to completely relax your body, from the top of your head down to the toes on your feet. Let this feeling fill you up until you can feel nothing else. Now I want you to stare at the pendulum on my hanging clock. Now I'm going to count down from five, and when I reach one, you will be in a state of deep sleep, and when I clap my hands, you will awaken. Five, you're getting tired, your eyelids are starting to get heavy. Four, you notice you are having a hard time keeping your eyes open. Three, your body is now fully relaxed, and sleep is starting to consume you. Two, your eyelids are too heavy for you to keep open. One, you are now in a state of deep sleep. Seth, are you still with me?" Seth, with his eyes shut, said in a very distinct voice, "Yes, Doctor, I am here." The doctor, sitting with one leg over the other with Seth's folder on clipboard resting on his knee, said, "Very good. Now I want to take you back to your childhood. Take me back to when you were ten." Seth, a little uneasy, began to move around a bit. The doctor, still jotting down notes, said, "If you're there, Seth, I want you to explain what is going on around you." Seth, still moving about, said, "I'm in my bedroom playing video games with my brother. I can hear my mother leaving the driveway." Seth's heart began to beat heavily. "What's wrong, Seth? Why are you breathing so heavily?" Seth's breathing was getting faster and faster.

"Because I know he's coming for me. I know that once my mother leaves for work, then I have to deal with my step-father. I try and guess what today will bring, to prepare myself, but every day, it changes and I can never make myself fully aware of what I must endure. Yesterday was ants. Today I can only hope for verbal abuse, but he hasn't used that in months." The doctor got fearful and excited—fearful for the story he was undoubtedly going to regret hearing but excited because he was finally getting some progress. "Ants, Seth? What did your stepfather do to you with ants?" Seth started to sweat. "Shh! He can hear you! Let me go hide in the closet, and I will tell you." The unconscious Seth was taking a few moments. "Okay, I will tell you but you have to be really quiet or he'll know I'm in here. Yesterday, I was playing out in the yard. Me and Stan found a lizard that changed colors, so we were going to keep it, but we'd have to keep it a secret. Mom don't like creatures of this sort. I held the lizard while Stan went to go look for something to keep it in, but before Stan could get back, a hand grabbed me on the shoulder. I looked up to find my stepdad with an evil grin on his face. By then, I was used to all the name-calling, but that never stopped him. 'What in the hell do you think you're doing, young man? Don't you know you're my little bitch until your mother gets home?' He then grabbed my shirt and yanked me inside so hard that I dropped the lizard. He pushed me to the ground and then kicked me in the stomach so hard I almost lost my breakfast. I looked up to find him grabbing a jar full of little red insects. I wasn't sure what they were, but I knew it wasn't going to be good. He then picked up a spray bottle full of clear liquid. He picked me up and forced me to undress right there in the dining room. When I was fully unclothed, he grabbed my arm and with a forceful thrust jerked me to the basement where he built a small wooden room with a lock on the door. He sat me in a chair and sprayed the liquid on my testicles and penis and then threw me into the small room. He laughed and said, 'I will make you a deal. If you don't scream or complain about being in here, I will stop.'" The doctor jumped in the middle of Seth talking. "Your stepfather called the abuse he dealt on you games?" "Yes. But before he shut the door, he took the jar from upstairs, shook it a few times, opened the lid, and threw it at me. After he shut the door, I didn't feel anything but lonely and a little afraid of the dark but then the biting started. All I can remember is that I kept feeling a sharp burning sensation on my lower body, and then I realized what was in the jar—ants. I cried and screamed for help, but no one could hear me."

Ian was writing down little bits and pieces of Seth's story. "Why could no one hear you scream, Seth?" "He made the room so that sound couldn't get out and told my mother he does very loud things with power tools and didn't want to disturb the neighbors. I tried to fight, but it was no use, for every time I went to brush them off, the angrier they got and the more pain I was in. I then could hear him on the outside say, 'Well, I tried to give you a fair deal and you just couldn't handle it. Too bad. I guess you remain my little bitch.' After a while, the pain begins to become so constant that you learn to just deal with it. The only thing that breaks this is an even worse pain." The doctor tried to hold himself together. "Are you still in the closet, Seth?" "Yes, but be quiet. I don't want him to hear us."

The doctor was still writing. "Seth, you have nothing to worry about. With me here, your stepfather can't hurt you. Now I want to bring you back to present day. Tell me when you're back." Seth, now sitting straight within the chair, said, "I'm back, Doctor." "Now, Seth, I want you to take me back to the day you first met your stepfather." Seth, with his eyes still closed, said, "My brother and I were playing upon the hill beside our house, and from this spot, you could see the whole house and some of the neighbors' houses as well. That day, we played tag for what seemed like hours. The sun was going down, so we decided to start heading home when we noticed mom's car pull up in the driveway, so our walk turned into a run. We would always make a game out of everything we did, so our running turned into a race to greet our mother. But before we could reach the car, I stopped dead in my tracks at the extra person in the passenger seat of the car. Mom never brought home strangers, so I knew something was wrong. Our mother got out of the car along with the stranger and, with a smile on her face, simply said, 'How are my boys doing?' But before we could respond, the man got down on one knee so that our faces could be on the same level. 'Hello, boys. My name is Steven, and I'm a friend of your mother's. She said I could stay here for a little while until I can get my living arrangements in order. Is that okay with you two?' I'm not a huge believer in trust, so I immediately backed away, but my brother, on the other hand, is very gullible, partly the reason why my mother is always so protective of him and, without pause, said yes. That night, we all sat around the table waiting for my mother to bring in dinner. My brother and I sat silently, staring at the new stranger who called himself Steven. The awkward silence seemed absolute until Steven commented on how nice our house was, with my mother saying thank you from within the kitchen. Finally, the wait was over and my mother brought in the dish filled with meat loaf, the steam rising from the meal as if it just came out of the oven. The smell was so intoxicating that I can't wait to eat. Steven just sat there staring at my mother . . ."

Silence overtook the office, the doctor a little baffled. "Seth, you still with me?" Seth got out of his chair, opened his eyes, and stared at the room as if this was the first time he was in it. The doctor, not entirely sure what's going on, said, "Seth, what happened? How did you get out of deep sleep without my guidance?" Seth was now staring at books on the bookshelf. Seth's voice changed to a two-toned voice, almost as if two people were talking within the same body. *"Doctor, why do you insist on helping this poor pathetic boy?"* The doctor, now standing, said, "Seth, whatever do you mean and what's wrong with your voice?" *"You keep calling me Seth, how amusing. I should be thanking you, Doctor. You allowed me to see what his world has become, and as long as I am here, Seth must suffer my world. What a poor helpless fool!"* The doctor was now realizing he must be dealing with a different personality that Seth might not have known he had, which wasn't too uncommon for someone who had been abused as a child, which, of course, would explain a good amount on why Seth couldn't remember things from his childhood. But still, the doctor must get to know this other self in order to fully help him. "May I ask who I'm speaking to?" The figure that resembled Seth turned toward the doctor. *"You may call me Hanuse, or maybe God might suit me better or at least it will once I am done with this one."* The doctor was now writing so fast to keep up with this new character that he had begun to get a cramp in his hand. "Okay, Hanuse, does Seth know you're here?" "Do you take me for a fool? I don't take to insults so you need to watch your tongue." The doctor, backing away ever so slightly, replied, "I'm sorry. I meant no offense. What I meant was, do you and Seth know each other?" Hanuse, seemingly getting frustrated, started walking toward the doctor. *"How amusing of a question. Yes, I know Seth. I actually know him better than he himself does or ever will. I've been torturing him for quite some time now, and those useless pills that he thinks are helping him control the nightmares are actually doing nothing. I decided to let him be. For what I have planned will be worth the wait! And with him dead, I will be free to kill all of you!"* Giving up on writing, the doctor got out his video camera and pressed the Record button. "So you're saying that if you kill Seth, then you can be free?" *"I grow tired of your lip. You will speak no more."* Hanuse stretched his hand toward the doctor, and within an instant, the doctor's lips melted on top of one another, leaving him unable to open his mouth. The doctor, with a quick panic, started moving about the office as if he was on fire. Hanuse was standing calmly with an evil smirk. All you could hear were constant mumblings and objects being frantically thrown about as the doctor tried to make sense of what was happening. With the camera still rolling, Hanuse started walking toward the panicking doctor. *"Shall we play a game? I know. How about we see how long you can last?"* Hanuse picked up the doctor with one hand by the coat and tossed him across the room. Suddenly, the sounds of feet marched up the hall, and with a swift motion of the hand, Hanuse put an invisible barrier around the door, sealing it shut from the outside world. *"We have to make sure no one disturbs us while we play, and let me remove that barrier over your mouth. It just seems like much more fun with your screams of horror and pain."* And just like that, the doctor's mouth was free of any obstacles. "Why are you doing this, Seth?" Hanuse, in a fit of rage, picked the doctor up with just the power of his mind and said, *"Apparently, ignorance runs rapid among your kind, I guess I will have to teach all of you the hard way."* And with the doctor still in the air, he was flung across the room to hit the wall, leaving a massive dent that showed an imprint of the doctor's body shape. Screaming in pain, the doctor tried to get up, but the pain was too unbearable; the majority of the doctor's bones had been broken, so any movement was met with sheer agony, but he managed to get on his knees. "Please don't kill me. I have a wife and kid!" Delilah knocked on the door. "Seth, is everything okay? Open the door!" The outside world was wishing to come in while the person on the inside was trying to get out. Hanuse found this extremely enjoyable and amusing. Hanuse, with an evil grin, began to chuckle. *"I know exactly what to do with you. I find sight to be the most beautiful of senses. Don't you agree, Doctor? I guess that's why it gives me great pleasure in ruining it for most people."* Hanuse reached down toward the doctor, placed his hand upon his head, and with a shocking glow, made the doctor blind. *"I also gave you another gift, something now you and Seth share. You can thank me later."* For what the doctor didn't know was that Hanuse created a link between himself and the doctor, so now he could invade his dreams.

The outside was scrambling, trying to find a means to break down the door. Everything was tried, and everything had failed. All seemed hopeless until Delilah noticed a small window touching the ceiling of the office. "Officer, do you think someone could get in through there?" The policemen turned to look at what Delilah was pointing at. "Nice going, kid! Hey we think we found a way in. We just need a ladder." Delilah nervously waited to see her beloved Seth, hoping that everything would be okay, thinking that maybe this wasn't such a good idea, that maybe he was right in wanting to just run away. Delilah ran up to one of the officers about to climb the ladder. "Please, sir, my boyfriend is in that office. Please make sure you don't hurt him!"

Still in the office, Hanuse paced back and forth in front of the young doctor. *"Oh, how I've missed the sounds of my victims screaming in pain. You may want to pray for the end, but it won't do any good."* Hanuse was now standing over the doctor, his eyes started glowing red and his laugh growing stronger and stronger. An officer from outside the office walls climbed the ladder and, with tranquilizer gun, began to make his way to the small window overlooking the office. Delilah, in the background, was still pleading for the men to not hurt her precious Seth, that he doesn't know what he was doing. The man finally got on top of the ladder, propping the gun onto the window seal. He was eagerly looking for an opportune moment to shoot Seth, but before he could pull the trigger, he witnessed a horrific scene. Seth picked up the doctor with one hand over his head, sounding as if her was speaking in tongue. The officer's only thought, *I'm going to need more juice for this gun.* He placed a heavier dose into the barrel, lined Seth within the sights of the gun, and before Seth could hurt the doctor any longer, the officer pulled the trigger, and Seth dropped like a rag doll.

The door dropped to the ground from the amount of abuse being issued before. The doctor curled up on the floor, bloody and broken with Seth's seemingly lifeless body lying directly to the right. Before anyone paid any attention to Seth, the paramedics came in with a stretcher and cared for the doctor, who had to be airlifted to the nearest hospital. Delilah ran in to hold her love. "Oh my god, I should have listened to you. Why didn't we just run away together?" Within minutes, the new set of paramedics rushed in to finally care for Seth, an officer behind them making sure he could lock Seth down to the stretcher. "I don't care if this is against hospital policy. I want to make sure this little bastard can't hurt anyone else." The paramedic was doing all their basic procedures on him until one of them yelled out, "What dose of tranquilizer did you give him? His pulse is almost nonexistent and his breathing is extremely low." The police officer who shot him was standing against the wall. "I don't know. He seemed like he needed a larger dose seeing as he was picking up a man twice his size with one hand, so I guess it was the largest we had." The paramedics were screaming and rushing Seth out of the building. "Everyone, get out of the way. We have to get this young man to the hospital as soon as possible!" Delilah started to freak out in the background; in her mind, everything was going to shit. Delilah was thinking of nothing except Seth's well-being and the thought of never being able to see him again. She walked up to one of the paramedics. "Please tell me what's going on. Why are you rushing him to the hospital?" The paramedic, trying his best to get Seth within the ambulance but between the police officer refusing to put away the handcuffs and Delilah bombarding him with question after question, simply said, "He has been shot up with too much tranquilizer. We have to get him to the hospital. That's all I can tell you right now!" Delilah began to cry; she asked if she could accompany Seth within the ambulance but was given only the hospital he would be going to and the excuse that they needed all the room in the ambulance to keep Seth alive.

The ambulance was racing off with lights and sirens blaring. Delilah dropped to her knees and began to weep heavily. The police officers tried their best to comfort her, but nothing seemed to help for the very thought of her losing her one true love crushed her life into pieces. "Please don't leave me, Seth! Why did I not listen!"

Chapter 5

*D*elilah sat at the hospital bed with her head by Seth's side, the tears running from her face, soaking the bed into a wet stain. The doctors said Seth was shot with three times the normal amount found in any human tranquilizer, but instead of killing him, he sat in a vegetative state, his mind and body still trying to fight but would most likely lose the war. Delilah never left his side and the nurses couldn't blame her, for they knew that he would most likely not make it for very long and wanted her to have as much time with him as humanly possible.

The nights were the worst; a man down the hall was constantly screaming in his sleep. Woken up for the last time, Delilah marched down the hall to find a nurse or to see what exactly was the matter with this one person, but what she found was the psychiatrist Seth had put there. She slowly went to his side to comfort him, but the screams never stopped. He would eventually awaken only now his once brown eyes now completely white with no sign of color. Delilah, a little scared but slowly coming to her senses, said, "I am so sorry for this entire situation, Dr. Ian!" The psychiatrist, with his full body cast, replied, "I don't know what it was I was dealing with, but that wasn't Seth. He took my sight and my sanity, my dreams filled with nightmarish sights. I no longer wish to live." Delilah, somewhat shocked, said, "What are you trying to say, Doctor?" "That whatever was in the room with me is dangerous, and if Seth can't control it, then you and everyone around him is in danger!" You could start to see the pain show through the psychiatrist's face, with both arms and legs in splints and a chest cast; you knew not much was left of him whole. "I'm in such pain. All I want to do is sleep, but every time I do, I see things not meant to be seen by anyone." Delilah, speechless, stood near just to witness the agony and pain before her eyes could take no more.

Standing within a mound of dead corpses, Ian horrified while trying to find ground that wasn't covered with the rotting bodies surrounding him. He was beginning to panic, sweating heavily and his breathing getting shorter and shorter almost to the point of passing out. He was looking around to see if there could possibly be anything more to this land besides what he saw. Miles upon miles of nothing except the dead as far as the eye could see. Puddles of blood and bones fill the landscape; burnt and torn clothes that once held a person now littered the ground with no owner.

With clouds overcast to no light, it was hard to tell what part of the day it had been. Still, the only thing Ian could think was of a way to get out of the massive graveyard he found himself in. "This can't be happening to me. What brought me here? I have to find a way out." Suddenly, a hand reached out and grabbed his leg, and with a quick jump, he pushed it away. He looked down to see a dead body, which had somehow come back to life, or at least enough to grab his leg and with a creepy moan, it said, "Pray for us all!" Ian, beginning to freak out, started walking the opposite direction of the living corpse. Another arm reached out, this time from a completely different body. "Pray for us all!" Ian, now officially scared, started running in any direction to just get away, but no matter which way he turned, a hand would be there to grab his leg until one actually tripped Ian to the ground. Trying to get up but it was no use, their numbers were too great and Ian too weak. The chanting got louder and faster, "Pray for us all!" "Pray for us all!" "Pray for us all!" "Pray for us all!" Ian, still fights his arms and legs, punched and kicked to be set free, pain setting in to the burden of being contained.

A light shone from the farthest reaches of the land, a tall figure with arms stretched out in a V, the light glowing from all around him. The bodies being pushed away were discarded with no care. Soon Ian was free and the tall figure standing was above looking down upon him, the light still emitting, keeping the stranger with no identity. The stranger was still standing over Ian. "I never expected anyone else here. The only reason you could possibly be here is if you speak to Hanuse." A blood-soaked Ian, unable to move and his speech beginning to slow, said, "How . . . do you . . . know . . . that name?" The stranger sighed. "So much you don't know and so much I need not bother telling you." Ian now curled up in the fetal position. "I feel . . . so numb . . . What's happening to . . . me?" The light that shone around the stranger began to vanish; he then stepped forward toward the man who lay bloody on the ground. "The numbness you feel is your life draining. You are dying. I can't help you no matter how much I want to. This will have to take its course." The light was fully gone and the face had a name that only Seth would know; the face belonged to Robert, a.k.a. Ewar. "You've mixed yourself up with something you can never understand, something you won't want to understand. Just be thankful it's almost over, and you will be set free." In a slow breathing, Ian began to weaken and then suddenly seized to be.

The next day, Delilah woke to the same normal tear-soaked spot next to her love. With sleepy eyes adjusting to the morning light to see the same sight as before, Seth sat in the hospital bed, hanging on for dear life. A doctor rushed past Seth's room, enough to notice but not enough to cause attention. Suddenly, several doctors ran past the room; Delilah, being very curious, got up to check out the scene. It was the psychiatrist in the corner of his room, curled up in the fetal position, with his casts torn and split. *Pray for us all* written all around the room in blood—the psychiatrist's blood. A doctor pushed Delilah out of the room as if this crime scene was not meant for human eyes; her only thought, *Nightmares actually drove him insane.* Going back to Seth's room in a dazed and confused state, she said, "How could Seth possible do that to someone? What if that weren't Seth in the room. After all, he did try and tell me some strange story the other day. Maybe this has something to do with it." Delilah turned just to stare at Seth's helpless body.

Seth was lost within a world that seemed familiar, nothing but white surrounding him. A distant echoed voice of a woman called out to him, *"I'm finally looking upon the last of the bloodline. Although I see you're not ready to face Hanuse, that's okay. Ewar has trained you well, and with what you learned from him and what you learned on your own, then it shouldn't take long."* Seth looked around to see who that voice might belong to, looking everywhere, but nothing around but pure white. Walking around, Seth looked to try and find an end, but with no luck; this room appeared to go on forever. The voice came and went. *"You cannot begin until the ones you love let you go from the other world. We will train you here, but until death becomes you,*

you can never face your destiny." Seth, with a puzzled look on his face, said, "So you're saying I am already close to death?" The voice was getting closer until the sound appeared to be right on top of him. "Right now you are in a coma. Your body and mind are fighting to keep you alive but are losing. Soon Delilah will have to choose on whether or not to let machines keep you alive or to let you go. As of now, there may be no hope, but I trust she will make the right decision." Seth, standing in amazement of the thought of his own death, said, "I have been through so much that I don't know if I even want this war. What if I don't want this anymore? What if I say the hell with it? I've already lost everything in my life. What does it matter now?" The voice was now taking shape; a young female now stood in Seth's presence. "My name is Nephia, and I know how you must feel. A lot has been taken from me as well. Hanuse took my twin brother, and I had to witness my mother being tortured and later had to help with her sacrifice. There is so much you don't know, and I'm not going to promise you anything, but I can say that if you fight and succeed, then there is a chance Rezorin can help you." A confused look came over Seth. "Rezorin?" Nephia, realizing that this name hadn't been spoken in many a year, replied, "Rezorin is the one all people in your world call god, or at least the ones who believe exist. He created me, Delilah, everything you've seen, and even you. Besides you, he is the only other being that can destroy Hanuse." Seth was beginning to become upset. "Well, if Rezorin is so fucking powerful, why doesn't he do his own dirty work? If he is truly real like you say, why didn't he save me from my shitty life?" "The answers aren't so easy to answer, Seth. Rezorin sacrificed himself to save your world. He promised he would send his own blood to fight for him, but Hanuse had a few tricks up his sleeve. But Rezorin did everything in his power to make sure your planet and its entire people survived, and now it's up to you to make sure it continues that way." Seth walked away. "This was never mine to accept. Why can't you understand that? I don't want this. I never did! So take this fucking war of yours and leave me be. I want what I can't have. I have what I don't want. My life is pure shit, and I thank Rezorin and the rest of you for all of it, so just let me die!" Nephia, shaking her head in disappointment, said, "I wish you wouldn't talk in such a way. Ewar thought so much of you. I can't make your decision. Only you can decide the fate of Earth and your beloved Delilah." Seth stopped and turned with a look of depression. "All I wanted was to be with her, to live a normal life with someone I love, but it was taken away like everything else in my life." Nephia walked up to Seth as his hands constantly touched the half-heart necklace; she placed her hands on his face in comfort. "If you don't accept this, she will die along with everyone else. You may not care about the rest of them, but at least think of her. From what I've seen, she loves you with whole heart. Now it's time to show her how much you love her." Seth's face dropped. "I don't want this, but I can't ignore my love for Delilah." Thoughts rushed through Seth's mind, leaving all his bad memories alone and focusing in on all the good thoughts, like every holiday with his mother and all the activities he would play with his brother and then the happiest of them all—the times he spent with Delilah. "I have no choice but to fight, if not for Delilah but to kill that motherfucker who killed my mother and enslaved my brother." Nephia, still standing next to Seth, said, "Excellent. The rest of your training begins immediately."

Delilah, speaking with the doctors about Seth's fate, "You can't just play god and determine who lives and dies! It isn't up to you on when to pull the plug!" One of the doctors placed his clipboard to his side. "I know this must be hard, but it's been a month, and he hasn't shown any improvement. He's showing very little body function, and his brain has given up. He may have a slim chance to make it out of this, but as of right now, it's not looking good." The tears rolling down Delilah's cheek. "So a slim chance to you should mean that he will die to me? I'm sorry, Doctor, but I won't give up on him as easily as you have." "Look, Ms. Delilah, we will leave the decision up to you, but you have to understand that you've already lost him. Maybe it's time to just let go. I trust you'll do the right thing for his sake." Delilah, still shedding tears of the thought of a world without her precious Seth, looked over at her love. "There has to be something I can do. I can't just let him die. I would do anything to save you, Seth. Anything!"

On the leftover remains of Vianna, Hanuse and Eiades began a conversation. "We don't need to involve her, Hanuse. With your strength, I can and will destroy him. I have already tricked him into believing his mother's death and made a convincing show with his brother. He is weak, and I will destroy him." Within Eiades's mind, Hanuse contemplated the next plan of action. *"Don't be a fool, Eiades. I can use her as a weapon against him. You say he's weak, but I'm just trying to have some fun with my last obstacle, and I will have fun even if that means replacing you."* An angry Eiades said, "We're a team. You can't do this! I have done things for you that I've known to be wrong, but I made that sacrifice and now you want to discard me like I don't matter. I thought we were in this together until the end. Please don't relinquish my power. You need me just as much I need you." Hanuse, laughing a sinister laugh, said, *"Such a sentimental speech, yet I see a lack of meaning. Without me, you are nothing but a weak young boy with a taste of revenge from that day. Don't think that anything you did could have been accomplished without me. You need me and that's a shame because I am letting you lose."* Eiades, dropping to his knees, said, "All I wanted to do was kill the monsters responsible for the death of my love, and yet I'm the one who has become the monster." And with a swift dark energy escaping Eiades's body, Hanuse set himself free.

Upon a hill, the wind was blowing Delilah's hair in all crazy directions; a gravestone lay in front of her that read, "Seth, friend and lover." The wind calmed a once-crying and upset Delilah; feeling torn and lost, she wondered what could have been.

A strange man in an all-white suit appeared next to Delilah, standing next to her, saying, "You miss him dearly, don't you?" Delilah, looking up at the man, replied, "Yes, I don't know what I'm going to do without him! Did you know him?" The man put his hands in his pockets. "Why yes, I did. I knew him all too well. Listen, if there is anything you need, don't hesitate to ask, and by the way, my name is Hanuse." Delilah, looking a bit uneven, replied, "Hanuse? I've never heard that name before. How did you know Seth?" Hanuse, with a smile, replied, "I've known him since he was little. I only wish his brother could be here to pay respects." Delilah, taking her eyes away from the stranger and back unto Seth's tombstone with tears rolling down her face in a constant stream, continued, "I would do anything to be with him again!" Hanuse, with an evil smirk across his face, said, "What if I was to tell you I can make that happen? Would you be interested?" Wiping her face with her hands, Delilah looked up at Hanuse. "What do you mean?" Putting his arm around Delilah's shoulder, Hanuse said, "What I am saying is that I can make it happen, but it's a bit tricky, and you have to trust me but I can make it happen." Her thoughts were racing. "Like I said, I would do anything, so of course I'm interested. What would I have to do?" Hanuse brought her closer. "This may hurt, but I promise you, you will see your Seth again."

Delilah woke up in the exact spot she fell asleep next to Seth. "What the hell was up with that dream? I think I'm losing it. Maybe I should get some fresh air." Getting up from her chair at the bedside of Seth, Delilah walked out of the room and into the hallway to speak with the nurses. "I'm going out to get some fresh air. Please look after him until I get back." The nurses nodded in agreement.

Walking along the sidewalk and into the local park, she thought about the dream and what it could possibly mean; on one side, it could mean that Seth was going to die and she must accept this fact, or the man could represent her determination to not give up. Either way, there was something definitely going on with her subconscious to dream something like that. Walking along, she gazed at some ducks swimming in the nearby pond; she smiled as they play within the water. Suddenly, a small light appeared in the distance, at first dull and almost invisible but with time, it gained strength. Curious, she walked toward this strange light, thinking the sun may be playing tricks with her eyes. The light was showing no signs of stopping; she was determined to figure out this mystery. The closer she got, the brighter the light became, getting closer and closer until Delilah stood right in front of the strange light that lay directly behind some bushes. Delilah parted the leaves and branches from the bush to reveal an orb floating three feet off the ground; still a bit curious, she reached out to touch what she didn't understand. With the slightest touch, a surge of energy released and engulfed Delilah, sending her floating in midair. A force penetrated her inner soul; a voice called out, "Be careful what you wish for! You want to see your darling Seth? Well, your wish is my command!" The energy still making its way into her until, in a sudden burst of light, she vanished in midair.

Seth was still waiting for his chance to settle the score, with Nephia still training him. "How much longer must I wait?" Seth asked in an angry voice. "First off, you have to be ready, Seth, and also it's not up to me on when you start the battle. It's up to whoever is watching over your body. They have to let you go as I've said before. Be patient. The time will come. Now please pay attention. I am teaching you this move so that when you're up against more than two opponents that you can handle yourself."

This training would go on for several weeks. Seth learned many a new techniques that Robert never mentioned, which raised the question, "Why didn't Robert teach me any of these moves? They seem more useful than all the other things he taught me." Nephia looked at Seth with a very puzzled look. "Robert? Oh, he must have used that name so Hanuse wouldn't find out who was teaching you. My father probably taught you how to survive rather than how to fight. His philosophy is to make sure you can survive in harsh conditions, which is what all of Vianna is, and he probably went into the basics with you on fighting. I can only guess he wanted to teach you more, but Hanuse found out his identity, and now you're with me." Seth stopped to face Nephia. "Your father was Robert?" With a smile on her face, Nephia made her way toward Seth. "You know my father as Robert, but his real name is Ewar. I wish he would have gotten a little further with your training. I would hate for them to pull the plug before you were ready. And he's right. You were reluctant at first, but once you put your heart into something, I can see the dedication." Seth stepped back. "You said that like Robert is still alive. How can that be? I watched him jump off a building. I was the one who buried him." "There is so little you know about our world. Ewar and I can't die by suicide. We can sacrifice ourselves with the help of Rezorin, but neither you nor anyone you know can kill us. There are specific rules about my world that you will learn very few in due time, but you must finish your training." And with that said, not another word was spoken and the training continued.

Back at the hospital, weeks had passed since young Delilah went out for some fresh air. The doctors and nurses waited impatiently for any sign of her or anyone from Seth's family, calling numerous times to the last known number from where Seth lived but with no luck; the number was disconnected with no forwarding address present. With no sign of anyone, they decided their only other option was to call Delilah's father. At first the only person they could reach was his secretary, but once Delilah's father learned of her disappearance, he quickly sprung into action and arrived at the hospital within mere hours. "Who's in charge here?" Delilah's father demanded to know. "I want to know when the last time you saw and spoke to my daughter." The doctor he was speaking to placed the pen he was writing with within the left pocket of his white coat. "It's been about a month since I last spoke to her, but the nurse at the counter saw her a few weeks ago. Listen, before you go, I have to speak with you about something. Your daughter came in with a young man who is still in a coma. Now we can't find any family from his side, so we are leaving the decision entirely up to your daughter or you." Having no idea what was being spoken, Delilah's father looked with a face of confusion. "Listen, Doctor, I have no clue what you're talking about. All I want is my daughter. Now if you'll excuse me, I need to speak with that nurse." Delilah's father turned away from the doctor and began walking toward the nurse, but before he left, within hearing distance, the doctor spoke, "If you don't decide, we will be making the decision for you, which is stated by law of this state." Delilah's father turned one last time. "Fine. Do what you need to do. It's none of my concern."

Seth was within his last days of training. Nephia lifted her hand, a glow coming from her palm and two chairs appearing from nowhere. "Seth, please sit and rest. It's been a long day, and I know you're tired." Seth took a seat with what must look like a large abundance of questions on his mind. "I need to know something, Nephia." Nephia now looked directly at Seth. "I will answer almost any questions you ask, but there are certain things I can't speak of, but I will do my best with the rest of your questions, so ask away." "First I need to know, why have I not been hungry or thirsty while I've been here? And more importantly, why haven't you either? We have been here for more than a month, and the only thing I have been able to feel was the occasional warm feeling, almost like a hug, but more intense." Nephia, with a smile, said, "The first one is easy. You are hooked up to a machine back home. You get all your nutrients from there. Since you're not dead on Earth, what remains here is just your conscience. You don't need a body here, just your mind. I can't answer your second question. All I can say is that I'm different, and let's just leave this and my origins alone. And the warm feeling is, more than likely, Delilah. Look, I'm sorry you're being pulled away from her. I know she loves you dearly." Seth, with a warm glow, suddenly sank to a sad expression. Nephia looked worried. "What's wrong, Seth?" He was looked up at Nephia with a single tear running down his face. "I haven't felt that warm feeling in a few weeks. I think she may have left me."

A new voice entered the room, this of a deep-toned male. *"Seth, I know it's hard, but you must continue. This will get worse before it gets better."* Seth, standing in excitement, said, "Robert, is that you?" Nephia, now beginning to stand as well, said, "It's about time you showed up. We have very little time. We must prepare him!" A bright orb floated from the ceiling down to the ground, taking the shape of Ewar. "You've done well, my daughter, but I think he's ready enough. The last remaining lessons will have to be taught on Vianna." Nephia marched toward Ewar. "I hope you know what you're doing. This could be suicide!" Seth, with his back toward both Nephia and Ewar, said, "I think Robert is right. I need to learn the rest on my own, and I have nothing left, so it's better this way." Ewar walked toward Seth, placing a hand on his shoulder. "Listen, in this whole war, I've seen many men march to their death, and with all of them, I have felt a strong sadness, but with you, it's different. My heart is breaking over the very thought of you fighting. I would trade with you in a heartbeat if I could. You're like a son to me!" Seth stepped away. "Please stop. I've lost you once, and I can't do it again. Every time I open myself up to someone, my world comes crashing down. I would rather have nothing, so I can no longer lose anything. The pain of everything that has come forth in my life has left a hole within my soul. I just can't do this anymore!"

By law, a hospital can only keep a brain-dead patient on life support until a family member gives the okay to pull the plug, or in the event a family member or friend can't be obtained, then the hospital has a grace period of two weeks before making the decision. Based upon a council of doctors from within the hospital, it's been fourteen days since Delilah's disappearance. A panel of doctors sat around a table, discussing the life of Seth; a few decided on keeping him on life support, but the majority ruled in favor of pulling the plug. Many had this to say, "His brain no longer functions, so the only thing we are doing is delaying the inevitable." Later that evening, three doctors entered Seth's room along with two nurses; one doctor reached over to turn off the machines and took the respirator out of Seth's nose. "All we can do now is wait for the body to give up." Seth, still standing in front of Ewar and Nephia, suddenly dropped to his knees. "What's happening to me? I feel so weak and numb." Ewar, standing over Seth, said, "They pulled the plug, and this is death. This will be painful, and I wish you didn't have to go through with it but you have to." Seth, grabbing his chest in agony, said, "Please make it stop. This hurts so much!" And within minutes, Seth's heart monitor reflected flat lines; the doctor with a clipboard said, "Time of death, 6:26 PM" and then wrote down the time in Seth's file. At that very moment, Seth sank down into the floor, the ground giving way to swallow Seth whole.

Delilah was now standing at the balcony of Hanuse's castle in the middle of the desolate and barren Vianna; Hanuse's voice echoed from within Delilah's mind, and a two-toned voice was coming from Delilah's lips. *"It won't be long now. I can taste his presence. I can't wait for the young Seth to finally meet us!"* Delilah was covered in a black shroud and, with both her hands, lifted the hood over her head. And with a sinister laugh, she said, *"You were such a fool, Rezorin. All you've hope to do is prolong what must happen, what will happen. He will never find Audia!"*

Chapter 6

*S*eth was falling through the sky, his back to the ground and face to the sky. If he were a conscience, he would see a sight to be seen, the land barren and dry. Everything was with a dead sense of isolation except a small portion to his left, which looked black and creepy with vines and a small amount of fog hovering over the area. In a castle toward his right formed entirely of rock and vines, except the large door at the rock gate, you could see firelights surrounding the place, which gave off an evil vibe. He was still falling, getting closer and closer to the ground. Thousands upon thousands of beings stood around waiting for something to happen, whether to take orders or even orders already given. Seth's landing would most definitely be directly within the middle of this horde of creatures. Falling even closer, Seth began to come back to consciousness, not entirely sure what was happening or where he might be. His vision was coming back; but with nothing to view but dark gray skies, Seth was still in disarray. With the ground becoming closer, Seth started to turn involuntarily, placing his back to the sky and face toward the ground. What would scare any normal person, Seth, in such a dream state, made himself unable to fully conceive what exactly was going on around him. Finally, Seth turned into himself, standing up straight before hitting the ground; he hit the ground with such force that it would make a large crater in the ground where he landed. Down on one knee within the newly formed crater, Seth stood up straight now, fully awake and aware. He saw nothing but creatures surrounding him. These monstrosities were huge in numbers, what looked like thousands but could be more; their numbers vanished from view the farther you looked within the distant land. These creatures once invaded his dreams were now standing in full force around his feet.

Seth stood with a sight of confusion. "There is no way I can take all these creatures on with just hand-to-hand combat. My skills are good but not that good." A single dark cloud hanging overhead branched out, thunder and lightning stretching with a violent force, almost like it was trying to convey a message. A jolt of lightning danced through the sky, jumping from cloud to cloud until finally settling directly above Seth to strike the ground nearest to his feet. The ground glowed with bright red heat; the smoke began to clear, and from the middle of the lightning strike, two blades appeared. A voice from within the clouds began to speak in an echo, *"Take these at your disposal. Use all we have taught you, and remember, this ends with you."* The two blades were sticking out of the ground at Seth's feet, but these were no ordinary blades, for the handles were replaced with a collar of some kind. Each sword had two blades on each side with hinges so that the blades could be flipped up for easy use of the hands. Seth walked toward the blades, a confident feeling coming over him. His hands slid into the collars of the blades, and with a quick snap, the collars closed around his wrist with a sharp penetrating sensation digging in his wrist. Seth screamed in agony as the pain from the collars of the blades entered his flesh, digging deeper and deeper until finally the blades and Seth became one with each other; a feeling of great power came over him.

Walking out of the crater, Seth heard the voice within the clouds again. *"Hurry! Their guard is down! This is the beginning!"* Seth looked all around him, noticing all the creatures doing nothing. Standing there without a care, Seth thought, I thought this was supposed to be some unstoppable army. And with a burst of rage, he ran toward the right side of the wall of the creatures and began his attack. His swords sliced through their skin like butter—a leg here, an arm there; nothing was getting in the way of his killing spree. Blood flowed like a river. A great scream came from a distance, sounding like an attack call. It looked like Seth would be getting a challenge after all. The creatures were now fighting back but nothing was stopping Seth; his anger and fuel for revenge kept him going strong no matter how many of the creatures throw themselves at him. A giant group headed toward Seth, and with a burst of energy, he charged, but before impact, Seth jumped over the groups to behead two of them. Doing a single flip in the air, Seth fell to his feet. The running continued, each arm a weapon of mass murder; body parts now littered the ground where they once occupied a being. His killings were becoming greater by the second; puddles of blood were like holes in the ground, gathering rain. As fast as Seth was, he knew he couldn't keep this up for long. The blades may be giving him some special power of stamina, but they couldn't keep him going forever. Seth knew this much. With one monster killed, it seemed as if another took its place, and with no end in sight, this battle would wage in a never-ending cycle.

Suddenly, a small mobile structure was coming to view; a humanlike being covered in a black shroud stood on top with four of the many creatures on each corner carrying the structure. The black shrouded character raised a hand, and the creatures stopped the attack. Seth stood, still staring at the structure that was coming his way. *"I gave you a choice and you denied me! And so now we stand here in the midst of a battlefield. You could have saved your precious Delilah, but now it seems she is doomed just like the rest of them! It's a pity, really. After all, you are my favorite,"* said the being in the black shroud. The anger growing too strong to control. Seth ran and jumped on the shrouded stranger, placing a blade on the throat that would speak ill of his love. The stranger gave out a sinister laugh while removing his hood. *"Go ahead, young Seth. End this now if you can! If you end me, you end her!"* Young Seth took the blade off its neck as the stranger revealed its identity. "How could this be? Delilah?" *"I knew you were weak. I gave you a chance to end this war, and you failed like the rest before you. What's a matter, darling? You don't like how I and your love are now one?"* Seth dropped to his knees. "Why? Why would you join him?" Delilah stood above Seth. *"Oh, she was quite eager. All I had to do was promise she could see you again and she was more than willing."* And with an evil laugh, he added, *"Would you like to speak with her?"* Delilah's eyes went from black to brown. "I'm so sorry, Seth. I didn't know what else to do, I desperately wanted to be with you. Please don't hate me! Please just kill me!" Delilah's eyes changed back to black. *"People shouldn't make deals with strangers! Now in order for you to end this war, you have to kill your true love!"* And with a swift raise of her hand, Delilah pointed to Seth while giving out a horrible scream. The creatures were now going crazy, running and rushing toward Seth in a fury of violent slashing, clawing their way into his skin. Seth got up to run as fast as he could, trying to escape their attacks, slicing a few that stood in his way; his blood slowly flowed out of him, and his strength was beginning to come to an end. He was running faster and faster until he found himself on top of a hill, looking down upon them; they seemed to have given up, or maybe this was just part of the game. Either way, they were walking back to their castle, and Seth was bloody and tired on top of this hill.

Seth, alone with his thoughts, pondered, *I can't do this!* The clouds in the sky lit up with thunder, and the voice spoke, *"I told you he would use any means to get to you. This was never going to be easy, and I think deep down inside you knew that."* Seth, now sitting, leaned up against a rock. "But I love her! You can't ask this of me. I'm too weak!" *"If you give up now, then all that has come before you will have been in vain. You must look past this. She no longer resides as Delilah."* Seth looked up. "That's a lie. She spoke to me." *"You misunderstand me, Seth. Delilah's body is still intact, but her mind is gone. What you talked to was the last remnants of her. The only way for her to be released is by Hanuse's own accord or death."* Seth got up. "Then I shall make a deal with him. I will join his ranks if he lets her go. She's the only thing that matters." *"I don't think you get it, my dear Seth. Even if you join him, she will die. Her death is inevitable either way you look at it, and right now, she has seen into Hanuse's mind, and any normal person can't view that without going insane. She has seen every evil act he has brought upon many nameless victims, city burning to the ground, mothers who were protecting their young brutally murdered. Everything Hanuse has shown you pales in comparison of what she has seen. I know this is hard, but you have to accept this. You have to accept that she will die one way or another."* Seth leaned against the rock as before. "You never told me this could happen. This changes everything, and you know it." *"My dear Seth, I know it seems like we are asking the impossible of you, but this must be done. You are not alone. We will be with you always!"* And as quick as the voice came, it vanished, along with the dark cloud that brought its way to Seth.

Journal entry: Day 3

What's wrong with me? I was actually having fun killing. The very thought in the past made me sick at my stomach, but watching all those creatures getting sliced in half made me feel alive. The anger in me grew and the rage showed itself as a murderous rampage although can you really call it murder if the victims have no soul? I can still see the leftover remains piled up on the ground, the blood now dried black within the soil. These creatures are like the ones from my dreams, almost identical in every way, which leaves me to believe that I've been here before. Is the inside of me changing, or are the blades doing this to me? I felt so alive out there that it's almost scary. What's happening to me?

My heart hurts with the feelings of what I must do. I've come so far, and I'm almost at the finish line, and I don't think I can do this. How can they expect for me to kill the one person I love, the one person who showed me love within a world full of pain and anguish? I didn't ask for this, and I have a feeling I will disappoint all who have their faith in me. They keep telling me that Delilah doesn't exist anymore, but I just can't believe that. She has to be in there somewhere. I have to find a way to free her. If only I could sacrifice myself to gain her freedom.

I love you, Delilah, and I will set you free!

Seth was still standing on top of the hill, looking over the barren wasteland, nothing to be used as shelter and nothing for his nourishment; a swamp nearby was the only thing that could resemble anything useful. He looked up to the sky. "I haven't anything here. What exactly should you expect I do? You taught me how to survive, but I never practiced what I've learned." A giant rumble came from the ground, soil cracking and splitting, knocking Seth on his back; a rock formation came up from the ground. He watched a large rock being pushed up from the soil, and when all was done, a cavelike structure formed in front of Seth's eyes. A small garden began to grow with basic essentials for Seth's health, the dark cloud appearing again. *"We give you shelter and food. We have already taught you how to filter water, so the swamp will be your well. If there is anything else, pray and you will receive."*

Delilah stood on top of the castle gates, staring at the hill miles away at the small glow of a fire. *"You will be mine very soon, my darling Seth. I've controlled your dreams, now I will control your fate. Number 13 come hither!"* A tall muscular man walked up to Delilah. "I'm at your command, my master." "I want you to stay out of this war until the very end. I want him to see you last. You'll be my secret weapon." "But, my master, I am the best you have. No other is equipped to handle this last soldier." *"Don't question it. Just do as you're told! Don't worry, my pet, I will send out the others in your place. They should be enough to keep him busy."* "As you wish, my master." *"You will soon learn Seth, you will learn the true meaning of pain and torture. As of now, you've seen what I've wanted you to see, but from now on, you get no mercy. This is only the beginning!"*

Journal entry: Day 8

It's been a week since I last came here. Every time I shut my eyes to try and sleep, I'm awakened by the sounds of howling, but I have noticed that my dreams in this world are safe from him. My dreams are no longer controlled, but my dreams are set into a nightmarish flow. Delilah sticks into the back of my head and what they say I must do. I think I would rather have my old dreams again; at least those didn't involve my love. My own mind-set is in autopilot of that dreadful day, the day I had learned Delilah to be the one I must kill. The memory is still fresh in my mind—me standing over, looking down upon her with my blade on her neck, she with that evil grin and that two-toned voice. Every time I think of this, I can't help but feel confused; the anger is building up, but the sadness is taking its toll. I don't know what I'm going to do!

The screams constantly keep me awake; the shrieks pierce my eardrums enough to keep me from sleeping. I'm not sure if they are trying to intimidate or just scare. Whatever plans they have won't chase me off. I'm in this till the bitter end. No matter what it takes, I just hope I can free her.

Nephia spoke to Ewar, "Do you think he'll find Audia in time?" Ewar looked down upon Seth. "I don't think we have much of a choice in the matter. If he does, then my only hope is that he knows how to use it and can handle it." Nephia stared down along with Ewar. "That's the one thing I fear. I don't know if his body can handle that much power and energy surging all at once." Ewar looked up at Nephia. "We just have to have faith that he'll pull through and save us all."

Delilah screamed. Seth jumped out of the bed and ran into the other room where the screams echoed from. The hallway was half normal and half another world of desert, tumbleweed rolling along the sand across Seth's feet. In front, a large group of monsters from Vianna were standing in a circle. Seth, only thinking of Delilah's well-being, ran closer to the group in an effort to save her. His blades appeared on his arms as if to tell him to kill every last one of them, and with a quick swing, Seth took out the first few standing in his way. Suddenly, something came over him, the same feeling of tunnel vision in the alleyway back home. Control was now lost within the flying body parts and blood, which now lay on the ground at Seth's feet. The murderous rage showed no signs of stopping until the head of Delilah rolled and stopped at Seth's heel, the last look of horror and despair with the final tears rolling down her face. Tunnel vision was now gone, and the shakes setting in. Seth dropped to his knees in a weakened state. "What have I done!" Stan, now standing above Seth, said, "I knew you were weak. You've killed the one person they wanted you to, and you're still wallowing in self-pity. Cry, my brother, for there will be no salvation for you or your precious love. I will make sure of that!"

Waking in a cold sweat, Seth said, "I thought he couldn't control my dreams anymore?" The clouds opened to reveal a ray of light down upon him, the voice of Ewar. *"His control has seized within this land, but that doesn't mean you can't have nightmares here. Whatever you've seen came from you and you alone."* Seth stared up at the clouds. "So even in this new land, I can't escape the nightmarish dreams?"

A shrieking scream echoed the landscape, the clouds closing with the light disappearing; the screams began to become louder until Seth witnessed a man running up the hill toward him. Readying his blades for a confrontation, the man ran wildly until he tripped on his own accord at Seth's feet. Seth looked down. "Who are you? Answer me before you find your end!" A blade now stretched across the stranger's neck. The strange man, bloody and beaten, said, "Must find Audia, must find Audia. Puri knows. Puri knows where Audia is. Find Puri, find Audia!" Seth, looking confused, said, "What are you talking about? Listen, I don't have time for your games. Tell me who you are, or I will separately pick you off piece by piece!" But before Seth's words could show meaning, two other male figures ran up behind the stranger still kneeling. "There you are, Eiades. Hanuse is very upset with you. You know the master told you to never leave the dungeon. Oh, and I see you found Seth! He can't save you, Eiades. No one can!" Seth looked at the two men standing behind the man they called Eiades. The two looked a lot like the army Seth had fought before but a little more human and muscular than the others. "I'm going to ask this only once. Who is this man kneeling before me and who are you two?" The two men chuckled. "You dare command us, the ones who've come before you. Come number Three. We don't have time for this. Grab Eiades and let's go." The men grabbed Eiades and started walking down the hill. Seth, still standing, began to walk after them. "Don't walk away from me! Stop or I will kill you all!" The two men stopped in their tracks. "Do you hear that Twenty? He wants to fight us." Twenty and Three put down Eiades and faced Seth, "But, Three, Hanuse doesn't want us to kill him, and he's saving that for you know who." "Don't worry, I don't want to kill him. I just want to show him the true meaning of pain. No more dreams, no more illusions, you will suffer!"

Seth was standing ready with blades at his side while Twenty and Three began walking back up the hill with Eiades on the ground behind them. Seth ran toward the men, and with a battle cry, swung his blade toward the throat of the man at the right named Three. The man blocked the blade with his forearm and began to laugh while grabbing the blade. "You honestly thought killing us would be that simple? Ewar hasn't taught you nearly as much as we've thought. No matter, this shall be fun!" And with a quick toss, the man threw Seth over the hill. Landing on the rock formation that he called home, his back making a crashing sound while hitting a stone and then a sudden thud to the ground. The two men now walked over the hill back toward Seth's beaten body. "I told you this would be fun!" Time slowed, making the beatings last more than what Seth was willing to endure. He laid bruised and bloody against the rock wall; the men wiped the blood from their knuckles. "See you soon, Seth!"

Journal entry: Day 70

I've become tired of fighting in this war. There seems to be no end in sight. Robert tried to explain the hierarchy of all Hanuse's army. The creatures I've been fighting are called the Evower Army, which are the evil that lives within any person, and when they die, they become part of the ever-growing horde. The more humanlike but still resemble the Evower army are the protectors who have come before me in the bloodline. They no longer have names, just numbers, but even those are split into two groups; the ones who tried to fight but lost have the same strength as me, but the ones who gave themselves to Hanuse gained some of his power, which is why I couldn't take on those two from a few months ago. And there appears to be one more that I haven't seen yet; he is Hanuse's go-to guy for everything. His power is off the charts and is the one whom Hanuse has destined to take me out. I don't know what Hanuse is waiting for. If this thing is as powerful as they claim, then I don't know why he hasn't come to take me out. This must be just a game, or he's waiting for something.

I tried to ask about this thing called Audia but wasn't given a clear answer. Robert told me that it's something or someone I must find in order to defeat Hanuse but didn't go into further detail. I wonder if that strange man knows anything about Audia. I believe his name was Eiades.

My dreams keep me in constant state of disarray. I thought coming here would keep my nightmares at bay, but it seems my mind is starting off where Hanuse left off. All I do from day to day is sit and wait; waiting gives way to memories I can now access without him blocking them. I now can remember my loving mother and the days me and my brother used to play in the yard and wait for mom to come home. Every time these thoughts come to mind, they usually lead to the thought of the stepfather and all the torment I had to endure as a child. I should just leave these thoughts to rest within the back of my mind, but they get me to remember the pain, which I can use as a weapon; my anger allows me to train harder and longer.

I still remember some of my journal entries from the days of my stepfather, the days when I truly believed there would be no escape from him, my personal favorite:

I've learned that fear and pain can be controlled, that as long as you dull your senses to the point of numbness, then you can take anything. You just have to give up. Death is only a burden if you allow it to be; death can drag you down if you want it to. Once you learn that death is inevitable, you can deal with anything and everything, even the tragedy that has become my life.

Wise words from a boy who shouldn't have had to grow up so quickly; as long as those words remain in my spirit, I can handle anything.

Chapter 7

*D*ays dragged into weeks, into months, and finally into years. The thoughts and feelings never left Seth; he felt the pain within his heart every time the thought crossed his mind over having to kill Delilah. Every day, he would talk to Robert over the same situations plaguing his daily life, but Robert had the same comments as before. "Robert, there has to be some way to help my Delilah. I can't sit here and allow that monster to keep her prisoner within her own body. Help me find Audia, or at least give me something I can use to help me find it. I am lost with no one to guide me over something I know nothing about." *"My dear Seth, please listen, for this is the last and final time I say this to you. I can't help you find Audia no matter how much I truly want to. I wish there was something I could do to help you with Audia and Delilah, but I'm afraid my hands are tied. You just have remember how much pain Delilah is in right now, the agony of not being capable to control all that you see, hear, feel, and do. The only one who can save her is the one who won't let her go. He needs her."*

Journal entry: Day 812

They want me to fight this war, but it seems I will be getting no help; my body littered with the scars of fighting. The Evower Army are more like a machine than a creature; they never sleep or eat, and they seemed to be able to find me no matter where I hide, although I have noticed they have a bit of trouble finding me as of late. I can only hope that remains unchanged. The traps are set in the swamp, and all my hiding places are concealed again from the last encounter. I've found that taking them out stealthily is more challenging and up my training more than it ever would when I was taking them on in large numbers and plus it's more fun.

Tomorrow, I plan on sneaking near to the castle. I have to talk to Eiades, and if that's him screaming, then there must be a window to his cell. I can only hope he can give me some form of help in finding the elusive Audia I keep hearing about.

I feel so lost and without purpose; nothing seems to matter to me. Everything I fight for means nothing. I continue only for the one remaining person I still care about and even that isn't looking so good at the moment. I have two choices, it seems—I can kill Delilah and end her misery or let her live and whatever pain she is in will continue for all eternity. I only wish there could be a third option, why can't there be one that allows me to save her from the monster, one that allows us to be together. Happiness isn't a luxury I've endured in my life but I actually felt happy when I was with her, if only it could have stayed that way.

The next day Seth waited for the sky to turn dark before he made his move. Before leaving for the castle, Seth smeared swamp mud on his skin, thinking this would hide his body heat just in case the Evower Army could detect heat signatures. Plus, when dry, it gave off a nice look that resembled the ground.

Standing at the edge of the hill, Seth waiting, thinking of his beloved Delilah and how he wondered if he had the strength to end her life, wondering if he could save his brother or if it was already too late. He contemplated the simple fact of just giving up or going through with the plan at hand; on one hand, Seth would be letting Robert down, but on the other would call for the murder of his one true love. *Decisions shouldn't be this hard,* Seth thought.

The sky suddenly filled with dark black clouds, lightning branching out from all directions; and with a sudden burst, rain began to pour. The wind picked up, pushing the rain sideways, and all the thunder and lightning made it seemed eerie with ever flash of light and crack of sound; Seth grabbed his dagger made from the bone of a fallen Evower soldier. Seth was thinking,

Hopefully my cover will still allow me to be unseen but also the storm should cover any kind of noise I might make, so I guess it's an equal trade-off. Keeping a low stance and only running or walking when any form of thunder cracked within the sky, the rain washed away any evidence of Seth being there, and the Evower Army stayed busy with the violent gust of winds. Seth made his way to the castle wall, making sure the guards up above didn't make his presence, looking around to find a path over the wall but nothing in sight. Not giving up, walked along the wall, and each pass of lightning showed more and more at his disposal; finally a single dead tree embedded into the castle wall was made visible from the south of the castle. A huge burst of thunder gave Seth just enough time to make his journey, climbing with caution, knowing that if he was to be discovered, he wouldn't have a fighting chance in the lion's den. Finally reaching the top, seeing no one in sight except a few soldiers off in the distance, Seth took advantage of his situation and climbed down the other side to hopefully find Eiades.

The screams were beginning to grow louder and louder toward a small window of light coming from within the distance; the screams screeched in the air between each crack of thunder. Seth walked ever so slowly toward the dim ray of light, making sure to keep the noise he made to a minimal for if the slightest sound was heard, he knew it would be all over for him. The rain and wind made it extremely difficult to move without an arm or hand in front of your face, but Seth knew if he was having a hard time, then so were the soldiers that occupied the area. The light was becoming closer and closer until Seth was finally within range to see what lurked inside, and as he predicted, Eiades was sitting on the mud-caked floor, with water coming in from the window, keeping the poor prisoner soaked. Eiades was still screaming and speaking in tongue; nothing that came from his mouth made any sense to Seth. He knew this would never be an easy task to fulfill, but he still needed to try, if not for Robert but for Delilah. "Eiades! Hey, Eiades, it's me, Seth! I need to speak with you about Audia. I need to know how and where to find it. Do you know where it is?" Eiades, still screaming but made eye contact with Seth, said, "Please, Eiades. I have to find this. Can you help me?" Eiades reached out to Seth as if to ask for something, but Seth took this as an act of aggression and pulled out his dagger. Eiades reached out even farther toward Seth with his hand trying to grasp the sharp object. With a small pause, Seth finally gave Eiades the knife to only tell himself, *I have nothing left to lose.*

Eiades pulled away from wall to face it; with the knife in hand, Eiades began writing as best he could with his handcuffs and the chains to his legs. Writing and screaming, the wall read, "What you seek is not really an object but a being; she was the mother of my beloved to whom Hanuse brutally beat. I can't tell you how to find her because to each of the descendants of Rezorin, the hiding spot was always different, but I do know that it was always meant to be difficult to nearly impossible to find Audia. Something about the most important thing in one's life gives way to true power." Seth, getting the most of what's written but still not understanding, said, "I don't understand, Eiades. You mean to tell me that whatever is the most important thing to me in my life is where Audia is hiding?" Eiades looked at Seth and then back to the wall to write, "Giving up what is most important will then reveal Audia." Seth was beginning to comprehend, but still a little confused. "But I have nothing in my life that means anything to me, so how can I find Audia and how can a person still be alive after all this time?" Eiades wrote, "Audia wasn't just a person. She was a *spirit* and *spirits* live forever or until a god destroys them." "Not that I don't thank you for all the help you are giving me, but why help me?" Eiades, with a look of sadness filled into his eyes, turned around again toward the wall. "Hanuse promised me that if I shared my soul with him, he would grant me my wish of seeking revenge against the ones who murdered my Puri, my love. I've seen so many horrible things, most of which I unwillingly helped act out and for those actions I bear the burden of knowing. When Hanuse released me, all I can think and see in my mind are all the horrible things I've helped do; every day is torture and every second I pray for death. I only hope that the new body he is now occupying can handle the visions and experiences he will most definitely show her. She is pretty much dead like me; she just doesn't know it yet."

Seth stepped back slowly from the news that rendered him speechless; each step back grew a hole into his soul. The very news that Delilah couldn't be saved echoed into the back of his mind, a numbing sensation filling his heart. His vision was beginning to grow narrow, and then suddenly Seth dropped to his knees. With a tear rolling down his cheek, he stared into the darkened cloudy sky; the rain poured over his face, mixing the rain with tears. Eiades was still screaming in the background; lightning flashed every few seconds, giving birth to light for just moments in time.

And without warning, a large howling scream that did not belong to Eiades screeched through the sky. Seth looked toward the loud noise to notice his presence had been revealed. Getting back to his feet, he began to run toward the wall that held the tree from within the background that brought him here. The Evower Army picked up pace, running faster and faster until Seth and the army were mere feet from each other. Scratching and clawing at the back of him, the army gave no sign of stopping. From within the distance, fires had been lit from all around the castle, making Seth's presence known through the entire kingdom.

Hanuse stood on top of the castle gates looking down upon the distance of a fearful Seth being chased by the very army Hanuse controlled. *"Your stupidity knows no bounds, young Seth! To come within the gates of the lion's den is either very fearless or extremely unwise. Who shall I punish for allowing him to invade my domain? Number Three and Twenty, stand before me!"* The two numbered soldiers slowly made their way toward the towering Hanuse. "Yes, my master." *"I asked you to do one simple thing. I needed you to keep Seth busy, not to kill him, not to let him walk right onto the very soil that I allow you to so willingly walk upon. So why is it I am looking directly at the very person who has the power to win this war? ANSWER ME!"* "We are sorry, my master," said number Three. "With the storm overhead, it was difficult for us to watch over the land. We will do better next time," said Twenty. *"Interesting that you point out the possibility of a next time. What makes you think I will allow for a next time? You make it seem as if I were a merciful god. I don't need excuses. I need my word followed and nothing else."* And with a swift movement of his arm, Hanuse lifted number Twenty off his feet and into the air without touching him. *"I grow tired of your failures, and I will no longer allow you to disappoint me!"* The sound of cracking and snapping could be heard from within him. Hanuse was apparently crushing every bone from inside his body. His yells and screams echoed throughout the land, but nothing would save him. Blood was beginning to pour from every orifice. *"Let this be a lesson to anyone who wishes to anger me. You will meet the same fate as your brother here."* And with Twenty still in the air helplessly dying right in front of their very eyes, Hanuse looked over at Three. *"Bring me Eiades. I'm sure our dungeon friend was eager to speak with Seth. Bring him to me! And do not fail me again!"* And without haste, number Three cowardly ran toward the dungeon to gather Eiades for the big confrontation.

Eiades, now kneeling in front of Hanuse, never looking within the eyes that once held his very body, but still seeing all that he had willingly and non willingly done within his years of being connected to Hanuse. *"So, my precious Eiades, should I even ask what you told Seth? Do I want to know how badly you betrayed me? Oh, Eiades, you disgrace me! No matter, though. He will still fail. He can't possibly obtain Audia if he can never let his Delilah go. I don't know why I even have you around anymore, Eiades. Your usefulness has run its course. I shall show the rest what happens when you betray me, and if you think your mind is the worst kind of torture, then I have so much to teach you. My full potential has never been fully realized from in front of your eyes, but that will change very shortly. You will wish to die before I'm done with you, and I will never grant it."*

Hanuse, still looking above, stared at the misadventure that was Seth's escape, and with a creepy smile and a laugh, Hanuse pointed down to his soldiers. *"You may hurt him, but as for the killing, I will have the pleasure."* The blood ran like a river down Seth's arms and legs; the clawing was catching up to the running, but nothing was stopping the tearing of skin. The rain and wind blinded his vision, the mud dragging Seth down with every step. You could hear the demonic laughter within the background coming from Hanuse, almost as if to taunt Seth. As if the time would never come, he finally made it to the wall, but the end was still not complete; Seth would have to find a way up the wall and quickly. The army carelessly slipped through the mud, giving him just enough time to use one of the many bodies from their massive numbers to give more reach to the edge of the top of the wall. And with a step down from the wall, Seth would only have to deal with a few instead of the horde. Hanuse, with a look of disappointment, said, *"I expected a show! But no matter, this is far from over. Come, my army and soldiers. You shall prepare a show in Seth's honor."*

Seth reached the top of his hill completely drained. The blood still flowing while the rain diluted with every drop. The wind still blowing violently, making everything seem alive with movement. The mud caked onto his skin and, at the same time, being washed away from the rain. Lightning was still flashing here and there, giving the landscape brief moments of visible light with every strike. The only thing left for him to do was to patch himself up with what he had available at the time as best he could and try and get some sleep; in the morning, he could fully assess the extent of the damage.

The next day, the black clouds had given in, and the sky filled itself with the same light gray clouds, giving only a dim essence of light, like every day before it. Seth gathered the same leaves to fix his wounds; this time it would take a lot of time and a miracle for the carnage that covered his body to fully heal, but he got what he searched for. Now it was time to take the next big leap and officially find Audia so he could finally end this nightmare. "Robert, are you there? I need to talk with you." The clouds began to separate from the light shining through. *"Yes, my child, what do you need of me?"* Seth covered his eyes from the brightness. "I talked to Eiades about Audia. Is it true that Audia was once a *spirit*? That I might be looking for a person, not an object? And what's this I hear that every time one of the descendants fought, Audia was something different? I just need a few more explanations before I begin my search." The light vanished, and the clouds took back the sky. Seth, frustrated and ill, said, "I don't know why I even try. I am left with this task all on my own, and they expect me to win!"

Ewar and Nephia spoke with each other. "I don't know, Father. He seems to be losing faith. Are you sure we can't help him in some way?" "I wish we could, my dear child, but he will just have to go through it alone on this. Like I said, if I could help him find Audia, I would in a heartbeat. The only help that we may provide will come soon enough. He is our last hope, and the time will come that the rest of us will join in the fight as one." "Don't you think that's a little dangerous, Father? He is, after all, not of our world, and the very thing you speak of could destroy him!" "We don't have much of a choice, daughter. If he begins to fail, that would be our only option, our last and final act for this war."

Journal entry: Day 814

After finally talking with Eiades, I found out that Audia was a person—well, sort of. She apparently is a *spirit* that sacrificed herself to become something completely different. The only question left is where and how do I find her. Eiades mentioned something about for every one of the descendants who have come and gone that Audia took the shape of a different object or something to that effect, so I'm thinking that maybe Audia resides within something of personal value, but I'm not entirely sure.

I've come to the conclusion that it won't matter, that I will have to end Delilah's life. As much as it pains me to even think of such a thing, I guess it must be done. Every time I look at her, I become weak, but then I look into her eyes and I see something different, something that shouldn't be there. It's the strangest feeling. On one side, I love her, and then the other, I want to hurt her. If only I could make sense of this, but it seems I'm destined for this anguish.

Every day I have to make up my mind on whether or not I should just give up; as much as I would love to, I know I can't. Having a simple decision in life is what I long for, and yet every obstacle that has come my way has been nothing but hard and complicated drama, and it shows no sign of slowing. Maybe I should look at the bright side; if I lose, I die, and if I win, then I can finally end myself since my services will no longer be needed. Oh, how I desperately want an end to this nightmare!

Seth held the necklace Delilah gave him on that fateful day—the half-heart necklace. Seth stroked his fingers on the word ever, staring into the void, thinking of nothing but the happy moments that he so badly wanted to relive again and knowing it could never happen; he was also wondering if the other portion of the necklace still remained on the neck of Delilah. If he couldn't save his love, the least he could do would be to rip the other half of the necklace, protecting the very meaning the necklace represented. "I don't want to kill you, my love, but I may have no choice. If I want to save you from the torture you're in, I must end your life. I will try and make it as painless as possible."

Months had passed and Seth's wounds turned into scars. The Evower Army making sure his recovery would take as long as possible just to torture him. The army would attack on random nights without warning, causing the wounds to reopen, making sure a quick recovery was impossible. Seth looked down upon the hill, staring at the bleak castle, with all the evil subjects watching and keeping guard. "This must end. Audia or no Audia, I must try."

Nephia gave Ewar a shocked look. "We can't allow him to go through with it. Without Audia, he will die!" "We can't stop him, for he chooses his own path. All we can do is guide, and if all else fails, then we will sacrifice ourselves." "Wait, Father. If we do that, then no one will be left to protect Earth from the Evower Army!" "I'm afraid if we don't, all will be lost. You seem to forget he is the last, and there are no others within the bloodline to take his place. We don't have any other path to follow. God help us all!"

Hanuse, at his throne, said, *"I call for entertainment. pique my interest!"* The remaining forces of the twenty-five descendants took stage with props and costumes. One soldier stepped in front of the stage facing Hanuse and the Evower Army. "On a glorious day much like this one, the masses gathered for the arrival of the last. We all stood around waiting, waiting for the words to be spoken by our loving and gracious lord to welcome our new guest to this world. The young Seth dropped from the sky and hit the ground in a heap of dust and debris. The sky would break to send a gift that would be used to unsuccessfully defeat us." A soldier, playing the part of Seth, acted lost and confused to show weakness. Hanuse grew very pleased with a smile upon his face, and the Evower Army, who were restless, began to calm down and pay attention. "The scared and weak Seth looked all around, knowing he is no match for the massive army that lay at his feet. Our beloved god, sitting at her mobile throne with all her beauty, gets up to point at the young Seth. *'Kill the mortal who dare step foot in my presence!'* Young Seth stood in one place, fighting off each being as it clawed into him. The fighting would last mere minutes until Seth began making his way to the front of the crowd, seeing his dear Delilah and our now-lovely goddess."

Hanuse seemed to become distracted by something close by; the soldiers who now played actors stopped to make sure they weren't upsetting their lord. *"Continue, my subjects!"* The soldiers moved back into place and began reenacting each scene from that fateful day. The character playing Seth walked up to the character playing Hanuse/Delilah and placed his wooden sword against their throat. "I shall end this now, you devilish fiend!" Then the character playing Hanuse removed her shrouded hood to reveal that she was actually Delilah. The character playing Seth dropped to his knees. "Damn you! You've beaten me without throwing a punch!" One of the actors picked up a wooden plank shaped like a horn and made the motion of calling out through it. The rest of the characters were running amok as to show the chaos being drawn to the character playing Seth; but before the scene could finish, Hanuse stood up and pointed for everyone to be silent. *"He's here!"*

Chapter 8

𝓗anuse stood upon the gate's wall, staring at the solo figure of Seth walking down the hill. They were patiently staring each other, knowing that this day would be the end of it all. Wind blew with a constant force that made everything flow with a feeling of life. Hanuse, still staring, kept his eyes directed toward Seth as if he was waiting for this moment his whole life. And without warning, Hanuse pointed his finger toward Seth. *"I grow tired of this game, no more holding back. Kill him, and bring me his head!"* Number Thirteen grew confused. "My lord, I don't understand. Why save me for last if your plan is to kill Seth now?" *"You will still have your chance, my child. I just want to watch this one die more than once."* A large rumble began to shake the very foundation of the soil; Seth looked around, trying to keep his balance before taking sight of the chaos being unfolded. The gates to the castle opened slowly, with the Evower Army pushing and shoving each other to gain exit, and when patience ran thin, the army began climbing the wall over the castle gate like a swarm of insects. Seth braced himself for the massive onslaught coming his way, knowing this moment would define the end of what would become and what would ever be.

Seth fighting the army off as best he could, knowing he bit off more than he could chew. "They seem stronger than before, much stronger." Each hit ripped flesh from bone; Seth's blood emptied out of his body in a never-ending flow. Seth, still slicing with the blades, took a few out with each swing, but the more he killed, the more hits were taken upon him. Then without warning, Seth fell to his knees with the Evower Army on top, ripping what remained of his flesh from his body; all that remained was a single hand standing out from the army, devouring him. While waiting for death, he thought to himself, *Finally, my day has come. All the pain and suffering I felt my entirely life will end, and I may rest in peace. I just wish I hadn't let Robert down. If only I could have saved Delila . . .* And with that last thought unfinished, Seth's heart began to rest.

On top of the castle gates, Hanuse was still standing within the same spot as before, only this time with a smile upon his face. *"I've waited for this moment for so long. It almost feels surreal. Rezorin, you should have fought me when you had the chance. You would have been wiser to just have given up your kingdom and heaven, but it worked out for the best since I had so much fun killing all your worthless children!"*

A clash of lightning struck the sky, breaking Hanuse of his speech. Thunder filled the sky with sounds; everything grew darker and darker until day became night. Besides the inner circle of soldiers still feasting on Seth's corpse, the outer circle backed away, staring at the sky with amazement. Lightning was streaking across the sky in a chaotic fashion; the wind picked up, blowing with such intensity that staying afoot proved difficult.

Up above, the *spirits* were conversing on the only move they had left. "Ewar, are you and your daughter ready for the last sacrifice?" Ewar stared down at the army that were still picking off small pieces of Seth. "I never thought it would come to this, but yes, we are ready. Let us all join together for the final stand!" The remaining forces of Rezorin's elite *spirits* gathered in a circle. "May this be the true divine light that will guide Seth to the righteous path!" A bright light began to glow from each *spirit*; they all held hands and raised them above their heads. The light was getting brighter and brighter until a white glowing ball of light was the only thing to be seen.

Meanwhile, back down on Vianna, Hanuse started to celebrate his victory by planning the massive takeover of Earth. *"First, I will pick out the few chosen to stand by my side, then I will enslave all the woman and children. I can only hope there are followers of Rezorin around, for torturing them shall bring me great joy."* Hanuse glanced down at the devastation of his army still devouring on Seth's corpse. *"Feast, my children, for today we celebrate victory!"*

Overhead, the storm showed no signs of slowing. Hanuse greeted the chaos in the sky as a sign of victory and celebration, but the bright light that was beginning to grow within the sky was about to show signs of a much different event. Horizontal streaks of lightning flowed from the north, south, east, and west in the sky, leaping and looping only to meet in the middle, forming a large ball of light and energy. The outer circle of the army were still staring in place as before, but this time, the inner circle backed up as well to gaze upon the miracle; Seth's mangled body showed more bone than skin or flesh. He lay heaped over lifeless on the ground.

The light gained brightness and strength until small streaks of lightning shot out from the ball to overtake the inner circle of the Evower Army, bringing them off the ground and into the air until they explode in place, leaving nothing but the floating remains of Seth that were just devoured. Finally, a large streak of lightning struck down from the middle of the ball to engulf Seth, bringing his corpse off the ground to float in midair. The floating remains began to spin in place like a tornado, spinning closer and closer toward him. Hanuse, up above, stared into the scene in front of his eyes. What once was a smile upon his face turned into anger and frustration. The voice of Delilah was speaking out in Hanuse's head, "I knew he would find Audia. I hope you're ready to die, Hanuse!" Hanuse, holding his head from the sound of Delilah, replied, *"You will shut your filthy mouth, you stupid bitch! This can't be happening. He was dead. I just watched him die!"* Seth's body still floated in midair, the pieces swirling until they finally reached their destination; blood flowed back into his body, the flesh and skin remolding and reshaping onto his very bone. The light was gaining brightness, swallowing his body whole until nothing could be seen except the blinding light. A shock wave rushed down from the ball, merging into Seth, and with a sudden burst of energy, he began to grasp for air. His lungs were now feeling with life, his heart beating with immense force and the blood now circulating throughout his veins.

Hanuse, shielding his eyes from the light while trying to command his army, said, *"Don't just stand there. Kill him!"* The army, now standing in full circle, looked a little confused as to what to do. Hanuse, looking down upon his disciples, continued, *"Did you not hear me? I said kill him! And this time finish the job."* And without pause, the army began to run and attack Seth, who was still engulfed within the blinding light. Each attempt at attack was met with the same inevitable demise, for each time someone tried to slice or claw their way toward him, they immediately burst into flames, and their bodies were mere ashes within seconds, leaving nothing but a pile of dust.

The light suddenly vanished, and Seth dropped to one knee, his blades rested at his sides and were still attached to his arms. Seth looked up with a glare and sign of anger in his eyes; every scar that he had accumulated was now gone. He thought to himself, *What just happened? I feel so full of energy, and the anger inside burns with intensity. All I want to do is kill!* And without hesitation, Seth jumped from his last stance and began slicing within arm's reach. The scene changed from before when he was losing without mercy; now he was the one showing no mercy. Seth ran through the massive army, slicing limbs and heads from the very body they were attached to. Blood sprayed like a fountain, turning Seth's skin a dark red; only this time, the blood didn't belong to him. He moved faster and killed with such fury that the Evower Army couldn't catch up or keep up, and it seemed as if there wasn't any form of slowing in sight. He was still running, slicing anything and everything within distance, but it wasn't really the army Seth was concerned about, for each step gained him closer to the castle where the very person that desperately needed to meet his blades resided.

Hanuse, knowing exactly what Seth was thinking, called for one of his twenty-five soldiers to call on the horn to have the castle doors closed, leaving Seth to deal with the army that lay outside. Seth was still running toward his destination, trying to pick up pace, when, suddenly, it occurred to him the army he was so eagerly ripping to shreds wasn't fighting back; in fact, they were all running alongside him. So instead of fighting the army, he pushed himself a little harder, making sure he could get past the doors before they closed, but no amount of running could slow down time, and sure enough, he would get there in front of the gates in just enough time to see them close and lock right before his eyes.

On the inside, a different story was unfolding. Hanuse was surrounded by the very army he used to control. *"I still control you. Mind me or be destroyed!"* Hanuse said in an angry voice. And with just enough energy, Delilah spoke within Hanuse's mind, "You're losing control. They must know that you have a little fear toward Seth. I see no other reason why they would turn on you besides that. And the fact that Seth no longer fears you must be killing you inside!" *"I still have a secret that I'm just dying to unleash on your precious Seth, and then when I'm done with him, I will make sure your life is long and painful. You will beg for death, so you best watch your tongue!"*

Hanuse commanded what remained of his twenty-five protectors, *"Control them! Push them back. We need room for our special guest."* The soldiers pushed back the army as best they could, moving them farther and farther back until almost the whole area within the middle began to clear. Hanuse, trying to control the small amount of fear that lurked inside, kept the thought of his secret wide open; and suddenly, the Evower Army began to settle and then became neutral. The remaining forces of the twenty-five put their hands down and stepped back, knowing they wouldn't have to control the army any further. Hanuse then commanded the Evower Army with what little power he still had left over them, *"Block that gate. I want Seth out there as long as possible. I need this moment to last longer!"* And with that said, a large group of the Evower Army walked over to the gate to keep it secure.

Seth, standing outside the castle gates, said, "You think this will stop me, Hanuse? I will rip every soldier apart, crush every stone just to get to you! I WILL DESTROY YOU!" Every angry sentence being spoken created a pulsating glow coming from Seth. Each word made the glow brighter and brighter. Seth was still yelling outside the gate, becoming angrier and angrier with each passing second. Then finally, the anger grew too strong and the light coming from Seth grew too powerful, and one massive power surge emitted out from Seth's body, ripping the front gate off its hinges, crushing several Evower soldiers in the process. The door scattered into several pieces; the Evower Army kept distance along the inner castle gate's walls. The remaining forces of the twenty-five were still standing idle, keeping guard over them.

Standing in front of the castle, Hanuse waited patiently for this very moment. *"I've waited so very long for this moment! This game has gone on long enough. I think it's time we end it. Although you still haven't met my special friend. Or have you?"* A giant beastlike creature emerged from the front castle door, muscles upon muscles; this being stood a staggering ten feet tall. Seth stared at the behemoth not because this monster was huge, but he resembled the face of his stepfather. Hanuse, planning on this to break Seth's spirit, did almost the opposite. *"You see, Seth. I've been with you your entire life, in more ways than one. I taught you what pain and emptiness feels like and how no one can be trusted. So in a way, I could be considered your father."* Hanuse glanced at number Thirteen. *"It's time. I'm granting your wish, but leave him a life enough so I may finish the job!"* The monster began to charge toward Seth, the ground shaking and rumbling from each step. Gaining speed and momentum, the monster balled up his fist. Seth was standing within the same place, giving off no effort of moving. Now within mere feet, Seth dropped to one knee, placing one blade at the floor. The monster, still charging, ran past the blades, dismantling his feet from his body, and with quick reflexes, Seth reached out with the other blade to cut off the monster's head while he fell. Three different sections of the beast now littered the ground, the blood still flowing fresh from the body. The once-mighty number Thirteen was no more.

Seth was now standing, staring at Hanuse. "I told you I would destroy you. Now it's time for me to keep my promise. Your soldiers can't save you, and the Evower Army are no match for my newfound strength, so do yourself a favor and take your punishment." *"Seth, there is still time to join me. All you have to do is say the word."* "Even with your back against the wall, you still try and recruit me? What surprising ignorance that you won't accept defeat." *"What do you want, Seth? I can give you anything!"* "Can you give me back my Delilah? Can you give me back my childhood? What about my mother and brother? Can you bring them back to life? There is nothing you can do for me and you know it. You're only buying time until your demise." *"You want your precious Delilah. What if I say I can give her back to you? Would you join me and leave this tragic war behind you if I gave her back?"* "What, so she can end up like Eiades? I know all about what happens when you take over someone's body, so save it! You can give her back to me, but she would much rather die than live like that. All I want from you is the necklace she gave me. Give it to me before I kill you and take it anyway." *"Don't make me laugh, my dear Seth. You may have his power, but even with that, you have to know how to control it. But fine, take the necklace. It means nothing to me."* Hanuse then ripped the necklace from Delilah's neck, breaking the chain, scattering the metal loops across the ground, then threw it toward Seth.

Seth ran toward where the necklace was thrown, diving in midair to try and catch it, but before Seth could reach out to put his hands on the half-shaped heart, the thrown piece of necklace started flying toward Seth, almost as if something was pulling it. The half piece Seth still wore on his neck was now sticking out from within his shirt, pulling itself toward the other half as if they both were calling to each other. Finally, the two pieces met in midair, and a spectacular scene began to take place. A flash of light and mesmerizing glow engulfed the now-complete necklace. Seth stood in front baffled as to what was happening. Hanuse, knowing exactly what was going on, let out a terrifying howl of anger. *"NO! But if you didn't have Audia, then what . . . I should have known. Ewar, this is your doing. How could I have been such a fool? Ewar and the others must have sacrificed themselves."* Still staring down at the brightly shining floating necklace, Seth began to wonder if this necklace could be Audia. "Could this little thing be the one true weapon that can kill Hanuse?" Suddenly, a faint voice echoed within the back of Seth's mind. "Yes, this is Audia. You had to give up the one thing that meant the most to you, which, in this case, is Delilah. So take our power and kill Hanuse once and for all."

The necklace gently touched Seth's fingers, which broke out into a bright light. The light overtook Seth completely, lifting him off the ground. A string of energy spread from the necklace, which stretched across his entire body until entering into Seth himself and then finally into his very soul. What once looked calm and peaceful turned into something violent as the energy began to rush from the necklace and into Seth, making him scream in agony. The very sight seemed extremely painful until finally he dropped to the ground in a fetal position.

A seemingly calm Seth rose to his feet, his veins glowing with a bright white all across his body. With the very sight of this, Hanuse dropped to his knees. *"This can't be!"* In the background, you see the remaining twenty-five being ripped to pieces by the Evower Army, limbs and blood spewing all along the landscape, creating mounds of body parts and puddles of blood. When all the soldiers had been destroyed, they began making their way toward Hanuse, but before they could reach their destination, Seth yelled out in a two-toned voice, "You will stay your place. I shall deal with him. Keep your distance . . ." A giant flarelike stream spread from Seth's arm, ripping a great divide into the soil. "What's happening to me? I can't control it!" Hanuse, now with a creepy smile on his face, said, *"You can't handle the powers given to you.*

Before you could possible defeat me, you have to control what lurks inside. To think, any of you mortals could possibly handle the powers given to you. You will die before you control it!"

A faint voice began to call out within the back of Seth's mind. Robert began to speak, "This power will consume you. Don't fight it. Use all your anger and unleash the power inside. You've come this far now. Finish it. This is the beginning." On his knees, with his hands covering his head, Seth said, "This isn't the beginning but the end of it all!" Flares shot out from all over Seth. Everything within their path would be destroyed; nothing was safe.

Seth got up from his knees, still holding his head, but eventually, he stood up straight and began walking toward Hanuse. In the background, the Evower Army were still holding position but eagerly waiting on something, as if fear was a meal and Hanuse was the main course. Standing before Hanuse, Seth, with blade in hand, said, "For so long I've waited for this moment. I told you I would never surrender and I would eventually kill you. Well, today is that day. Do you have anything to say before you meet your end?"

A conversation began between Hanuse and Delilah from within Delilah's mind. "Tell him you still live inside this body, that if he destroys me, he destroys you!" "Hanuse, give it up. You lost, and there is nothing more you can do to save yourself." *"There is always a way to overcome odds of this nature. NOW TELL HIM!"* "If I tell him and he spares us, then you have to promise me that you will allow him to live, and not the torture that I know you're thinking of but actually allowing him to live out his days in peace." *"Fine, as long as he kneels before me and joins my side, then he can live beside me, but you must convince him to relinquish his power over to me and kneel."*

The blades were now crossing over Hanuse's neck. Seth stared down into his eyes, waiting for the last comment; the last thing Seth would ever hear would come from his dear Delilah. Seth, now waiting, said, "If you have something to say, now is the time. You won't get another chance." Hanuse, still on his knees, said, *"I have something of yours!"* Then suddenly, Hanuse's voice changed to Delilah. "Seth, nothing could ever be enough on how sorry I am, both for the way your life turned out and for me being here. I can't imagine how hard it is for you. Maybe this is just the beginning of something wonderful for you, and you have to live through this to get to it. I don't know much, but I do know that this is something you have to do. You have to kill me." Hanuse was now screaming from within Delilah's mind, knowing he had just been tricked. And with those words escaping Delilah's lips, Seth's blades, with a quick twist, dug into Delilah's neck only to have Delilah call out to Seth, "I love you!" With a tear rolling down Seth's cheek, the blades finished the job, and the now headless Hanuse/Delilah began rolling around on the ground.

Seth dropped to his knees. "I'm finished! I've done what you've asked. Now grant me death! Just let me go. End me and let me go!" A large quake shook the land; the castle started to crumble and crack within the soil. The castle slowly shifed, the ground swallowing the castle whole, rocks stumbling down and breaking apart, scattering itself along the ground. The scenery began to change; the gray clouds began to break, and the sun shone through. Trees and grass grew within seconds, creating a lush beautiful landscape. The Evower Army was still standing together within the castle gates; a large thunder echoed from underneath their feet, and the soil gave way, and the army vanished into the ground. Water began to sprout from the swamp and turned what once was an ugly landscape into a glorious mesmerizing lake. People in white ropes began to appear out of thin air; they surrounded Seth, hundred upon hundred gazing upon their hero, all with smiles of joy on their faces. Seth looked up; the battered and torn shard shell of a man basked in the sunlight that he hadn't seen in so long. A voice called out from within Seth's own mind, "Let go!" Seth was still on his knees, with the strangers still hovering over him; suddenly, he stretched his arms in a V. "Let me go!"

Bright lights branched from Seth; the power he kept inside sought an escape; strands of white glowing light came from all over him, twisting and turning. A voice called out without a trace of where it's coming from, *"You've done what no one could, what I once thought I did many millennia ago. There is nothing I can do to fully repay you, but I will spend the rest of your life trying."* Within seconds, Seth was suddenly being lifted from the ground, a calm wind relaxing every muscle in his body while many different voices began to call out to Seth. Among the many voices, Seth could recognize at least one. "Robert! I felt you inside my soul. You helped me control the monster inside. If only I could have saved Delilah!" Seth was now overlooking the land; what once looked dead and barren was now streaming with life. Animals and people scattered throughout. The mountaintops were glazed with a snow-topped layer. The lakes and rivers, which used to hold nothing but rock and dust, now twinkled in the sun, filled with sparkling water and life. Children played on top of the very same hill Seth had slept, ate, and planned his next move of attack. The same strange voice as before spoke once more, *"Gaze upon the world you helped restore. You have given my first people their home back. There is now a heaven for them and your world to claim after death."* Seth looked up toward the sky, trying to speak with the stranger. "Rezorin, if that's you, grant me my wish of death. I've done everything asked of me and more. Now let me go!" *"I see inside your soul and I know what you truly desire. I will grant you this. I am the light, I am your guidance, and I will watch over you always!"*

The light surrounding Seth became bright enough to blind, and within a flash, everything turned white; and time stood still for a mere moment. And as if dropped out of thin air, Seth now stood in the middle of a familiar but still vaguely strange room—a rocking chair in the corner in front of a window, pictures of Seth's family hanging on the wall. Feeling confused, he turned around to face the mirror, and to his amazement, the reflection staring back at him was none other than himself at the age of eight. The door behind him began to open slowly, and the voice from before started again, *"You only think you want death, but I know what you truly desire . . ."* The door was now fully opened to reveal Seth's mother and brother coming into the house with bags of groceries. Seth's heart beating rapidly, not knowing if he could trust this vision to be reality. "Mom, Stan, is that you?" Seth's mother turned to look at him. "Well, of course, it is, honey. Who else would it be?" *"I'm granting you a second chance!"*

Edwards Brothers,Inc!
Thorofare, NJ 08086
27 September, 2010
BA2010270